SAY GOODBYE

Autolemy

A True-to-Life Musical Fiction

First published in Great Britain in 2023 by AU Recordings & Publishing Limited.

www.aupublishing.co.uk

First impression

A CIP catalogue record is available from the British Library

ISBN (Hardback) 978-1-7399618-0-0

"Give me a child until he is seven and I will show you the man."

- Aristotle

PREFACE

Dear Reader,

For a long time, I have had certain musical ideas spinning around my head. For years I walked the pavements of my home town knowing they were connected in some way, without knowing the true reason why. As time moved on further, the vision of what the story should be, began to crystallise each and every day until I finally decided to do something about it. It's been thirteen long years in the making but I have vowed to myself to see this through – no matter what.

This story is the first of three that is set in the mid-to-late 1970's, based in the south of England. England had only recently entered the European Common Market and the nation had just got used to currency decimalisation. 1976 was the year of the endless summer, and the nation's economy had begun to dry up like the riverbeds. Strike upon strike brought the country to a standstill, along with raging inflation; a pint of beer was 32p and a loaf of bread was 19p. Whilst this was supposedly a new era, remnants of a World War II mentality still remained; you just had to make do with what you had.

If you were exceptionally lucky and had a steady job, you could afford a colour television and a telephone in the house. The television had three channels, some of which broadcast on a part-time basis, and telephone answering machines weren't available to the average family. There were, of course, record players, cassette tapes and the radio for music, but this was as technologically advanced as the country had got; computers wouldn't exist in the common houschold for another ten years, and fax machines had yet to permeate the workplace. Very few people owned their own home and there were nowhere near as many cars on the roads as you're used to seeing, because people just couldn't afford them. Children played in the streets and adults actually talked to their neighbours during their spare time.

People found their way around by road signs, paper maps or word of mouth. As a child, if you were in trouble with no money, you had to find a phone box somewhere and hope your parents would accept the reverse charges, which were incredibly expensive. If your parents didn't have a phone, you were in real trouble. Even though children weren't supposed to wander too far from home, they often did. But as long as they were home at the right time, it was no bother. It was rare for kids to be wrapped in cotton wool; not because parents didn't care for them, but having street smarts and a thick skin were essential to being brought up in the working classes from a young age.

The quickest way to get a photograph developed was to own a Polaroid camera and the expensive film that went with it. Otherwise, getting pictures developed required sending the film negatives away and it took weeks to get back. If you wanted to share a picture or document, it had to be done in person or by post.

Imagine your life now without technology. How would you get messages to your loved ones or files to your work colleagues? How would you know the correct spelling of a word or whether something was fact or fiction? How would you validate the knowledge you have now? How would you pre-plan a journey or find out where you were if you were lost? How would you arrange to meet up with friends or family if none of them had a telephone? These are just a few of the challenges a person in the modern age barely needs to consider. But this was normal life in 1970s Britain.

I hope you enjoy the combined adventure of sound and thought.

Autolemy

PART 1

(Late January 1978)

CHAPTER 1

THE BRIDGE

NE SAUTEZ PAS!

Lee Walker looked with a side glance at the police car as it passed him, but maintained his walking pace so as not to look suspicious. The car continued at the same speed, but he stopped anyway as a precaution, and opened his suitcase. He quickly shed his coat, took the gun holster from the case, placed it over one shoulder and put the coat back on. The combination of the cold winter day and his state of nervousness made him shiver. It was something he'd become accustomed to, so Lee picked up the walking pace to try and take his mind off the discomfort. He was too exposed here and his chances of disappearing would be far greater if he could just reach the cover of the riverbank on the south side. His mousey blond hair, sharp blue eyes, oversized coat and trousers tucked into his socks really set him apart from the other pedestrians. As he paced along the bridge, Lee's fear was just realised. The police car had pulled over at the end and two people had stepped out and were heading in his direction – a woman and a police officer. A shot of adrenalin coursed through his body, making his right arm shake. Thinking that it was the weight of the suitcase, he swapped it to his left hand and shook out his right. The gun in the holster was heavy, and if he needed to point it at someone he certainly didn't want them to see him tremble.

Lee turned abruptly, and began walking even quicker in the opposite direction. The police sirens in the distance were getting closer so he jogged as best as he could. But within twenty seconds his escape route was blocked by two police cars with flashing lights at the other end of the bridge. Lee stopped. He was trapped with the police closing in on his position from both sides; a sense of hopelessness washed over him like an inescapable asphyxia, as he thought about the inevitability of his situation if they caught him. He wasn't going back - not if he could help it! Lee looked around; he needed a height advantage. The only option was to climb the heavy girder behind him, so he scrambled his way up and turned to face his pursuers.

"Leave me alone!" he shouted in both directions, hoping this would at least give him some time. On TV, people would try to talk down the person who was threatening to jump; but these people clearly hadn't read the script, because the four of them took no notice and continued to close in. Reluctantly, he took the gun from the holster belt and pointed it in an arc at anyone who approached. Lee shouted again as two bystanders quickly ran as far away as they could. The advancing police slowed, but not enough for his liking. The two officers from the north drew their weapons and pointed them at him. *Four police and six bullets*. This was getting serious now as his arm began to shake, but he kept the gun pointed at them – if he had to shoot, he would.

"LEE!"

The woman who'd approached from his right with the other officer shrieked out his name. He looked at her momentarily but didn't recognise her at all. *Is this a trick? Maybe a distraction?* He quickly turned back to the officers on his left with their guns still pointed at him. They edged closer. Lee's eyes welled up knowing this was it; this was the end. If they were going to shoot, he didn't want to see it and he was going to go out on his own terms. Lee turned around slowly to face the river and looked at the dark grey flowing water below. Without hesitation, he put the gun to his head, knowing what was to come, and pulled the trigger.

* * *

PART 2

(August 1976 - January 1977)

CHAPTER 2

GANG OF TWO

Lee said goodbye to his best friend, Richard, and his dad. Richard's dad had offered to walk him to his front door, but as they lived in opposite directions Lee was happy to walk the short distance on his own. Besides, he needed the time to prepare himself. He let out a short sigh and opened the door.

"I'm back!" he yelled, setting his bag down. Laura instantly appeared from the front room and shouted up the hallway stairs.

"He's filthy dirty again, mum!"

Here we go again, Lee thought, as he scowled at his sister. *How do you play football and not get dirty?*

Within seconds, a pale, slender figure with long, centre-parted and straight black hair skipped down the stairs in her usual bell-bottomed jeans and tight-fitting shirt. Despite her 5ft 4in frame, Louvaine was not a woman to mess with. Never slow to make her feelings known, Lee knew that he was in trouble – again.

"You were told not to get dirty! Just look at your filthy clothes!" She went to smack Lee around the side of the head, but missed when he fortunately dropped down to one knee to start untying his shoelace. Instead, she hit Lee around the head with her right hand, and then the left – an extra punishment for not having the decency to be standing up the first time.

"Now look what you've done!" she shouted, showing Lee the smudges of the newly applied nail varnish on her long slender fingers. Lee's eyes welled up and he literally couldn't see what she was talking about. Even though his mother barely weighed 7 stones, she could still pack a wallop to a young boy.

"Take your clothes off here and then go upstairs to clean yourself off. And don't use the hot water either!"

Still standing by, watching everything unfold, Laura smiled at Lee and walked off back into the front room. Louvaine stomped back upstairs to reapply her nail varnish, leaving Lee to undress at the bottom of the stairs by the front door. Hot water was the last thing he needed on yet another scorching day anyway.

Once clean and dressed again, he went back downstairs to the front room where Laura lay on the floor in front of the television, reading a book. The television was on in the background and Lee went over to change the channel. A choice of three channels wasn't much, but anything would be better than watching Black Beauty.

"I'm watching that!" Laura said, her nose still between the pages of her book.

"No, you're not. You're reading a book," Lee said, as he changed the channel anyway. Laura was three years older than her brother, three inches taller and very much the image of her mother. She got up, pushed past him and changed the channel back. Lee ducked around behind her, picked up the book, removed the bookmark and threw it carelessly across the room. Laura shouted to her mother; there was no reaction this time from upstairs, so she picked up the book and tried to hit Lee with the spine as she chased him around the house. Becoming quite used to her moves now, Lee ducked and rolled through the swipes, smiling as he did so.

"See, you're not watching Black Beauty after all!" he shouted. Another swipe glanced his arm and he pretended to be hurt. "Next time it'll be harder," Laura warned, as she went back in the front room and resumed her position. Lee was just happy that she'd had to find her page again – he had to take the small victories when he could.

Lee sat back on the sofa and occupied his mind by thinking of all the annoying things that he could do to his sister. This was starting to cheer him up immensely when he heard the familiar sound of the front gate creaking. Lee ran to the front door and opened it just as his dad was about to put the key in the lock. He jumped up and hugged his dad, who had just managed to take the cigarette out of his mouth before spilling ash on the top of Lee's head.

"Hello, Badger," he said with a chuckle. Lee clung on to him for as long as he could before Laura arrived to try and push him out of the way. Lee made himself as wide as possible to make it difficult for her to grab hold of her dad. Laura tried to wrestle Lee out of the way, but he was having none of it.

"Come on, you two! You going to let me in?" They both slowly let go of their dad's legs so he could now walk through the front door.

David was easy-going and generous by nature. Originally from Malvern in Worcestershire, he'd lost his strange mix of a folksy European accent at senior school when his mother moved them to Tonbridge in Kent. He had kind brown eyes and had crafted a look to the latest style with shoulder-length thick and wiry dark hair and a full beard. Although he was six foot tall, he was not the type of person to stand out in a crowd; but he had a winning smile that could make anyone feel relaxed. These days, though, he really didn't seem to have too much to smile about. The pay strikes had meant that he was effectively covering two jobs at the factory, with long hours and no extra pay. Not wanting to work on the shop floor all his life, David also attended night school to study for a Diploma in Management three nights a week. That was going to be his ticket out of the grime and dirt of manufacturing to a world where he would have his own office, desk and maybe even his own secretary. But there was a cost; by the time David got home of an evening he never had much time for his wife or the children. He rarely seemed the man he once was, feeling constantly washed out and tired.

David exhaled the last of his cigarette as he walked through the door, dragon smoke extruding from his nostrils. Lee turned his head away and waved his hand back and forth like a fan across his nose. He didn't like cigarette smoke. They all looked up the stairs at the same time to see Louvaine hurtling down them in her slippers.

"David, put that cigarette out! You know there's no smoking in the house!"

David patted both children on the shoulders, encouraging them to move away.

"Not today, Lou," he said, clearly restless and exhausted. "I've had a long day and I don't need this as soon as I walk through the door!"

"Put the cigarette out!" she demanded, this time with eyes narrowed and through gritted teeth. David did what he was told. He opened the front door and flicked his cigarette out on the front footpath. Closing the front door, he put his bag down and asked Laura to take her brother outside into the garden.

"I'll be out with you both in a minute."

Laura went to grab Lee by the arm to escort him out into the garden, but Lee instantly pulled away.

"I know where the garden is!" Just like her mother, Laura gritted her teeth and said in a low voice, "Get outside!"

They both walked down the hallway, through the kitchen and out the back door, with Laura making sure it wasn't fully closed. She started listening through the crack. "What do you think they'll be talking about this time?" Lee said.

"Shhh... that's what I'm going to find out, if you'd shut up and be quiet!" Lee shuffled in to listen through the crack as well. Laura tried shoving him away, but he kept coming back. She eventually had to relent, knowing the noise would expose them both. They could hear their mum protesting.

"Why is work always so important to you? You're never home."

David responded in a caring tone. "I'm here now, aren't I? Do you know what it's like covering for these strikers? You do want to get out of this place eventually, don't you?"

Louvaine was still angry and stomped up the stairs. "This isn't fair!"

David began to walk towards the kitchen. All he wanted when he got home was some time to unwind and relax; he hated the constant animosity from his wife. He just wanted to go outside, play with the kids and forget about work pressures – and the nag upstairs. Seeing him approaching, Lee and Laura darted towards the rear of the garden to make it look like they'd both been playing for a while.

Upstairs and angry, Louvaine continued making herself up, preening her hair to ensure she looked her best. As part of the agreement for

David to better himself at night school, Louvaine was able to take a part-time job, so long as it didn't interfere with the children's schooling. She originally met David when she was twenty-one whilst working behind the bar of the local nightclub. She'd noticed him when he'd come in on the odd Friday night with his friends. He wasn't like the other guys with all the bravado and inane chat-up lines; he just paid attention to her and took the time to remember their conversations. He'd seemed so mature in comparison to all the other 'lads' at the time, even though he was only two years older.

Louvaine had seen an opportunity to better herself with David, and she'd made sure to keep him on the hook. In what was a whirlwind romance to the local community, they got married within six months of meeting. She'd fallen pregnant with Laura soon after the wedding and, instead of applying for a council house, she'd convinced him that they should privately rent a home in a better area because it would be better for his children. David had done his best to ensure that Louvaine didn't need to work, which had suited her for nearly nine years. Now with two children in tow and thirty years old, her life was ebbing away; Louvaine felt David had become ambivalent towards her; she wasn't sure he was even attracted to her anymore. She needed something else. So, every Thursday, Friday and Saturday night, Louvaine would do a six-and-a-half-hour shift behind the bar of the same nightclub where they had originally met, from 7:30 in the evening to two in the morning. With additional clean-up duties, this usually meant her getting home at around 3.

* * *

CHAPTER 3

DECEIT

Summer stretched into autumn and as a favour to David for helping him get his job back, Richard's dad offered to take the two boys to a professional football match that coming Saturday. Ecstatic, Lee was surprised that both his mum and dad agreed to the idea so quickly. Not that David ever had a problem with allowing Lee to have fun; it just always seemed that his mum preferred that he was second in the queue for happiness after Laura.

Saturday morning had come, and Lee practically jumped out of bed; there was nothing quite like the anticipation and build-up to a football match. He put on his best blue and yellow t-shirt, along with his favourite faded jeans. His mum had even made him some sandwiches, wrapped in cling film, for the match. David was scheduled to work that morning, but said to Lou that Richard's dad would be round for Lee at 10 o'clock before rushing out without waiting to hear her protestations. This was the exact same time that Laura had to be at ballet class, so now Lee was an annoyance again and his mum barely spoke to him at all, except to give him an order to wash his breakfast bowl up. David had taken the car, so now a five-minute drive would be a twenty-minute walk for Louvaine and Laura; both of them were now seemingly mad at Lee for the inconvenience. Before they left, Lee was warned not to go anywhere except with Richard's dad, to switch the television off before he left and to make sure the front door was closed on the way out. Lee nodded to all the commands. As soon as they'd gone, he ran back to the front room to watch Swap Shop.

Ten minutes later, the telephone rang. He wasn't normally allowed to answer it, but he took the risk.

"Hello?" he said.

"Oh, hi, is your mum in?" a female voice said on the other end.

"No, she's not in at the moment."

"Is that Lee?" she asked.

"Yes," Lee said, in a slightly hesitant voice.

"Oh, Lee … it's Richard's mum here. I'm glad I've caught you. I'm afraid I've got bad news. Clive's really ill and won't be able to take you both to the football match."

Lee sighed out loud.

"I'm so sorry, my love. We'll make it up to you, I promise."

Lee thanked her for calling and put the receiver down. His day was in tatters - what was he going to do now?

* * *

Louvaine walked Laura to her ballet class at the local community hall. She always liked to watch the start of the class to see Laura do her warm-up stretches; it was just one of the things that made her so proud of her daughter. Laura was the ideal build for a ballet dancer: slender, straight-legged and with the right bone structure, so the teacher said. After watching for about fifteen minutes, Louvaine spotted who she was looking for outside in the car park. A man had just got out of his car and was walking towards the main entrance. At twenty-six he was fit and reasonably muscular, wearing tight-fitting clothes so that everyone could see his physique. His blond hair was high on his forehead, below which were blue eyes and a chiselled jaw. He wasn't that tall, about average, which was just as well given the car he had just turned up in – a small Hillman Imp in a very noticeable cobalt blue colour, similar to the three-wheeled invalid vehicles Louvaine had often seen in town when she went shopping.

"Sh*t!" she muttered under her breath. She waved to Laura with a quick smile and made her way to the front entrance, making sure to walk past the man whilst discreetly gesturing for him to follow her as she did so. *Not the smartest cookie in the factory*, she thought, as he did an about-turn to follow her.

"Jon, I thought I told you to stay by the car!" she scolded through her customary gritted teeth as she walked towards his vehicle. "This yours, then?" she questioned. Jon was a little embarrassed; if yes, then why did he buy such an ugly car? And if no, then why didn't he have his own car?

"No," he said, deciding honesty was the best policy. "It's my dad's car. I'm saving up for my own, so he lets me use it on the weekends."

Jon had met Louvaine behind the bar of the nightclub a few months back. He'd seen she'd been getting a lot of attention, but that she looked down in the dumps. He'd been cheeky enough to tell her to snap out of it and give him a smile. Her initial reaction was to tell him to grow up like the others, but she actually quite liked the look of him and said, "Sure, if you buy me a drink!" After a few drinks they'd hit it off quite well; flirtatious remarks batted back and forth like a shuttlecock across the bar. As the weeks went by, he met her outside the club after her shift, where they'd kissed and ground against each other. He'd offered to give her lifts home, but she'd politely refused. She hadn't wanted him to know exactly where she lived, but had eventually agreed he could come round to her place for a couple of hours on this particular Saturday, when her husband and children would be out.

Jon unlocked the driver's door, got in and leant across the passenger seat to unlock the door for Louvaine. She crouched in, sat on the PVC passenger seat and looked around the car.

"I'm guessing your dad isn't exactly James Hunt, then?" she said sarcastically.

"You can walk if you like?" Jon pushed back gamely.

"I'm sorry. That was a bit below the belt, wasn't it?" She gave a little smile and placed her right hand on his upper thigh. "How's this for below the belt? Come on. Let's go back to mine – we don't have much time."

Jon tried to start the car three times before it finally spluttered into action. They both looked at each other, Jon with embarrassment and Louvaine ready with a disparaging comment. In the end, she decided it was better not to say anything other than give him directions.

* * *

Sitting in his usual spot by the bay window, Lee was enjoying the time to himself and was about to get up to change the television channel when he noticed a car pull up diagonally opposite the house. Always observant, Lee looked through the crack between the net curtains. The colour reminded him of those invalid cars he'd seen around. Everyone called them 'Spasmobiles' at school, but he'd never actually seen anyone in one. *Who would drive a crappy car like that?* He expected to see an old-age pensioner shuffle out of the driver's side, but it was his mother who stepped out of the passenger side door, quickly followed by a muscular man with blond hair.

"No touching until we're inside!" she whispered.

Lee couldn't believe what he was seeing. Who the hell was this guy and why was his mum bringing him home? He had a bad feeling about this so, like any good detective, he made a note of the car registration number in his head: UMF 456M. Once it was in his mind, Lee could remember anything.

Louvaine opened the front door and quickly ushered Jon inside. Even before the front door had closed, Jon pushed her up against the hall wall and pressed himself against her, kissing her passionately. Groin against groin, Jon pulled Louvaine's shirt out from inside of her jeans and ripped it apart, pinging buttons in all directions in the hallway. Louvaine wasn't wearing a bra, and for a split-second Jon admired her beautiful C-cup breasts and pert nipples before placing both his hands on them, feeling their warmth and suppleness.

Having kicked the front door shut and been briefly caught up in the moment, Louvaine could now hear that the television was still on in the front room. *That little sh*t!* She manoeuvred her way out of Jon's grasp to go and turn the TV off and stopped dead in her tracks. Lee stood in the hall facing his mother and the strange man. In what seemed like the longest second ever, time stopped as they all just looked, dumbfounded, at each other.

Louvaine's first instinct was to cover herself up and shout at Lee so loudly that even Jon jumped.

"WHAT ARE YOU DOING HERE?" she exclaimed. "WHY AREN'T YOU OUT?" she continued, as her voice broke. Small tears welled up her eyes, a combination of fear and too much adrenalin now in her system. "GET UP TO YOUR ROOM! NOW!"

Lee didn't say anything; a look of complete disdain said enough. He thumped upstairs, making sure every step could be heard before slamming the door to his bedroom.

Louvaine sat at the bottom of the stairs, her whole body shaking. Jon sat beside her, placed his arm around her shoulder and motioned for her to place her head to his chest.

"I don't believe this," she whispered.

"What can I do?" Jon asked in a concerned tone.

With a sniff, Louvaine replied, "I think you should just leave. I'll see you soon, OK?"

Jon kissed her head and forced an encouraging smile. He made his way out of the house and quietly got into his car, praying that it would start first time. It didn't.

Louvaine thought for a few minutes. She wondered how much Lee had actually seen, but then realised that anything would be damaging. She composed herself and headed upstairs to her bedroom. She took off her shirt, counting the number of missing buttons, and then put on a new top. She then went across to Lee's room, leaving her old shirt on the banister. She had thought about taking a softly-softly approach, but quickly realised that Lee would always have a hold over her, even though he was only six. *No, that won't work,* she thought.

Lee was sitting on his bed when his mum quickly pushed open the bedroom door. She walked straight up to him with her hand about to strike his face. He flinched, expecting a stinging right-hander.

"You dare say a word about this to anyone, you hear? You weren't supposed to be here. It's all your fault! If you say one word, I am going to make your life a living hell! Do you understand me?"

Lee began to sob, his bottom lip quivering. A day that was going to be such fun had now become the worst of his life. In frustration and sheer anger, Louvaine smacked him around the side of the face anyway. "DO YOU UN-DER-STAND?" she shouted again. Lee just nodded. He knew he couldn't say anything without bursting into tears.

"You're staying in your room until I say you can come down. And don't think there'll be any dinner for you, because there won't!" she exclaimed as she walked out of the room, slamming the door behind her.

Louvaine walked down the stairs, taking the shirt from the banister with her. Four buttons were missing, so she made sure she found all of them. She looked at her watch. There was just enough time to sew the buttons back on before she would need to go back to collect Laura.

Lee sat on his bed, still wondering who the strange man was and how he knew his mum. He then thought about his mum, her deceit, the threats and then the punishment. He was angry now. *She's being disloyal,* he fumed. *Going behind Dad's back like that! It's her that should be punished, not me!* His mind was made up.

"Don't you dare come out of your room!" Louvaine shouted as she went to go and pick up Laura. After hearing the door close, Lee waited for what he thought was about five minutes and then went downstairs and grabbed the sandwiches that were meant for football. *I'll need those later.* Then he took a pen and some paper from the kitchen, and went to his room to write a letter to his dad.

Lee soon heard the front door opening; an anxious feeling pulsed through his body, causing him to involuntarily shake. He tried his best to contain it by controlling his breathing, a lesson he had been taught by his nan during the previous winter, when bronchitis had taken hold. He headed back over to his bed as he heard the familiar footfall of Laura running up the stairs.

As she reached the top stair she could see that Lee's bedroom door was closed. Fully expecting the room to be empty, she opened the door to rearrange his toys and maybe take one of them just to annoy him.

Both were caught off-guard as she went to enter the room. Lee quickly hid the letter under his pillow and shouted, "GET OUT!", which briefly startled Laura before she closed the door again and went downstairs.

"Mum, why is Lee in his room? I thought he was going to the football?"

"He's been naughty again, so I said he wasn't allowed to go to the match."

Louvaine had had some time to prepare an answer but, even to a nine-year-old, this was a little at odds with logic and timing. *How did Lee manage to get into trouble when we weren't even there?* Laura knew this was not the time to dig any deeper.

As the day wore on, Louvaine remained on edge as she thought through scenario after scenario. In the end, she decided that if Lee ever said anything to David she would just act completely flabbergasted that he would come up with such a story. It would certainly be game over if she came clean by herself; whilst she felt trapped, she realised things could become much worse. Other women in the neighbourhood didn't have it quite so easy. With the local male population mostly on strike, many of them had to take two jobs just to put food on the table. Thinking about her husband for once, she was grateful that he was able to grind the difficult days out for her and the family's sake. Knowing that David would be home soon, Louvaine told Laura to go and tell Lee that he could come out of his room now. He came downstairs in a timid fashion, like a prison inmate who'd just been released. He could barely look at his mother when he walked into the back room. She decided to try and act like she usually did after Lee had been punished. With a stern voice she said, "You can go in the front room and read a book, quietly. I'll bring you a couple of slices of bread."

Lee wasn't like Laura in any way. They didn't look alike, they shared absolutely no interests whatsoever, and he certainly hated reading books. Strangely though, Lee had been the first in his class to pass the elementary 'Red Book 1' reading test. He was never sure why; he could just absorb the words quicker than the others, he guessed. This was the one and only time his mother had been proud of him. She'd given him a cuddle and gave him the choice of any cake from the bakers on the way home from school that afternoon. Lee had chosen the one that resembled an ice cream which was actually made of marshmallow.

Upstairs, Laura sneaked into Lee's room. She had seen him hastily shove something under his pillow but had decided not to say anything at the time. She was not going to let him keep anything from her. Laura always seemed to have the upper hand on her brother. Those three extra years and her academic intelligence made a big difference. She removed the piece of paper and went back into her room to read the letter. Her jaw literally dropped.

Dear Dad,

Today I was supposed to go to the football match. Mum went to take Laura to ballet so I was waiting to be picked up. Richard's mum called to say that his dad was ill and could not take me to the match. When mum got home she bought a man in the house. He had blond hair but he was not as tall as you. They were kissing and doing naughty stuff by the front door and I saw everything. He has a blue car but I don't know what it is called. It is the same colour as those invalid cars if that helps. I did get the registration though it was UMF 456M.

I promise I am not lieing and that it is the truth.

Your loyal son

Lee

Question after question flashed across her mind. Was this true? Was Lee imagining this, or was this some kind of fantasy? Was he lying and trying to get their mum in trouble for sending him to his room? Laura wasn't sure what to think or what to do, but she was sure that she couldn't allow Lee to keep this letter. She put it in the drawer of her bedside cabinet and headed downstairs with a book. Lee was sitting in the front room with the only book he could find. It was a large animal encyclopaedia that he had already read cover to cover.

Neither of the children spoke to each other whilst Mum cooked dinner in the kitchen. After what seemed like an age, but was really just after 4pm, David arrived home. Louvaine was surprisingly kind to him, offering him an alcoholic drink and telling him she was making his favourite for dinner – steak & kidney pudding, no less.

Lee put his book down and went to leave the front room, but Laura stood in his way. "You heard what Mum said!" she snarled.

"DAD, LAURA WON'T LET ME GO TO THE TOILET!" Lee shouted.

"Leave him alone, Laura," came the response from David. Lee pulled a face at Laura, accompanied by a rude finger gesture. Laura narrowed her eyes and pursed her lips, but didn't dare say anything back. Whilst David was Lee's only ally in the house, this only worked when he was physically there. It was never often enough for Lee, and he always missed his dad when he was away.

Lee shot upstairs and headed to the toilet. When he came out, he went to his room to see if he could find a toy to play with, despite what his mother had said. He also wanted to get the letter he'd written, but it was gone. He instantly knew who had it and cursed her under his breath. Lee softly trod along the landing to Laura's room. He knew he didn't have much time and searched in her bed, under her bed, near her toys and then finally in the bedside cabinet. *Found it*, he thought with relief. He quickly folded the letter, put it in his back pocket and went downstairs. He went into the front room where both he and Laura stared at each other for a while.

David noticed there was a bit of an atmosphere at the dinner table, but it usually blew over after a couple of hours or so. After dinner, they all sat in the front room to watch television. After ten minutes or so, David said, "Hey, Badger, I forgot to ask you – how was the match today?" Louvaine and Laura both stiffened.

"I didn't get to go to the match because Richard's dad was too ill," he replied, looking directly at his mum. Thinking quickly on his feet, Lee then added with a smile, "Can I watch Match of the Day with you tonight instead, Dad?" David agreed with a smile.

"That's way past your bedtime, Lee," his mum protested, but David just said, "One late night won't do him any harm, will it?" It was a rhetorical question and one his wife felt best not to press any further. Louvaine and Laura were now both angry at Lee – his mother because he had scored one against her, and Laura because she would end up going to bed before him that night.

Lee went over and sat down on the sofa next to David, who put his arm around him. Laura cast a look over in Lee's direction, but he just looked her right in the eye as if to say, "Got you this time!"

When Laura went to bed that night, the first thing she looked for was the letter. With it no longer there, she was furious that she'd been bested by a little kid. But she was stuck; she couldn't say anything to anyone. She hoped that Lee wouldn't say anything to their dad about it; he had no idea what the ramifications would be.

Sunday morning arrived and after having to go to Sunday School, which Lee detested, the best part of the day was about to begin. It was time to go and visit Nan.

David's mother Nancy lived on her own in a large four-bedroom house about eight miles away from where he worked. In her early sixties, she was a kind and feminine lady with old-fashioned views. David had clearly inherited her eyes, along with her sense of duty. She was about average height and every morning she would be up at 6am sharp to brush her greying hair to ensure she looked respectable. Lee never quite understood why she had this routine, which she duly carried out without exception, even on the weekends.

Lee had never known his grandfather, but there were pictures of him around the place and Nancy would often recite stories to him about what he did in the war. Nancy's husband had died in 1960. The circumstances of his death were never discussed, but it had had a far-reaching effect, leading her to question her Church of England upbringing and any belief in a god and forgiveness. She looked forward to having the family around whenever possible, especially engaging and spending time with the children. She loved her 'little detectives' as she'd call them, giving them puzzles and psychological tests to solve to expand their horizons. Her relationship with Louvaine could be a little testy sometimes; she never won an argument with Nancy, who had pin-holed her type and how she operated very quickly. Louvaine was jealous of this superior intellect and would often like to exert her own form of power by not letting the children visit when David was working.

Being a young detective was a great escape for Lee and he adored his nan immensely. They had worked out their own secret codes for words that required a combination of a physical movement with a specific facial expression. So far, she had taught him codes for Yes, No, Help, Danger, Anger and Fear. It was during a game of *Dominoes* that Lee tilted his head to the left and pursed his lips to the right. *HELP!* Nancy gave an imperceptible nod, and when they had finished the game said, "Oh, Lee, I forgot to tell you that I picked up a bag of plastic soldiers from a jumble sale, if you're interested? They're upstairs. Come on, you can help me bring them down if you like?" No-one else was really interested in plastic soldiers. Upstairs in one of the spare rooms, Nancy pulled out the bag from under a bed. It was indeed full of green plastic men. *Not all in the best condition*, Lee thought, *but definitely usable.*

With his left hand, Lee pulled out the letter he'd intended to give his dad from his back pocket and handed it to his nan. With his right hand he put one finger over his mouth. Nancy quickly read it and looked seriously at Lee with eyebrows raised.

"True?" she said. Lee just nodded slowly three times. "Don't do anything. Leave this with me, OK?" she said. Lee nodded just once. Nancy ushered Lee downstairs whilst she made sure to put the letter in a safe place.

* * *

CHAPTER 4

THE DETECTIVE

Come Sunday evening, David and the family eventually headed off home. Nancy hadn't seen the children for what seemed like ages, and truly missed their company. To her, they were chalk and cheese, so completely different in every way. Laura was probably a year or so ahead at school, but was being held back and should really have been pushed up a year. She was linear, a thinker, a strategist and could play chess to a very good standard. Lee, on the other hand, wasn't like this at all. He was all about having fun, taking risks, seeing what was on the other side, and observation. They were both fast learners, but in different ways. Laura used books to absorb material, whereas Lee only needed to see or be told something once.

After tidying up after everyone and making sure her home was back to immaculate, Nancy re-read Lee's letter. Trying to separate her emotions from her professional training, she contemplated the options. She could do nothing, tell David, confront Louvaine directly or even have the woman killed if she desired. Telling David seemed the most sensible next step, so she called him at work the next morning to ask him to pop over on the way home that day to help unstick her garage door. When David arrived, she made him a cup of coffee and they sat in the living room.

"David, I need you to be calm, but I have some bad news. I have a letter that you need to read, and I will tell you more once you've absorbed it." David read through the devastating letter and tensed. Nancy could see his fingers tighten around the edge of the paper.

"How did you get this? And in fact, why do you have it?"

"Lee gave it to me yesterday. My guess is that he didn't have the opportunity to give it to you personally, otherwise I think he would have ... it was written for you."

"That f*cking ungrateful bitch!" he exclaimed. "The sacrifices I make for her, for the family, to better ourselves!" Nancy wouldn't normally tolerate swearing in her presence and David knew it – but she gave him a free pass on this one. He hadn't deserved this deceit. She put her arm on his shoulder.

"What do you want to do?" she asked, keeping her voice calm.

David thought for a bit, taking his mind back to the atmosphere he encountered when he got home from work on Saturday. He stood up. Nancy knew this wasn't a good thing if she wanted him to keep calm.

"I'm going to confront her about it, show her the letter and make her explain herself," he said angrily.

"David!" she said sternly. "Look at the wider picture here. All you have is a letter from a six-year-old boy. Yes, he's provided some good information, but do you have any real evidence? Do you really think Louvaine will admit to it? Then what?" David sat down, completely deflated.

"So what, then? I should hire a private detective to get some evidence?" he questioned.

"Why not?" Nancy said. "It makes more sense to confront her with real evidence, doesn't it? At least you'll be 100% sure."

"There is no way Lee is lying about this!"

"I agree," Nancy said. "But any good divorce solicitor will dismiss this in a heartbeat." David was stunned.

"You think this will end up in a divorce?"

"What do you think? It's time to play the scenarios out, son. If it's not true, you'll always have doubts and you'll also have put Lee in a very bad position. If it is true, could you ever trust her, even if she swears never to do it again?"

Nancy stopped short of personally attacking her daughter-in-law. She knew that she was using David to better herself. She knew that there was no love in the marriage. She also suspected that Louvaine was mistreating Lee, but that was harder to prove. David turned away and stood motionless for a while. When he returned to face his mother, he agreed that she was right.

"But, Mum, I can't afford a private investigator right now. And, besides, Lou would know that I've taken money out of the account."

"There's someone I play bridge with who I think would be able to help you. I'll call her and get a meeting set up for Thursday or Friday after work. On whichever day it is, don't do any overtime. You'll need an alibi for being late home. And don't worry about the money for now. It's more important that we put your mind at rest, right?"

David's half-drunk coffee had gone cold. Nancy asked if he'd like her to make him another one but, looking at the time, he decided he needed to go home. They hugged one another, and then Nancy offered one other piece of advice.

"I know it's going to be difficult but try to act normally. I'll call you at work when I have more details."

David nodded and walked to his car. Once David was out of sight, Nancy closed the front door. She needed her address book; not the burgundy address book by the telephone, but a different black book that she stored in the safe in her bedroom. She took the book downstairs, laid it on the telephone table, thumbed her way down to 'K' on the alphabet cut-outs and called Kimberly Montrall.

Kim had only just finished the washing-up when she was surprised to hear her phone ringing. She didn't have a boyfriend and she'd only spoken to her parents the day before, so just after 9pm was definitely out the ordinary for receiving calls. Casually walking over to the phone, she picked up the receiver on the fourth ring.

"Hello?"

"Hello, Kim! It's been a while. I think I might have a job that suits your talents."

Kim instantly recognised who it was. When Kim had first joined 'The Service' ten years ago, Nancy had been her 'handler', but she now felt rather more like a former MI6 agent since her cover had been blown whilst posing as a nationalist supporter on a mission to undermine Francisco Franco four years ago. The amount of quality assignments she'd been given in the last three years could be counted on one finger. A good agent needs to constantly be in the field, and she'd worried about losing her skills. The Service still paid her a retainer, but this barely paid the bills. As a form of cover, she had set up an investigation agency, but this really wasn't pulling in the big cases she so desperately needed to pay the mortgage. She had effectively been ostracised. She was happy to hear from Nancy, hoping for something that would get her back into the good graces of those at Century House.

Nancy explained why she was calling and what was needed on this case. Kim didn't hide her disappointment. "Is this really a good use of my skill set? I'm better than this, Nancy."

Even in retirement, Nancy had been in receipt of service status reports every month for years and could completely understand Kim's frustrations. But what Kim hadn't realised was that the intelligence business could be very tricky and incestuous. It often took time and a significant change of appearance to redeploy a blown agent.

"I understand you're struggling at the moment, Kim, but I would see it as a personal favour if you took the job, and I will see if I can get your name back on the active roster."

So I have been benched! Kim thought.

"OK, I'll do it, but you'll have to pay my standard rates."

"Sounds perfectly reasonable to me. We all have to put food on the table, don't we?"

Nancy gave Kim all the details necessary for the operation: David's address (work and home), a description of his car, a description of Louvaine and where she worked, and the information about the man she was seeing. She dictated every line of Lee's letter and then confirmed with Kim which day she would meet David after work.

"And do not under any circumstances engage with the targets – this is reconnaissance only!"

"I know the job," Kim said stiffly. She knew that this was part of the reason her cover had been blown four years ago.

"I just want to be clear," Nancy said, and then hung up the phone. She would call David at work tomorrow to give him the details. Kim went and sat down in her living room. She lived in a small single-story apartment above her office, which sounded convenient but could also sometimes be a burden. She picked up her diary and began putting a plan together. She had agreed to meet with David on the Thursday, with her hunch being that Friday night would be her first actual day on the job. Her nightclub days had been pretty non-existent since leaving university. She hadn't gone to Oxford or Cambridge like many of the other recruits but had actually been courted at Loughborough. Her first few weeks in the job were quite difficult. The self-entitled nerds from Oxbridge had made sure she was treated as third class, not even worthy of being in the same room. But Kim had gone to Loughborough for a reason; she loved sports and was particularly adept at hockey and judo.

On a particular occasion when one of the 'guys' had continually prodded her on the way to one of their classes, Kim had snapped. She'd spun around, grabbed the man's finger and snapped it. When he had fallen to the floor screaming and cursing in agony, she had then driven her heel into his left eye socket. He never made it past training, but her card was also marked from above and she was nearly removed from The Service. It was Nancy who'd backed her at the tribunal. She definitely owed Nancy a few debts. Kim went to her bedroom wardrobe to see whether she had anything that could possibly pass for nightclub attire. She did have one dress she'd used on a case a couple of years back but it would stick out like a sore thumb now, such was the change in fashion these days. A shopping expedition would be a welcome distraction tomorrow.

By the time David got home that evening, both the children were in bed and Louvaine was just sitting with her legs up, watching television. She'd had the decency to ask how his day was and told him there was some dinner in the oven that could be heated up if he wanted it, but David was exhausted and didn't really feel like eating... or talking.

The next day Kim decided that, rather than waste time going to the nightclub three nights in a row and risk being exposed, she would find out the registered address of the vehicle Lee had seen. She made a call to a contact she had at the Driver and Vehicle Licensing Centre in Swansea, who said it would take a couple of hours and cost £50. With no other cases on, Kim went shopping – she had a dress to buy.

On the Thursday, as agreed, Kim parked herself outside the main gate of the manufacturing plant where David worked. She had an aging Morris Marina, which she hated, but it was all she could afford. Making sure she would be in a position to see all entries and exits, Kim waited patiently for David to arrive at the exit gate. She flashed her headlights at him and proceeded to turn her car around, gesturing for him to follow. He followed her for a couple of miles when Kim indicated left to enter a car park of a nearby pub. She got out of her car and walked over to David's, gestured for him to unlock the passenger door and duly sat herself inside.

"Hi, my name is Kim. Your mother has asked me to help you." They shook hands. To David, Kim's handshake and overall demeanour was very business-like. She was quite tall at about 5ft 7in, with attractive dark hair that had plenty of body to it. The way her hair moved reminded him of the models on the Harmony Hairspray adverts he'd seen recently. She wore tight-fitting trousers and a brown corduroy jacket that was only buttoned once. Her face wasn't anything to write home about, probably a five out of ten if he was talking to his mates. She had a sort of Mediterranean look and the pores on her cheeks were very large and open.

Kim wanted to get straight down to business. She asked him a series of questions, making notes as she went along.

"Is this week the first indication that something was wrong?"

"How long has Louvaine been working at the nightclub?"

"What times does she leave/get home usually?"

"Does she always get home at the same time?"

"How does she get to the club and home again?"

"Does the description in Lee's letter ring any bells to you?"

During this questioning, Kim was gauging David's reactions as well as his actual answers. He didn't seem like the type to over-react, but she had learned that some people were better at masking their feelings than others. Finally, she asked, "If I find out that she is cheating, what will you do with the information?"

David just stared off into the distance. Finally back in the moment, he just murmured, "I just don't know yet."

Kim briefed him on what was likely to happen but did not disclose the entirety of her plan. Sometimes giving too much information to a client could lead to over-expectation on results.

"I'm not going to give you my card, just in case someone finds it at home. I will be in touch through Nancy and I'll give her an update as soon as I have something. You <u>must</u> be patient. I promise you that if there's something going on, I'll find it. Meanwhile, try to act normally when you're at home. It is imperative that you maintain all of your normal activities. Do you understand?" David nodded despondently. Kim put a consoling hand on his as she left the car. "Don't worry, I'm good at this."

That night, Kim sat in her car fifty yards away from a cobalt blue Hillman Imp. Whilst on her stakeout she began to apply make-up, doing her best to remove five years from her appearance. In a bag behind her seat was the new dress and shoes she had bought. She hoped she'd at least get to use them again someday, and maybe even get herself a guy. *Not much chance in this line of work.* On the front passenger seat was her camera bag, complete with zoom lens. There was a remote tape-recording device in there as well, but it was unlikely to be any good in a nightclub. The dress didn't get any use that night, and so at 2am she headed off back home.

Friday night came and at 7pm Kim was in a spot approximately eighty yards down the road from UMF 456M. At 9:15pm, it was beginning to look like another boring night when she saw movement near the proximity of the Imp. A young-ish guy had got in the car but wasn't going anywhere. She could hear a car engine constantly turning over and realised that perhaps hers wasn't so bad after all. The description of the man matched what little the boy had provided, so she stood by on alert. Eventually the blue car pulled out and spluttered off down the road towards a T-junction. Kim started her car but was in no rush to be right on his tail. The target pulled into an underground car park to the north of the town centre, which she already knew was the nearest one to the club. He wore a tight green shirt and even tighter brown trousers; she could see why David's wife might find him attractive. Kim parked up and hopped into the back of her car.

The car park was dimly lit so she felt OK getting changed in her car. Making sure she was dressed and composed, she took her miniature Minox C out of her camera bag and slipped it into her small clutch bag. At about 4.5 inches long and 1 inch wide, it would be barely perceptible in a nightclub environment; in fact, Kim had perfected the art of taking pictures whilst making the camera look like a perfume atomiser. With everything set, she headed off to the club. At the entrance, the doorman had asked why she was on her own. Kim just said that she was meeting a couple of girlfriends, and that they'd probably already be inside by now. He let her in just before 10pm, so she didn't have to pay.

Inside, Kim had almost forgotten what nightclubs were like. It took a minute or two for her eyes to adjust to the bright flashing lights as the beams searched their way through the fog of cigarette smoke. She didn't really recognise the disco music they were playing, but it felt pretty good. She did a circuit of the club, taking the whole place in and scoping out which bar David's wife was behind. Nancy's description had been spot-on; Louvaine's bar was packed, and she was busy serving. Kim hadn't seen the blond guy yet, but there was plenty of time for that.

Kim needed cover. Being on your own in a club environment could be torturous, and eventually people would begin to notice. Girls would think she was a bit strange, and guys would start to flock in like vultures. She needed to be part of a group and saw three girls dancing at the edge of the dance floor to a funky track which the DJ introduced as Dazz by Brick. She went over and spoke in the ear of the one she suspected was the de facto leader.

"Excuse me," she said. "Would you mind if I joined you? I split up with my boyfriend yesterday and it's hard having fun on your own."

The three girls probably averaged about twenty years old, so adding Kim to their little group added another six years to that. But their 'leader' was cool and just said, "Of course you can! What's your name?" Kim introduced herself to all three. She had no need for any false name that night. Dancing with the girls was fun; she didn't know all the latest moves but did what she could to keep up with the other three. They went back and forth to the bar; guys glided in with their smooth moves and chat-up lines. The group giggled and gossiped about 'the talent' around the place, all making their choices of who they'd give the invitation signals to. Kim hadn't had this much fun in a long time; she actually felt much more relaxed here than when she'd been twenty at the University bars and clubs.

But throughout all of this fun, Kim made sure she had a line of sight to the bar where Louvaine was serving. It looked as though she was going for a break and, sure enough, Kim could see the blond man head round to the side of the bar to liaise; she still didn't know his name yet. Kim made her excuses to freshen up and headed towards the ladies' toilets near the bar. She took the Minox out of her bag, held it up to her throat with her right hand as if about to spray perfume, and quickly took two pictures of the couple as she walked towards the toilets.

Louvaine had given Jon the usual signal to say that she was going on her break. By the side of the bar, Louvaine was a little anxious. She apologised again about the situation they had both ended up being in on Saturday and for not telling him about having children. Jon said that it was just unfortunate, that was all. He then asked her a question that made her pause on the spot.

"Do you think you'd like to have any more children?" he asked, with a genuine look on his face. This was something she had definitely not wanted to do with David. She was about to open her mouth to say no, when she paused again. Louvaine smiled and drew Jon closer.

"You know, I hadn't really thought about it." She put her head in the nook of his shoulder and placed her arms around his neck. Jon put his arms around her waist.

Kim felt that two minutes in the toilet was long enough. As she came out, she could see the couple in an embrace. *Stay right there in that pose*, she thought, as if she was David Bailey on a photo shoot. She managed five shots this time, with the two lovers still none the wiser. *At least one of those will be OK.* She went back to the dance floor, where the other girls were really getting down to KC & The Sunshine Band. It was a great song and the dance floor was packed. The blond guy had moved away from the bar and Kim still had one more mission. She pointed in the direction of a group of lads and asked the girls if they knew who the blond one was. One said she thought his name was Jon, but couldn't be sure. The leader commented, "Get back in the saddle, darlin'!" Kim smiled. She had to take a risk and be sure of the name for her report.

Kim walked over towards the group, lost her balance and fell, knocking over a table where a few of them had left their lagers. Kim acted embarrassed. She'd made sure not to let the drinks spill in her direction, but when trying to get up she brushed herself down anyway. One of the men gallantly helped her up and asked if she was alright.

"I'm so sorry! Had a bit too much to drink and I haven't got used to these shoes yet."

One guy laughed. "My sister's the same."

"Do you want me to replace your drinks?" Kim asked. The group all looked at each other. The drinks had been nearly full, and they weren't made of money.

The man who had helped her up said, "I'm not that bothered, but the others will be; they were all fresh pints. I'll come to the bar with you, and we'll work something out," as he turned and winked to the rest of his mates.

Kim smiled. It was pretty decent of him. The bar was about two deep, so the man asked Kim what her name was.

"I'm Kim. What's yours?"

"I'm Trevor. But just call me Trev." Pointing at his friends, he said, "That's Dave, that's Mike, Jon and that's Ben - but we just call him Dover!" Kim looked at Trevor and they both burst out laughing. Trev was a bit of a wide-boy, but he definitely knew how to hit the funny bone.

They talked for a bit whilst getting the drinks, but Kim now just needed her exit strategy. She rifled around her bag and pulled out a £5 note. "Will this cover the drinks?" she asked. Trevor smiled. He was on to a winner here, a girl with her own money and didn't mind spending it. Kim made an excuse to go to the Ladies, but instead headed out of the main entrance and back to the underground car park.

Once inside her car, Kim changed back into her jeans, t-shirt and thick jumper. She was glad to be rid of the evening shoes, swapping them for a pair of black Gola sneakers. She placed her Canon F1 camera on the dashboard under a blanket, making sure the settings and focus length were all correct, and then just waited.

Although Louvaine's shift officially ended at 2am, all of the barmaids were still required to tidy the bar area afterwards. This was unpaid work and so they would only do what was absolutely necessary to collect their wages and get out of the place. At the rear entrance of the club, Jon was waiting. It was 2:20am and Louvaine was tired. Jon put his arm around her as they walked down to the car park.

Kim spotted them in the distance as they walked towards his car and clicked the shutter release a couple of times.

Jon and Louvaine got in the car. Louvaine didn't look at Jon whilst he got frustrated trying to start the motor. On the fourth turnover it spluttered into life. "You should probably get that seen to," she suggested. Jon gave her a knowing look. They talked about a number of things on their journey, the key conversation being whether they should continue seeing each other. Louvaine was very warm towards him when she said, "I'll understand if you don't want to have any more to do with me, what with two kids and a husband." Jon kissed her on the side of the mouth whilst driving.

"I can't speak for your husband, but I don't mind kids." He shrugged. "Let's just see how things go, yeah?"

As they approached within a mile of her home, she said, "Drop me at the top of the road; we can't be seen together by anyone."

Kim had kept a pretty good distance behind them as they headed off. From the route they were taking they could only be heading towards Louvaine's home. As they got closer and closer, Kim knew that things could get tricky for her. As Jon had taken a particular right turn and was briefly out of sight, Kim switched off her headlights. She continued to follow. Her hunch was correct, and they slowed down and pulled up at the top of Louvaine's road. Luckily for Kim, it was under a reasonably bright lamp post. Kim cut her engine and pulled to the opposite side of the road about one hundred and twenty yards back. Camera in hand, she zoomed in to focus on the silhouettes inside the car, making sure to also include the car number plate. She now had them kissing, and for extra measure took photos when Louvaine got out of the car.

A night's work well done, Kimi! she thought to herself as she drove home. The next day, after dropping off the films at a discreet photo developer who made a decent living processing 'adult material,' Kim wrote up her notes into reports for David and Nancy. The following Monday morning, Kim contacted Nancy and they agreed to meet at 12 o'clock over some lunch at Nancy's home. Kim put the reports on the table along with her invoice. Nancy put on her spectacles and read through one of the reports, glancing at the pictures as she went along. She sat and thought for a while.

"Thank you, Kim. This is very good work."

Kim smiled. "You will put in a good word for me, won't you?" she asked.

"A promise is a promise," Nancy responded. "But there's just one more thing I'd like you to do, if you wouldn't mind?"

"What's that?"

"Can you meet David and present the report to him yourself? I think he needs to feel that he's the client." Giving this sort of bad news to any client was always the crappy part of the job. Kim had yet to deliver any good news about a suspected cheating spouse and clients could be very unpredictable.

"Of course. Can you give me his work number?"

At just after 6pm that evening, in a discreet corner of the same pub they'd driven to before, Kim presented an envelope to David. She could see he was devastated as he looked at the pictures. "I'm very sorry," she said. She genuinely meant it but didn't want to get emotionally involved. David eventually thanked her and asked her to leave so he could gather his thoughts. He ordered another pint of 'Dutch courage' and rehearsed in his mind what he would say to confront his wife.

When David arrived home, Louvaine had the audacity to moan at him for being late. It was if he was the one having the affair, badgering him on where he had been. David finally snapped and shoved the envelope right under her nose.

"READ THAT!" he shouted.

"Don't shout at me!" she roared back. "You'll wake the kids up!" So angry now, David quickly raised his hand to hit her round the face.

She'd never seen him like this before and flinched instinctively. David stopped himself, instead shouting at her to get out of his sight and read what was in the envelope. Louvaine ran off to the kitchen and closed the door. She was seriously worried now. What the hell could this be?

David had made his mind up. He just wanted to be away from the unfaithful woman. He went upstairs, grabbed a suitcase from the top of the wardrobe and started packing clothes, shoes, suits and anything else he could see that would be useful. He walked across the landing to the bathroom and took a bunch of toiletries. Both of the children had been woken up by the commotion downstairs. As David made his way back to his suitcase, Lee popped his head out of his bedroom door. Laura had also got up but didn't come out of her room. She sat on the floor with her ear at the door to listen. David got down on one knee and put his arm around the boy.

"I'm sorry, son, but I have to go." Lee realised that his dad must've read the letter but was still devastated at being told the bad news. Any foundations he thought he had were about to be swept away. *Surely it's Mum who should leave?* he thought.

Louvaine had only needed to see the pictures to realise the trouble she was in as she came out of the kitchen. David turned and looked at her as she stood on the stairs.

"Your mother is a nasty piece of work and a whore – a dirty, filthy, ungrateful little whore!"

Louvaine didn't say anything. Lee didn't know what a whore was but, given the venomous way in which it was said, a dictionary wasn't necessary. He completely agreed with his dad and said, "Can I go with you?" Louvaine looked at him as though he was a traitor.

"I'm sorry, son, but not right now; we'll sort things out, I promise." David kissed Lee on the forehead and went back to the suitcase. Worried and afraid, Laura finally opened her bedroom door. When David had finished packing, he gave Laura a hug and a kiss and said, "Everything will be alright. I'll see you soon, sweetheart."

As David turned the corner to make his way down the stairs, Louvaine quickly headed back down to make sure she was not in his way. When he'd reached the bottom, she said, "I'm sorry, David. Please, let me explain. It won't happen again. Please let me explain!"

"The pictures tell me everything I need to know, and the fact that you brought him here into my home... you f*cking slut!"

Louvaine's face changed in a heartbeat. From passivity to anger, like a coiled rattlesnake she instantly verbally attacked him.

"It's all your fault, anyway. I wouldn't need anyone else if you came home at a decent time. I'm practically here on my own looking after the kids all the time! Yeah, that's right, go on and get lost. Go back to Mummy!"

David held his temper, put his suitcase in the car and drove off. Louvaine stomped upstairs. "Go back to bed, you two. I don't want to hear a peep out of either of you until the morning." Laura and Lee went back into their rooms, both scared and anxious about what they'd witnessed. Lee was crushed and a little angry that his dad had left without him. *Can't he see what they're like when I'm on my own with them?* That night Lee cried.

Laura also went to bed feeling crushed. She loved her father, but her thoughts had already turned to her brother. Lee must have given him the letter somehow. Her blood boiled. *What has he done?* Whilst he had always been an annoyance to her, she now vowed to make him pay for what he had done to her and her mother.

Louvaine sat in the living room in tears. *What have I done? How could I have been so stupid? What must the kids think of me now?* Thoughts swirled around her mind until they became vengeful, justifying her behaviour and seeking ways to make David and Lee pay.

* * *

CHAPTER 5

TWICE THE HEARTBREAK

Three months after David had confronted Louvaine with the evidence, things had not gone well. After turning up at his mother's with a suitcase, Nancy had been kind but admonished him for leaving the family home because he'd instantly put himself in a position of weakness. It wasn't exactly what he wanted to hear, but he knew she was right. What subsequently happened proved that point very clearly. He stayed with Nancy for a while, but in his mind he knew it would only be a temporary arrangement. As much as he loved her, his mother could also be quite difficult and strict at times, and he wasn't a child anymore. David eventually moved out just before Christmas into a very small flat by himself. Though not much, he preferred the solitude when he got home, rather than dealing with the searching questions from his mother. Of course, it didn't stop the thoughts of Louvaine's unfaithfulness chiselling away at the back of his mind, and he found that the only way he could deal with them was to bury his head in work during the week.

Louvaine restricted much of their communication to nasty letters via a solicitor, defining all the rules of engagement. David was able to see the children on the weekends and he was to pick them up and drop them off at specific times; the exception being Christmas when he was only allowed Boxing Day, which happened to fall on a Sunday. Louvaine had received this advice, and the recommendation of a slimy solicitor, from a friend who had really gone to town on her ex-husband. The solicitor had done this many times before and had even prepared a plan of action for her to achieve the outcomes she wanted.

Nancy ensured that Christmas was still a special time for the kids. Her decorations were up and, come Boxing Day, she prepared a wonderful table of chocolate squares, peanuts, crisps and clementines ready for when they arrived. David and Nancy had jointly bought presents for them, with Laura receiving a set of classic novels and Lee getting an Action Man soldier with accessories. They both received a customary annual – Jackie for Laura, and the Beano for Lee.

On weekdays, Lee began to feel like an outcast within his own family. Now completely out-gunned by the females, he had been restricted in what he was allowed to do. Unable to watch any of the television programs he liked, they would take turns in telling him off or ordering him around. Laura took a keen interest in setting him up for trouble. Whether it was hiding his stuff, planting her belongings in his room, blaming him for something being broken or just staring at him, she would constantly apply pressure to provoke a reaction; that reaction would then be punished by Mum. When word got around at school that David had left, Laura had put it about that it was because of Lee, and that his father hadn't really liked him. Lee knew better and would refute any claim with his fists to anyone that said otherwise. This of course got him in trouble at school and again at home. Lee's only solace had been to play down the park with friends when he was allowed, or to play by himself in his room.

Weekends were different, however. Lee would feel the great weight lift from his shoulders once his dad pulled up outside on a Saturday morning. He would run out of the front door and push past Laura to try to get 'dibs' on the front passenger seat.

David and Louvaine would barely speak to each other, with the exception of Louvaine barking out some kind of order or criticism. "You're late!", "You're too early!" and "I want them home by 4 o'clock on Sunday!" were classic examples. But it seemed that each week things would get worse. Louvaine would say that David was not allowed past the front door, then the next week not on the doorstep, the week after that not past the front gate, and so on. She was following her plan; each time David complied, not wishing to cause a scene or upset the children. It still made him angry. After all, he was still paying the rent for the damn house that he wasn't allowed in.

David would take the children round to his mother's. He didn't take them round to Louvaine's parents just on principle – that was up to her. It wasn't that he didn't like them, far from it; it was just the fact that he wanted to be selfish for his and Nancy's sake for once. Besides, Louvaine's parents could come and see the kids anytime during the week. The weekend was his time, and no-one was going to interfere with that.

Nancy loved having the children round. It was a healthy neutral ground for everyone. She made sure that Laura's divisive behaviours towards Lee were not rewarded and tried to instil less combative behaviours between them both. It didn't always work. Bright and early every Sunday morning, Nancy would be up making cakes. The sweet smell would engulf her home and it would be a fight as to who got up first and got to lick out the cake bowl. When David was able to take them out, the activities were centred mostly on male pursuits, although they'd sometimes go to the odd bazaar or museum. But Laura missed her dancing classes and mentioned this to her mother when she got home.

Through her solicitor, Louvaine ordered David to not pick the children up until 1:30pm on Saturdays, so that Laura could go back to her ballet classes. This rankled with both David and Lee. Jealous that Laura was getting to do an activity, Lee asked if he could do football training on Saturday mornings. At 15p a session it was nowhere near as expensive as ballet, but the answer from his mother had been a firm 'no' as they couldn't afford it!

During the time when the children were with David, Louvaine had begun to invite Jon round on a fairly regular basis. With the house empty they could and would do anything they wanted. For Lou, the carnal activities were particularly enjoyable. After nine years with David, the physical side of her marriage had virtually disappeared. On the rare occasion when they did have sex, Louvaine would find herself fantasising about other men. Things were different with Jon though. He was from a new generation and would often suggest things to her that she'd initially baulk at. But she liked the way he began to corrupt her.

Jon suggested the possibility of seeing each other during the week. Living at his parents had been suffocating for a while now, and so Louvaine agreed. Initially, she allowed Jon to come round after the children had gone to bed. The kids could hear his arrivals, as well as laughter and movement downstairs, but didn't say anything. Louvaine eventually invited Jon over at an earlier time so that he could be formally introduced. The first meeting had been a little awkward, as all forced meetings are. He arrived just as the two were going to bed and said 'hi' in a friendly way. Laura smiled at him and curtsied as if in 'fourth position.' Lee didn't smile. Confirming in his mind that this was the man he'd seen in the hallway all that time ago, he was not going to welcome him into the home with open arms. He said nothing. Jon decided not to really push the issue, but Lou ordered Lee to mind his manners and say hello. Lee had no choice but to capitulate. With the initial meeting out of the way, Jon became a regular visitor to the house, sometimes stopping by after work in the evenings for dinner before heading off home. Each time, Laura was the more accepting of the children, with Lee quite resolute that he was a usurper and doing nothing to encourage his further presence. It was during this time that something changed for Louvaine; she'd been to the doctors and a test confirmed that she was pregnant.

Seeking further legal advice from her solicitor, Louvaine began putting new plans in place, the first of which was to divide and conquer. In addition to ballet classes, Laura had previously shown an interest in learning the guitar at school and had enquired whether it would be possible to do a course of lessons. Louvaine had originally dismissed it because of financial constraints, but she now changed her mind and told Jon to give Laura the good news that they could enrol her in January after all. Laura jumped at the chance without realising the consequences. When she came home from school one day the week after, Louvaine happily told her that they had managed to get her into some classes. Unfortunately, however, they could only get Saturday afternoons due to Laura being at ballet in the mornings. Seeing that

Laura was torn between disappointment and excitement, her mother said, "Don't worry. You can just do the course of ten and see whether you like it or not."

The second part of the plan was to let Laura call David to tell him how excited she was to be taking guitar lessons. David found this hard to take, the pain transiting from his heart to his throat. On the one hand, he didn't want to shame his daughter into not doing something she was clearly eager to do, but he just wondered when he'd get to see her again. Laura sensed this and promised, "I'll be able to see you when I've finished the course, and I'll be able to play you a song!" David had nearly choked up on the other end.

Laura gloated to Lee that she'd now also convinced their mother to pay for guitar lessons, knowing full well that Lee hadn't even been allowed to go football training. Lee was understandably furious at the one-sidedness of life in the household, and just wanted to hit the big chin she was jutting out at him when she broke the news. But on reflection there would be an upside for him – he would get the weekend out of prison, and his dad, to himself!

The following few weekends were great for Lee. There was no atmosphere in the car journeys and he and his dad were free to do what they wanted, like drive well above legal speeds with the radio blaring and heads out of the windows and go to football matches. Lee also got the cake mix to himself. There were times when David had to go to work on a Saturday; on those occasions he either took Lee with him or dropped him off at Nancy's. Sometimes, and always separately, either David or Nancy would ask Lee questions about what was going on at home. Lee knew what they were doing; he even knew that Nancy was sometimes asking on his dad's behalf, but he chose not to disclose too much. After writing the letter, and his dad not taking him when he'd had the chance, Lee had seen what too much information could do and didn't want to make his own situation any worse than it already was. He thought that any information was bound to get back to his mother sooner or later.

It was a Friday night when the first bombshell hit. Lee was standing in the hallway and Louvaine was arguing on the phone with David again in her usual hostile manner. Like an airborne poison, it didn't really matter where anyone was in the house – Louvaine wanted to contaminate everyone with what she was saying. After a particularly nasty tirade, she casually tagged on, "Oh, and Laura doesn't want to see you anymore either!" It was as if she was so annoyed that she'd just blurted it out. This was really how to kill two birds with one stone. Both David and Lee had been on the receiving end of her toxicity over the past months, but this rocked them both to the core. On the other end of the phone, partially dumbstruck, David said, "Don't do this, Lou!"

Laura was in the kitchen when her mother ordered her to come to the phone.

"Tell your dad that you don't want to see him anymore," she said, handing the receiver to the young girl. Rather than say something that might anger her mother, she didn't fight the decision at all.

"I'm sorry, Dad, but I don't want to see you anymore," Laura repeated weakly.

Lee couldn't believe the betrayal he had just seen. He vowed there and then that he would not let this happen to him. The following day was a difficult one for David and the children. He came to collect Lee in a very sombre mood. David walked to the front door to try and get access to Laura and speak with her face to face, but Louvaine very proudly and forcefully barred his way. She threatened to call the police if he didn't get off the property right away. David had never been one for confrontation and Lou knew it. He backed down again and returned to the car with Lee. Lee knew what he would have done in that situation and couldn't understand why his dad wasn't the same.

When Louvaine hired the solicitor, David couldn't deal with the onslaught. Working twelve-hour days had taken a toll on his energy levels and morale. Though Nancy advised him to see a solicitor of his own, he initially refused. For one, he really couldn't afford it and, two, he felt that if he was reasonable and patient things would work out OK. He was incorrect on both counts, and now that Lou had the upper hand David had no leverage to do anything whatsoever. This caused some friction between him and Nancy, and for most weekends Lee would be taken care of by his nan with his dad making general appearances here and there. It was one of the reasons David rented the flat.

After David told Nancy about no longer being able to see Laura, she'd clearly shown her displeasure with him and his handling of the situation. He told her to stop interfering and to let him handle things. Luckily, Lee had been out playing because Nancy was a force to be reckoned with. She really tore into David and in the end he just walked out, not to be seen until it was time to take Lee back home.

On the Monday when she knew the children would be at school, Nancy called Louvaine. At first, she used kindness to try and persuade the woman to let David see Laura, but Louvaine was belligerent.

"She doesn't want to see him anymore. She already told him that on the phone!"

Nancy finally snapped. "I know that's a lie. You told her to say that, didn't you?"

"Don't you dare call me a liar! Count yourself lucky I let you see Lee. My solicitor told me that I will be getting the kids, and David will have to pay for it. Now don't call here again!"

Nancy was seething. Who the hell was this tramp to speak to her, and treat her son, like this? Nancy spent the rest of the day thinking about what to do about Louvaine. What she really wanted was for the woman to disappear from the face of the earth. She could definitely make that happen, but when thought through none of the potential interventions would really work. Whatever the plan, either David or the kids would be hurt in some way. Whilst she had access to resources she'd acquired over the years of active service, it was absolutely frowned upon to take personal matters into one's own hands.

Having seen how easy it was to stop David having access to Laura, Louvaine saw the opportunity to do the same with Lee. But Lee was a much tougher prospect. Knowing that Lee was closer to his father, she wanted to drive a wedge between them. As Jon had been staying over between three and five nights a week, it made sense to her for him to live with them. On a weekend whilst they had the place to themselves, and after some strenuous bedroom activity, Louvaine whispered in his ear to ask if he'd like to move in. Jon readily agreed to the idea but was wary of Lee's resistance towards him. Louvaine was understanding and suggested that maybe he could take Lee out for the odd day or afternoon to see if they could bond better. Jon said he'd give it a try, but inside felt that the boy just needed a bit more male discipline.

That Sunday evening, just before the children's bedtime, Louvaine announced that Jon would be moving into the home. Laura smiled politely, whilst Lee just looked down at the floor, not wishing to show the disappointment on his face. Jon offered to take the kids up to their bedrooms.

"You kids pop upstairs, and I'll be with you in just a tick," he said.

As the two children made their way upstairs, Jon went into the kitchen. Out of a duffel bag he pulled out a new Polaroid camera he'd bought to have some fun with. He went into Lee's room first and showed it to him. Lee grudgingly looked at it. As interesting as it was, Lee was still upset by the earlier announcement and found it hard to show any enthusiasm. He could see that Jon was trying, but to Lee Jon just wasn't his dad. Whatever the man did, his loyalty would always be to his father. Jon asked Lee if he wanted his picture taken, but Lee just politely declined. So, he bid Lee goodnight and headed into Laura's room.

Laura was fascinated by the camera. The fact that it had a built-in flash and could produce a picture on the spot was just amazing to her.

"Let's test it out," Jon said. He took a quick picture of her face and once the instant colour film popped out said, "Right, now you just need to wave it like a fan for sixty seconds." Excited, Laura waved as instructed. She smiled as her face began to appear.

"Can I keep it?"

"Of course. How about one for me?" Jon asked.

"Can I do one of my ballet poses?" Jon smiled.

"Sure… let me just step back a little."

Laura chose an 'Arabesque' pose, as this was one of the hardest and one she was most proud of. Jon took the picture and sat next to Laura on the bed whilst it developed. It was a little blurred around the raised leg, as Laura had not been able to maintain its height for long enough, but they both smiled. Laura asked if she could take one of him, but Jon said he didn't have much film left so they'd have to do it another time. Laura smiled and got into bed, and Jon put out the light on his way downstairs. Downstairs he showed Lou the picture before placing it on the living room mantelpiece.

Jon had been a permanent resident for three weeks when Louvaine announced the 'wonderful news' to him. He was over the moon that he was going to be a father. He'd been brought up in quite a strict Anglican family and Louvaine was Catholic by denomination. Though not quite as strict as their upbringings, they both agreed that they wanted to keep the baby. They also agreed not to tell the children yet. They went out to celebrate the next day.

Jon tried to do what Lou had asked of him and spend more time with Lee. But no matter what he tried, Lee saw this as a form of bribery to try and win him over. With only so much imagination and willingness to hit his head against a brick wall, Jon gave up on the idea of trying to win Lee around. Louvaine was angry at how ungrateful Lee was. As a punishment, Lee wasn't allowed to see his dad. She hadn't bothered to call David, who only found out when he'd arrived to pick Lee up on the Saturday. Both Lee and David were upset that day, but Louvaine was proud of herself and Laura was now happy that she was beginning to get Jon's attention.

The following week was a bad one for Lee. Forced to be separated from his father, he reacted badly at school and at home. At school he got into fights and was belligerent in class, answering the teacher back on a number of occasions. This necessitated Louvaine being called to the school twice. Having had to apologise for the boy's behaviour, she was more worried about her reputation. On the first occasion, Lee arrived home to be told to go straight to bed with no dinner. On the second occasion, Louvaine was told to take Lee out of school that day. When they arrived home, Lee received a heavy smack across the side of the face and was told that he would not be receiving any lunch or dinner. She also said that any more bad behaviour would lead to him not seeing his dad again the next Saturday.

When Laura got home from school she was told not to talk to Lee as he'd been naughty and must stay in his room. Not wishing to pass up an opportunity, Laura went upstairs, immediately opened Lee's door, popped her head through the gap and stuck out her tongue. Lee had heard her ascend the stairs and was waiting for her. As she stuck her head through the door, Lee barged at it with his shoulder. Laura's head bumped against the wooden door surround. She yelped in pain. As she tried to withdraw herself from the situation, Lee barged the door again, managing to trap her fingers. She let out a scream this time. Laura pushed back, managing to free her fingers, but the noise of the commotion had now sealed Lee's fate. Louvaine stormed upstairs and immediately went to Laura, conveniently forgetting what she'd just told her a minute earlier. After checking that her fingers were OK, she stormed into Lee's room like a crazed banshee and hit out at whatever body part she could connect with.

But the second blows hit twice as hard as the first. Early on the following Saturday morning, Lou called David. He hadn't made the last rent payment and she'd received a letter from the landlord stating that the family would be evicted if the payment wasn't received within seven days. When Louvaine complained, David tried his hand at playing hardball: "When you let me see the children, I'll think about making the payment!" Not liking being cornered, Louvaine only had vengeful thoughts on her mind.

"Lee!" she yelled out to the front room. Lee had been listening to one side of the conversation. He couldn't wait to talk to his dad and rushed to the phone.

"Tell your father you don't want to see him anymore." Lee paused. He couldn't believe what he was being asked to do. Louvaine stared at the young boy's face and pushed the phone receiver into it.

Tears welled in his eyes as Lee said, "No!"

Louvaine pulled a great clump of Lee's hair back, simultaneously threatening a smack around the head with the telephone receiver. With great difficulty Lee said, "I can't see you anymore." Seeing the boy distraught and in tears, Louvaine wanted to press home the message.

"Tell him you DON'T want to see him anymore!" Lee initially refused, so his mother followed through with her threat. Lee couldn't believe what he was about to say. "I'm... I'm sorry, Dad... I... I don't want to see you anymore." Louvaine snatched the receiver back from Lee's hand.

"There you go," she said. "That's what you get for not paying the rent!" She slammed the phone down on David and finally let Lee's hair go. Lee was devastated at what had just happened. He'd done the very thing he had sworn to never do and been as disloyal as his mother and sister. He wished he could stand up to his mother, stand up to everyone who had been pushing him around for so long. He hated her and everything she stood for. As he walked up to his bedroom in tears, Lee wondered if he'd ever see his father again.

David was completely devastated. He had played the one card his solicitor said would work, and it had backfired in the most dramatic fashion. He thought about going round to the house but knew that no matter what happened, Louvaine would call the police and he'd end up in a cell. He didn't want to set a bad example for the children.

Lee didn't come down from his room that day, other than for food. All of his thoughts were of hate and vengeance. He couldn't understand why his mother was doing this to his dad. But most of all, he couldn't understand why his dad was allowing this to happen.

* * *

PART 3

(February 1977 - November 1977)

CHAPTER 6

UPROOT

The fallout from the divorce was completely one-sided in the end. Louvaine's solicitor wiped the floor with David, painting him as an uncaring ogre who was never at home. The court granted her full custody of the children, along with a hefty maintenance penalty for David. His reward for all the money he had spent on his own solicitor, and effectively hers, was rent for a home he no longer lived in, child maintenance, a huge debt and no access to his own children. The decree nisi would just be a matter of process.

David broke the news to Nancy, knowing full well what her reaction would be. She was furious with him, naturally. He'd allowed the foul woman to get the better of him. She was concerned for the children and, though angry with her son, concerned for him too. David couldn't bear talking about the situation any more than he had to. He felt like a complete failure. He couldn't even stop paying the maintenance for risk of going to prison. The only way he was going to help himself was to earn more money to pay off the debt. With a potential promotion coming up, he made sure that his entire focus was on work and nothing else. This also meant staying out of his mother's way for a while. On the occasions when he wasn't working, he would sometimes just sit watching television, his eyes blankly staring at the box in the corner of the living room as he pictured the children playing in his mind. On the odd occasion, he would pop down to the local pub to drown his sorrows over a few pints.

When Louvaine announced the outcome of the divorce hearing to the children, there was no response from either of them. She'd told them that they would no longer see their father and, looking at Lee specifically, stated that Jon *will* be their dad from now on. Laura went upstairs to her room and sat on her bed. Looking at herself in the mirror, she knew that she was partially to blame by taking the guitar lessons. But she wasn't going to shoulder as much blame as Lee. No, it was him that was really to blame. If he hadn't written that letter, things would be different right now.

Lee went out the back door and picked up his small purple bike that was leaning against the wall. Instead of using the pedals, he just sat on the saddle and pushed off with his feet and coasted to the end of the garden. He hated his life and wondered how best to end it. At that point in time, he couldn't think of a single reason to live.

Louvaine was overjoyed when Jon came home from work. Seeing how relieved and happy she was, he went down to the local off-licence and bought them both back some celebratory lager, wine and Babycham. Lou had had time to think about what she wanted to say to Jon that day and, after a few relaxing drinks, eased into the subject.

"I'm sorry I haven't been as attentive to you for a while," she started. "This has been a really stressful time."

"Hey, that's OK. Now that it's over, we can do the things that we want, right?" Lou agreed and snuggled into his chest.

"Can I ask how you're enjoying yourself at the bakery?"

Although Jon had trained as an electrical engineer as an apprentice, he had never been able to find the right work locally and had ended up at a bakers local to his parents' home. He had to get up at 4:30am each day to make dough and bake bread, rolls and doughnuts to make sure all was ready for the shop to open at 7am.

"I hate it. These early mornings are horrible, but there's no other work around here for me," he said.

"Why don't we use this as an opportunity then? There's nothing that ties us to this place anymore, except our parents, and we can always visit. Why not look in other areas to see if you can find something you really like?"

"You'd be happy to do that, even if it meant moving away?" Jon asked.

"I'm game if you are!" Lou said positively. She watched as the cogs began to turn in Jon's mind.

"You know what? Yes, let's do it!" he said with a new vigour. They clinked their glasses and toasted themselves and their new plan.

For the next few weeks after finishing work, Jon would head to the library to trawl through the various Yellow Pages they had for all sorts of engineering companies. During his break times at work, he'd pop out to the nearest phone box to make calls to see if any jobs were available. Initially despondent due to the lack of any useful leads in Kent, Louvaine suggested it might be worth trying further afield.

Weekends and weekdays now dragged their feet for Lee. On weekends when he wasn't being punished for something, he was able to go down the park to play with Richard and one or two other kids from school. But Lee's bad behaviour had begun to spill over into his cherished friendships. Richard now rarely played with him, and when over at the park Lee would often just be left to his own devices. It wasn't much fun playing football on his own anymore, so he began exploring further afield. His new thing was to scope out the local shops to observe opportunities to pinch sweets or anything else that would catch his eye.

At school, he'd become very despondent, which manifested as disruptiveness in the class. He would answer back to any teacher that said anything to him, and if they weren't speaking to him he'd answer on behalf of other classmates. He continued to get into scraps at playtimes, which often led to him being segregated from the other children. It surfaced that Lee had also been caught stealing sweets from the tuck shop. Rumours caught like wildfire around the school, and eventually made their way to the other parents. Louvaine started getting strange looks from them when she was out and about, many not wishing to speak to her anymore. Having been sent to the headmistress' office at least two times a week on average, something had to give. His teacher had had enough of Lee, which left the headmistress no choice but to call his parents in for a meeting.

Only Louvaine turned up of course, which did not go down well with the headmistress. Lee had also been sent for so that he would also be present.

"Is your husband coming, Mrs. Walker?"

Already irked and defensive from being summoned to the office like a naughty child, Louvaine shook her head dismissively. "He won't be coming. We've divorced and he has left the home."

Lee bit his tongue. He wanted to tell the truth out loud.

Expecting some sympathy, Louvaine was somewhat surprised when the headmistress said, "Well, divorce aside, I shall direct this to you."

She went through an itemised list of Lee's misdemeanours and behavioural issues. Louvaine just stared at Lee. He knew what the stare meant and wasn't looking forward to going home that afternoon. The headmistress also stated that Lee's teacher no longer wished to teach him. Lee was a little surprised at how weak his teacher now seemed.

"This is a grave issue, Mrs. Walker. I'd like to know what you intend to do about it? This school does not tolerate this sort of behaviour. I don't understand why Laura is so well behaved and on track for an 11+ pass, whilst Lee has so many problems. Is there something else going on at home we should be aware of?"

Louvaine was not happy with the insinuation and the intrusiveness of the questioning. *Why is that boy putting me through this?*

Again, Lee was desperate to tell the headmistress what had really been going on, but he was more fearful of the repercussions. Louvaine had to think quickly on her feet.

"The only thing I can think of is that maybe the divorce has been harder on Lee than I originally thought."

"Well, there's something that both of you need to know. If Lee's behaviour doesn't improve soon, he will be expelled from this school." There was no mercy in the headmistress' voice, just a very clear threat. "I will be reassigning Lee to the other class that Mrs. Spencer teaches," she said, with a look at Lee. "Do you know Mrs. Spencer?"

Lee knew Mrs. Spencer. Everyone knew who Mrs. Spencer was.

"Can you wait outside for a minute, Lee? I want to speak to your mother separately."

With both women now alone, the headmistress then said in a lowered tone, "Have you thought about speaking to Social Services?

They can sometimes be helpful in this situation." Louvaine nodded appreciatively.

"No, I hadn't, but I'll think about it." And with that the meeting was officially over. Louvaine gave Lee the 'I'll see you later' look as she left, whilst he was then taken to Mrs. Spencer's classroom. When Lee arrived home later that day, he was sent straight to his room to go to bed with no tea. This had become so routine for him now that it was barely a punishment at all, and he had learned to withstand the hunger with the odd sweet he had hidden from his 'shopping' exploits.

Things got much worse when Jon came home. Louvaine told him about the meeting she'd had with the school and what Lee had been getting up to. She said to him that Lee needed punishment, and that David had never really punished Lee properly. Jon agreed that Lee was in need of some male discipline, but initially felt a little awkward. Jon's only reference point had been his own strict upbringing. He went out to the back garden to pick out a thin bamboo cane and then made his way up to Lee's room, his adrenalin mushrooming as he made his way up the stairs.

Pulling Lee from his bed, he then dragged him downstairs to the hallway. Making him hold onto the balusters, Jon pulled down Lee's pyjama trousers. In front of Lou and Laura, he hit Lee hard 1…2…3…4…5 times with the distinctive whip/crack sound. Lee squirmed and tried to pull away, but Jon was far too strong, his hands huge like a giant's. 6…7…8…9…10 – Lee now screamed a sound he didn't even know existed within him.

"This is what's going to happen if you keep misbehaving, boy!" his mother chimed from behind Jon. Lee was in agony. Striped like a zebra across his legs, back and behind, he pulled up his trousers in floods of tears.

"Now get back upstairs and start learning to behave!" she added.

As Lee walked shakily up the stairs, he caught a glimpse of Laura. She looked him in the eye and smiled. If he wasn't before, Jon was now the enemy in Lee's mind. He now lived in a home where everything and everyone was against him, and yet he didn't know why.

Later that evening at her bedtime, and already in her nightdress, Laura asked if it was OK for Jon to read her a story and tuck her into bed. Lou and Jon both looked at each other. Jon smiled back and said, "Aren't you a bit old for that?" Laura pouted a little. Knowing Laura was pretty smart, Jon said, "You could probably read the story better than me. How about you read me the story and I'll tuck you in?" It was a fair deal all round, so Laura accepted the offer. Jon got up from the sofa, "Don't let me catch you!" Loving the challenge, Laura shot round the corner and up the stairs as quickly as she could, with Jon in hot pursuit. Jon had much longer legs and could take two steps at a time, so by the fifth step he was right behind her. He shaped his right hand like a duck's beak and with a quacking sound tickled and pinched her legs and bottom all the way to the top step. Laura was in fits of laughter. She hadn't laughed that much in a long time. Neither of them gave a damn about the noise or whether Lee was asleep or not.

Laura jumped into bed and pulled the blankets up to her armpits. Jon retrieved the book and went over to the bed. "Move up, then," he said, as Laura scooched up towards the far edge. Jon sat on the bed with his feet up, leaning his back against the headboard. He put his arm around her as she read through the chapter she was on. Jon was impressed by the speed at which she could comprehend the written words and read them out without any mistakes. *I definitely couldn't read that quickly*, he thought. When she'd reached the end of the chapter, Jon said, “Right you, it’s time to go to sleep now.” Laura pouted and moaned a little and held on to his muscular arm, but Jon eased the book from her fingers and put it on the side. He then gave her a couple of quack-quack tickles around the neck, causing her to hunch her shoulders in laughter, and gave her a goodnight kiss on the forehead.

“Night, night,” he said as he closed her door and went back downstairs to Lou. Lee could hear everything that went on in his sister’s room next door. *Traitor!*

* * *

Having barely slept during the night because of the burning sensations, Lee couldn’t miss the purple and red lines across his skin when he looked in the mirror as he dressed for school. He knew he had P.E. that day and realised he would have to find a way to get out of it to avoid unwanted attention. Overnight, Louvaine had given more thought to what the headmistress had said about contacting Social Services. She made a phone call the next day whilst the children were at school.

Anne Dawkins was well respected as a case worker at Kent Social Services. She was tall, slender and always dressed in a feminine manner. Now forty-two, she had learned a lot during her twenty years of dealing with youngsters. Needing glasses, she wore sturdy rims that were fixed to a chain around her neck, and she made sure that her dark greying hair was always short, but stylish, in an A-Line cut. Her clothes were of a durable kind, but somehow she always managed to look like an artist’s sketch; some people were just born with the right proportions. The Department of Social Services worked on a rotation basis to allocate cases amongst the workers. Anne had been next in line and was passed an enquiry about a mother looking to put her son into social care. She read the information that had been gathered by the administrator twice because something struck her as a little odd – it seemed to be based purely on the child's behaviour and nothing else. If this was a teenager she could be more understanding, but this child was only six years old. Normally, a family might want to put a young child into social care if they were homeless, couldn't afford to keep them or the child had overwhelming physical or mental disabilities. But none of this, upon initial inspection, was the case.

She rang Louvaine to confirm the basic details that she had on file and asked Louvaine when the best time would be to come round. Normally with children this young, Anne liked to visit the home when they were present to get a feel for the situation, but Louvaine was very specific that Anne could not come round any later than 2pm on a weekday. Anne said she would do her best, to which Louvaine had given an awkward response: "Well, I may not be able to see you if it's after that time." Louvaine instantly regretted what she had said, and it was something that Anne made a note of when she put the receiver down.

On the day of the visit, Anne decided to push her luck. She could have easily met Louvaine at 12pm but decided to call the woman at 1pm to say that she was really sorry and was running late; she would be with Louvaine at 1:30pm. Before getting out of her car and knocking on the door, Anne drove down the street to give the house and area the once-over. The houses looked OK, and this wasn't a particularly bad area. She'd never been called out here before.

Louvaine had made sure that the house was the cleanest it had been for a long time, ready for this visit. Any clothes or washing had been dried and put away and the kids' bedrooms had been tidied. She'd even gone as far as spraying the place with air freshener to create a fresh scent. She had also found a few interesting things hidden away in Lee's bedroom, such as sweets and some Airfix model airplanes. None of these had been given to him, but that would be something to find out about later.

Louvaine opened the front door and was slightly surprised that she had to crane her neck up to greet the social worker, who stood at least 5ft 11in tall.

"Hello," Anne said, offering out her hand. "I'm Anne. We spoke on the phone?"

Louvaine shook the lady's hand. "Hello, and thanks for coming," she replied as she invited her in, guiding her into the front room.

"Would you like a tea or coffee?" Louvaine asked.

"I'll have a coffee, please."

She seated herself on the front room sofa by the window, whilst Louvaine went to the kitchen. Anne gazed around the room, taking in the detail. The cleanliness was the opposite of what she was used to seeing when investigating family issues. There were a couple of pictures of a girl, in cardboard frames, but she could see nothing of the boy. There was also a light stain on the wallpaper where a picture had once hung above the mantelpiece. *There could be pictures in the other rooms*, she noted to herself. She definitely wanted a tour of the home.

"Would you like milk and sugar?" Louvaine called out from the kitchen. Anne took this as an opportunity to see a little more of the house, so she headed out to the kitchen to join her host.

"Just milk will be fine," she said in a soft voice. "Thank you." Louvaine handed her a hot coffee mug and guided them back into the front room. Anne asked if she could put a small tape recorder out so that she could write up her notes later in the office. Louvaine was somewhat reticent about this until Anne reassured her that it would probably be quicker than her having to write everything down as they spoke. She asked Louvaine to confirm the initial information they had collected over the phone from the first contact. Louvaine agreed in a somewhat clipped tone. "I thought we'd already done this when you called to make the appointment?"

"It's just a formality," Anne said, again keeping her voice soft. "I take it Lee is not at home at the moment?"

"Of course not. They're both at school," Louvaine scoffed. *Does this woman know what she's doing?*

Anne asked Louvaine about Lee's height, weight, physical features, eating and sleeping habits, and if there was a picture of Lee she could keep for the file. Louvaine went to a drawer in the back room and brought a picture in for Anne. It was small, dusty and creased, but the one and only picture she had of Lee in the house. Anne asked about any hobbies, physical activities, his likes/dislikes, what he did outside of school, as well as how he was getting on at school and with his sister. Louvaine had been truthful in her own way about most things but had made sure to elaborate and exaggerate the issues at school and with Laura. Anne then probed further into home life and asked Louvaine about a spouse and why she addressed herself as 'Ms.' She snapped at Anne.

"What's that got to do with anything? You haven't even asked me why I called you in!"

"Ms. Walker, these are very standard lines of questions. We need to understand what's happening at home before we can make any kind of determination," Anne said in an authoritative tone. Louvaine sighed.

"I've recently got divorced from their dad, but he's too busy and doesn't see them anymore."

"And the father's name?"

"Why do you need to know that? I have full custody and he doesn't have anything to do with us anymore," Louvaine asked, whilst trying to buy herself some time to think. Anne sharpened her tone.

"Again, standard questions, Ms. Walker. I have to establish everything I can during this meeting."

"David... Walker," Louvaine said, expressing another sigh.

"I'll need his address and telephone number if you have it?"

In her mind, Louvaine stopped in her tracks. She'd just caught herself in her own web of deceit and was now about to pay the price. The last thing she wanted was for David to find out what she was doing.

"I don't know where he moved to," Louvaine protested.

Anne sensed this was a lie by the tone of the response and looked sharply at Louvaine.

"Honestly, I don't know where he's living now!" Lou said defiantly. "I'll give you his mother's address." Once Louvaine had given Anne the address details, Anne continued with her lines of questioning.

"And is there anyone else living here?" she probed.

Louvaine now felt pressured and trapped. She was worried that they might not help her if she lied.

"I have a new boyfriend who I met some time back. He's been living with us for a little while now. He's a nice man and my daughter likes him a lot. But Lee is awkward and downright rude when he's around. I just don't understand why." Louvaine made sure to keep quiet about the pregnancy. Although half-way to term, she didn't think she was showing yet.

"Does Lee misbehave a lot?" Anne enquired.

"All the time!" Louvaine was getting into her element now. "He's constantly causing problems at home and getting in trouble at school. We've been threatened with his expulsion if his behaviour doesn't improve."

Now that she could see that Louvaine had something she wanted to talk about, Anne asked her to talk through the timeline of things that had happened. This was very useful for a number of reasons. Not only did it help build up a picture of family life (albeit a one-sided one), it was also making the interview last longer. It was 2:30pm and Louvaine had started glancing at the small carriage clock on the mantelpiece. She was getting nervous. Sensing this, Anne decided that she would start bringing the interview to a close.

"So, what do you think should happen to Lee?" Anne asked. Louvaine paused as if reluctantly revealing a heavy sadness.

"I just don't think he's suited to this family."

Inside Anne was stunned. She had heard many different things said by parents, aunts, uncles and guardians over the years, but this was cold. She decided not to pursue the conversation any further, instead choosing to wrap things up.

"Well, thank you for seeing me today, Ms. Walker. I shall write my notes up back at the office. But there is one more thing I will need to do before I go."

"What's that?" Louvaine said testily. "I have to go and pick up the kids from school now."

"I just need you to give me a five-minute tour of the home, if you don't mind." Anne said this in such a way that it was not optional. As

Anne was shown around the house, her eye took in the things parents often overlook. There were no other pictures of Lee throughout the house. There were some of the daughter and some of Louvaine, but nobody else. Laura's room was pristinely decorated, and her bed was fairly new. Lee's room was starkly different. Although cleaned up and tidy, everything else was dark, dingy and distinctly second-hand. As she wasn't shown around the garden, the one thing Anne did not see were the two plant canes resting against the back wall of the house.

At the end of the tour, Anne thanked Louvaine again. "Just so you know, these things can take a little while as we have a lot of other cases on. Once I've typed up my notes and made a report, it must then be discussed with a number of my colleagues so that we can make a consensus decision. But we should be back in touch within about seven days, Ms. Walker."

Louvaine thanked her with feigned politeness and closed the door as soon as the woman had reached the front gate. She went to the front room and watched her walk to her car, nervously hoping that she wouldn't hang around too long. Anne knew she would be watched, and took her time getting things settled in her car. Eventually, she drove around the block and parked up the road from Louvaine's home where she could get a good vantage point, albeit from a distance. At about 3:15pm she could see children walking up the road. She recognised one of them from the pictures in the house. She was pushing the boy on purpose, with the boy trying to chase her down and kick out. *Lee.* So, the mother had lied about going to pick the children up from school. If that was the case, how much of everything she had just heard was also a lie? The boy looked pretty normal to her and in good health.

After completing her report and conferring with other colleagues over the next week, Anne typed up the letter to Louvaine and put it in the 'Outbox' for post.

* * *

Jon came home excited, but pensive. "You were right. I think I've found a job!" he said to Louvaine.

"Sounds like good news?" she said, reading into his pensiveness.

"They've asked if I can go and see them tomorrow, and if I'm successful they'd want me to get started within a couple of weeks."

"Oh wow, that's great! I'm guessing there's a catch by the look on your face, though?"

"It's for a company in Bracknell."

"Where's Bracknell?"

"It's in Berkshire," Jon said. "Here, I'll show you on the map." Jon had bought an Ordnance Survey map on the way home and circled where Bracknell was in pencil.

"Bloody hell, that's miles away!"

"I know, darling. But it's the only company I've had any interest from, and I've tried everywhere in between." Louvaine thought for a while. Jon waited, not sure what her reaction was going to be.

"Let's go for it!" she said, putting her arms around him. "We can't pursue your dreams if we fall at the first hurdle." Jon kissed her on the mouth.

"When I'm there, I'll take a look around for potential places to live as well."

The following day, Jon called in sick to the bakery. Louvaine made him some sandwiches and a flask of hot coffee for the trip. Jon just prayed that the car he was still borrowing from his dad would hold up for the journey; the fanbelt was looking decidedly ropey and the engine would overheat if not carefully managed. It was going to be a 140-mile round-trip, so Jon made sure to take some canisters of water, just in case. He set off early that morning before the children were up, with Lou waving from the front door. He'd agreed to meet with the head of engineering at an electrical assembly plant at 10 o'clock and really didn't want to leave anything to chance and blow this one opportunity.

The car did eventually make the journey but overheated three times on the way. The meeting itself went really well, and Jon had impressed the engineering head enough to offer him the position there and then. They agreed a start date in two weeks so that he could get himself and the family moved and settled. Jon had even been given a couple of contacts in areas near the town to look at for potential accommodation. As soon as he was out of the factory, Jon headed to the nearest phone box to give Louvaine the good news. He said he'd be home later that evening after he'd looked into the accommodation options his new manager had given him.

The second place he went to see had literally only just been built. It was on a new estate, and this house was on a hill that led to a dead end with open fields beyond. The rent was lower than what Lou was paying now and, although it was still a three-bedroom place, it was brand new, so everything worked properly. Jon agreed to take the place and gave all of his particulars to the agent so that they could arrange the leasehold. That night when he eventually got home, some four canisters of water later, Jon told Louvaine about everything he'd done that day. For once he began to feel like the head of the family.

"Do you know what primary and secondary schools are nearby?" Louvaine asked.

The colour drained from Jon's face temporarily. "Sh*t, I'm so sorry, but I just didn't have the time," he said apologetically. The truth was that he had simply not thought about it. Louvaine looked more than a little miffed.

"I'll make some phone calls whilst you're at work. What's the address of the house?"

"I'm really sorry, Lou."

"Don't worry, we'll get everything sorted out." They hugged each other. Louvaine then directed Jon's attention to a letter she'd received that day from Kent Social Services.

Dear Ms. Walker,

Ref: Care for Lee Walker

Thank you for your initial enquiry about Lee and for taking the time to meet me on Thursday 24th. I, along with my colleagues, have considered the merits of whether Lee should be separated from his family and placed into care. The type of action you are looking for must be considered very carefully when talking about the welfare of all concerned. We would generally only consider this if:

i. The child is at serious risk of abuse or suffering

ii. The child is a serious risk to themselves or other family members

iii. The parent(s) or guardian(s) are not able to take sufficient care of the child, or iv. The child has a mental or physical disability where the parent(s) or guardian(s are unable to provide the correct degree of care.

I appreciate the behavioural difficulties you discussed with me, but as I was not able to sit and talk with Lee myself, I cannot confirm their validity or the best action for your son. What I can say is that the divorce process can often take a toll on family individuals in many different ways. In my professional opinion, providing a foundation of nurturing support will often lead to behavioural improvements.

I did see Lee briefly as he was walking home with his sister on the day of our meeting and can confirm that he looks fit and healthy for his age. I can confirm that Laura also looks fit and healthy for her age.

Given the information provided, there is no legal basis to remove Lee from his family at this time. Please feel free to call me if you wish to discuss this further. I will be happy to revisit your home.

Yours faithfully,

Anne Dawkins

"I'm not sure I fully understand," he said. "Are you trying to give him up?"

"He's not one of us, Jon; look at how different he acts compared to Laura! You see the way he looks at us, don't you?" She didn't want an answer to this question. Jon shook his head.

"Come on, Lou. He'll come round in the end, I'm sure."

"I wouldn't count on it," she said. "He looked like he wanted to kill me when he wasn't able to see David anymore!"

Just over one week later, everything was arranged. Jon had given notice at the bakery and a removal company had been engaged to pick up their belongings for the coming weekend. The school had been notified that the children would be leaving, and the children were told to start packing their things into the boxes Lou had been collecting from the local supermarket. Whilst the whole thing was sold to the children as an adventure in the making, neither was particularly enthusiastic about the move. Both were upset that they were about to lose their friends; Laura was even more upset because she was going to lose her ballet and guitar lessons, as Mum couldn't guarantee that they had them where they were going. When Laura asked her mother about the school she'd be attending, Louvaine said she wasn't sure whether they did the 11+ there, and whether there was a grammar school in the vicinity. She became annoyed that her parents had just made arbitrary decisions about her life, her future, without even thinking of her needs. But she didn't dare speak of this aloud.

Lee was upset because he'd started talking to his best mate again and would miss celebrating the best goals of the week with him down at the park. He was also beginning to like Mrs. Spencer. Having been transferred to her class under a cloud, she had taken him aside one morning playtime for a chat. She'd treated him like an adult; rather than dictate what was going to happen and how he should behave, she'd actually had the decency to ask him about what he was motivated by. Lee had been envious of two of the other children who were allowed to skip class on a Friday afternoon to work with an art teacher. Lee wasn't sure whether he had the talent to draw, but absolutely wanted to learn.

They both made the deal that, in exchange for Lee's good behaviour, he could be included in the art class. The trade-off for Lee was that if he behaved badly in class at any time the privilege would be lost forever – there would be no second chances. They'd shaken on it, and anytime that Mrs. Spencer had started to see the signs that Lee might be getting a little 'over-enthusiastic' about anything, she'd just give him a knowing look over the top of her half-rim spectacles. This had begun to pay dividends with his attention span and grade improvements. But now Lee was about to lose all of this.

The only other people Louvaine informed were her parents, the landlord (to whom she'd given £20 not to disclose her forward address) and the divorce solicitor. She neglected to tell David and Nancy. As far as she was concerned, David could keep paying the maintenance wherever she was. When moving day came, they all piled into Jon's old banger and followed the removal truck. The truck actually had to reduce speed to allow the car to catch up, such was its lack of pace. The move went pretty much to plan. When they arrived, Jon took them on a quick tour around the place. There were no carpets, just floorboards. There were no light fittings, just bulb sockets, no furniture whatsoever and the distinct smell of fresh paint. Most of the furniture they'd brought with them looked decidedly old and out of place. There was room for three cars on the driveway, a nod to Jon to do something about his. The kids only really fought about which room they would have. Laura got first choice, being the eldest, but Lee wasn't that bothered as his new room was still larger than his old one. Louvaine definitely approved. It was a new start and a blank canvas to work with. She could do something more than just being a housewife.

Monday was a new beginning for everyone. Jon started his new job and Louvaine took Laura and Lee to get officially registered at the school. She'd called the local authority prior to moving to check and see if they could fast-track the enrolment of the children. The school had reserved places for them and said they would do what they could. In the end it had taken a full week to get the children officially enrolled, although the school had been very obliging by allowing both kids to take part in classes.

By the end of the week, however, Laura was depressed and unhappy. The new school was literally that, a two-year-old school building. They didn't do the 11+ and there wasn't a grammar school within twenty miles. She hadn't made any friends, the school didn't teach guitar and there wasn't anywhere to do ballet. Whenever she got home, she went to her room to read her books. She was about to turn ten years old, and her life was over already. Lee didn't mind her being unhappy; at least she left him alone for a while. He, on the other hand, had made a couple of friends from the estate. To keep out of his mother's way when she was doing up the house, he spent a considerable time getting to know the local area. He was told to stay within shouting distance of the house, but he figured that his mum could shout pretty loudly, and that she didn't really care whether he was around or not. So, he explored further each day, making sure to always stop every now and then to look back and take a mental snapshot of his surroundings, just so he'd know his way home. He again scoped out the various shops and stole sweets and toy cars when he could. He just had to make sure he was always home before teatime each evening.

At teatimes, neither of the children engaged with the adult conversations about work and home improvements. Lee wanted to get away from the table as quickly as possible, and Laura just pouted most of the time. Laura's unhappiness hadn't gone unnoticed, so Jon would often spend some time before bedtime reassuring her that they were going to see if there were dance and guitar lessons around. But the biggest disappointment was going to be the inability to achieve grammar school. Jon always cuddled her to try to give some level of comfort, but he knew that there really wasn't much else he could do. He felt guilty for the new job being so far away. He said he'd get Louvaine to call the local authority to see what the options would be, which gave her a glimmer of hope.

"Hey, haven't you got a birthday coming up soon?" he asked Laura one night. "Would you like to have a party of some kind?"

Laura was acutely aware of her low friend count and just shook her head.

"Bad idea?" enquired Jon. "OK, then. Is there something else you would really like?"

Laura paused for a few seconds. "If I can't have guitar lessons, could I maybe get a guitar and some lesson books for me to learn from?" Jon paused.

"Well, I'm not sure about that," he said. "Aren't guitars really expensive?"

Laura shrugged her shoulders, not wishing to commit either way. She'd been to the shops with her mother before and had a pretty good idea about the price of guitars.

"I'm not sure we can afford that at the moment, Munchkin, but we might be able to afford the books as a start." Jon could see the disappointment on her face, even though she tried to mask it. He said goodnight and went downstairs to Louvaine, not stopping to say anything to Lee. He spoke to Louvaine about the present Laura would like for her birthday. She initially baulked at the very suggestion because of the expense, but Jon said that he would pay for the guitar if Lou bought the books.

* * *

Nancy and David had not forgotten the children's birthdays. Nancy wrote her customary card for Laura and inserted a £5 note. She really didn't know what to buy for her, so this was the safest option. David thought that he knew what to buy, but when he stopped to think about it he realised he no longer knew Laura's shoe size. *She's bound to have grown.* He decided to take a risk and bought a pair of pale pink Bloch ballet shoes, two sizes bigger than what he'd last remembered. *Should be OK*, he thought. The tension had dissipated a little and he was now talking to his mother again. Nancy had asked David to pop round to collect Laura's birthday card.

"Maybe you should try seeing her?" she suggested.

"Let's not start an argument, Mum. You know Lou will call the police and just make things worse."

"OK, well at least try to call her."

"Yes, you're right. I'll try to call on Saturday."

"Thank you, David. I miss them too, you know. But whenever I call, she just puts the phone down on me."

"I'll try. But the last time I tried calling she threatened to get a restraining order."

It was midweek and David got up at 5 o'clock to drive round to what was once his home before going to work. He parked the car twenty yards further down the street and kept the engine running. He plucked up the courage and, with the package held under his arm like a rugby player, ran to the doorstep, placed the package down and ran back to the car. He didn't take any time to look through the front room net curtains; he was just intent on getting in and out of the situation as quickly as possible. When Saturday came, David did as he'd promised. He tried calling at 9am, 2pm and 6pm. Each time there was no answer.

Laura came downstairs, hoping to see a pile of presents in the living room. She was a little disappointed, but tried to put on a brave face, when she saw just three presents and some birthday cards. Jon knew she'd be disappointed, but that was part of the plan. She opened her cards first. Louvaine had made Lee write out a card she'd bought for him. He didn't have a problem writing the card as such; it was just the last words that stuck in his craw: *Love from Lee.* This didn't sit right with him. How could he possibly say something he didn't believe in? But his mum had made him write it; he really hadn't had the choice. What he really wanted to write was: *I hate you, from Lee.*

When she opened his card, she scarcely looked at it and tossed it to one side. Lee watched (smiling on the inside) as Laura had clearly been humbled by the few presents she'd been given - mainly story books and some cheap talcum powder. There wasn't anything from their dad. After she'd opened everything, Jon said to her, "Can you get me a black bag from the cupboard underneath the stairs for this paper, please?"

She opened the cupboard door and smiled. Inside was a very large wrapped present with her name on it, standing three quarters of her height and shaped similarly to an isosceles triangle. Open-mouthed, Laura pulled the large present out. She had no idea what it could be. She tore through the outer wrapping and read the name on the cardboard box - Ibanez. Laura still had no idea what this was.

"Open it, then!" Jon encouraged.

Laura did just that. Inside the box was a lovely new acoustic guitar along with three large instruction manuals. Laura was over the moon. She immediately hugged her mother and her new dad.

"I hope you like it. Perhaps you could get me that plastic bag I asked for now?" Jon said with a smile.

Laura's birthday was also a good day for Louvaine. She'd received the decree absolute via the solicitor, which now made her officially divorced. She never understood why this took so much time. *Probably a scam to make the legal profession seem more convoluted than it really was*, she thought. She showed the letter to Jon, and they hugged each other in excitement. On the spur of the moment and in front of the children, Jon bent down on one knee and asked Louvaine to marry him.

Surprised and almost emotional, Lou said yes immediately. She'd thought about tagging Jon along for a bit but decided that he probably wouldn't take it too well in front of the kids. Laura was very happy and hugged them both. Lee, however, was not.

"Aren't you going to congratulate Mum and Dad?" Laura asked, knowing how awkward this would be for him. Lee was sick of everything. He just wanted to punch her for putting him in a situation he couldn't get out of.

"No," he said. And with new-found strength added, "He's not my dad and you're a traitor!" Louvaine instantly went for him with a swipe to the head. Lee ducked and bobbed to his right. Louvaine had used so much momentum in the failed strike that she tripped and fell to the floor on her side, bouncing off the floorboards. Jon reacted decisively by grabbing Lee by the neck.

"She's got a baby inside her, you idiot!" he shouted.

He let go briefly to make sure Lou was alright and helped pick her up from the floor.

"I'm OK," she said with a tear in her eye. Jon had never seen her cry like that before, which flipped a switch in him. He grabbed Lee by the neck again. Lee tried to kick out but Jon's arms were longer. He threw Lee across the living room, where he skidded, tripped and fell into the porch doorway with a thud to the head. Lee was slightly dazed when Jon grabbed him again by the arm. He dragged him up the stairs and took Lee to his room, where he swiftly received three huge smacks to the rear. He sat Lee back up on his bed and was about to admonish him when he saw the huge bump on Lee's forehead about the size a of a golf ball. Concerned that Lee might need medical attention, Jon shouted down the stairs.

"Lou, can you get me some ice and a tea towel, quick?"

She brought some wrapped cubes upstairs and immediately saw where they would need to be applied. The last thing either of them wanted was to have to explain what had happened to him. Lee hadn't seen the lump; he could just feel the pain. Jon made sure that Lee didn't touch it. Louvaine placed the cold compress on to Lee's head for a short period and then told him to hold it there himself.

"You can stay in your room for the rest of the day now!" she said, as she and Jon walked out of the room, slamming the door shut. As they came downstairs, Laura looked at her mother, expecting some kind of explanation.

"Yes, darling, we're going to have a new baby," she said. Laura didn't quite know how to react, so she just smiled. This was obviously not the way Louvaine and Jon had wanted to announce the pregnancy to the kids, but it was out there now and there was nothing they could really do about it.

Lee walked across to the mirror. He could feel the compress was further away from his forehead than he would have expected. He looked at his tear-stained face and pulled the tea towel away from his head. *Wow!* He was both intrigued and angry at what had happened; intrigued because he'd never seen a lump that size before, and angry because he'd been hit for something that wasn't his fault. Lee went back to his bed and tried to get comfortable; this was going to be a long day! Thoughts did circle his mind though. *There's a baby in there!* he replayed over and over again. At the age of six, Lee didn't understand the facts, but he quite liked the idea of a new brother or sister.

Louvaine wasn't going to have Lee ruin the plans for the day. Leaving him at home, the three of them went out into the local town. Lou and Jon needed to choose the rings they wanted for the wedding in addition to treating Laura to a birthday lunch.

"Would you mind if we just have a low-profile registry office wedding?" Lou asked Jon. "I don't think we could really afford all the bells and whistles, and the money would be better spent trying to save up the deposit for a mortgage, don't you think?" This was music to Jon's ears. He knew that his parents would be disappointed, but it would be better if they could buy their own house. He also needed a new car.

"That's fine with me," he said. "I'll square it with my parents." Lou smiled and gave Jon a quick peck on the cheek. At lunchtime, after they had chosen rings and confirmed finger sizes, they all went to the local Wimpy. Laura had never had a cheeseburger before, so this and the milkshake were going to be a real treat. Jon went off to the toilet, which gave Louvaine a chance to talk privately with Laura.

"Do you think Lee is stealing?" her mother said. Laura shrugged her shoulders. "I found some sweets and airplane models in his room before we moved, and I know he didn't get them from David." Hearing her father's name spoken in such a distant manner jolted Laura for just a second. "I want you to keep a closer eye on him. We've only just moved here, and I don't want him ruining everything by embarrassing the whole family. We need to get him on the straight and narrow for his sake."

Laura nodded in agreement. This was her chance to legitimately enforce her delegated authority now, with carte blanche.

* * *

CHAPTER 7

CRIME & PUNISHMENT

The guitar present was nice, and Laura did appreciate it, but learning a musical instrument from books wasn't the same as with a tutor. She'd worked her way through them pretty quickly and, as far as she was concerned, knew every note on every page. Jon had promised to try and find her some dance classes, but nothing had been forthcoming as he focused on his job. Louvaine had also tried to find something, but nothing had emerged from that avenue yet. Laura needed more stimulation, and she wasn't getting it at school either.

The work in her class year was what she'd already covered in her previous school and therefore easy. She viewed everyone in her class as a form of pond life in comparison, which in turn set her apart from the other children. Having now alienated herself, she began to get picked-on by the other children. Her first reaction was to always tell a teacher or dinner lady, and that sealed her reputation as a 'snitch.' Word gets around, and Lee made sure to not extinguish that particular fire. At school and in front of his friends, Lee chose to call Laura by her new name, encouraging anyone else to do the same. He knew that she'd spend her time concocting some plan against him at home, but she'd been doing that for a while now anyway, and he was becoming hardened to it. In fact, Lee had also started to grow at a faster rate than Laura and there was now only a one-inch difference between them in height. Lee was also stockier and could now push her away more easily when she grabbed him.

After a four-week progress review with the school deputy head, Lou had been dumbfounded that it was Laura either having or causing problems rather than Lee. Although initially quiet, Lee had come out of his shell and made friends. The teacher had wanted to see how clever he was and had really pushed Lee to achieve good results. Yes, Lee could get overexcited, but his teacher made sure to keep the boy's mind occupied as much as possible. Laura, on the other hand, was a bit of a know-it-all. She could do the work, but she had an attitude problem and looked down on everyone, including her teacher.

"Well, why don't you give her harder work then? She was fully on track to pass the 11+ before coming here," Louvaine said.

"We have," the deputy said. "She can do the work, but her attitude needs to change, that's all. We can't put her up a year because she's in the final year, so perhaps you might want to think about some tutoring? As you know, Ms. Walker, we aren't geared up to teach for the 11+; we prefer a wider syllabus here."

Louvaine had wanted to explode at the woman for insulting her and her daughter's intelligence but chose not to react. The last thing she wanted was for the school to just say that she could enrol her daughter somewhere else; that really wasn't an option right now.

Louvaine had enjoyed spending time doing the house up to her specification. Jon was pretty relaxed about everything and appreciated what she'd done. They'd go out on the weekends to the DIY shop and pick out all the things Lou wanted, within reason. She would then paint, wallpaper, install fixtures and fittings, and even plant shrubs and trees in the garden. With Jon's higher wage and the money from David, they could now afford to make what was a shell into a home.

Louvaine was also in charge of their wedding plans. She had a hard time convincing their parents about the small and intimate registry office affair. In the end she'd compromised by arranging the ceremony back in Tonbridge, so they wouldn't have to travel far.

When Jon asked her about what they should do for Lee's upcoming seventh birthday, Lou was quite dismissive.

"Don't go spending your hard-earned money on him, Jon. He doesn't deserve it. Look at all the trouble he's caused! Anyway, we need to make the home nice for when the baby arrives, don't we? Leave everything with me. I'll sort it out," she said. "You need to focus on making a good impression at work."

"You know they've given me a warning?" he plucked up the courage to say.

"What? Why the hell is that?"

"That damn car keeps breaking down. I've been late for work twice now, and I'm still in the probationary period."

"Perhaps you should leave earlier then," Lou suggested.

With Lee's birthday coming up, David bought his son a Matchbox Superfast Track Set with some cars to add to his collection. He drove round to the home and dropped off the present in the same style as before. The only thing he noticed that was different about the place was that Louvaine now had some different brightly coloured curtains in the front. But they were closed, and he couldn't see anything through them. He didn't hang around. He just wanted both the kids to know that he still cared and thought about them.

It was one week before his birthday, and nobody had asked Lee what he would like. That wasn't out of the ordinary for this family. *'Be thankful for what you get' is the motto*, he thought to himself. His birthday had fallen on a weekday, so in the morning Lee came downstairs a bit earlier than usual in his pyjamas.

"Why aren't you dressed yet?" asked his mum. No 'Happy Birthday' or anything. Lee trudged back upstairs to get ready for school. When he came back down, none of the family were waiting for him; instead, they were all milling around doing normal school-day activities. Whilst he and Laura were eating breakfast, Mum passed him a couple of wrapped presents and a card. Lee smiled politely. The first present he opened turned out to be a couple of colouring books and felt tip pens. It was hard for Lee not to show some disappointment. When he opened the second present he was completely baffled. It was a thick, hard-backed green book – a 'New English Bible.' Lee was shocked. Laura sniggered. *What am I supposed to do with that?* he thought. Louvaine read him like the book he was holding.

"You read it and abide by it!" she said.

Lee opened the one birthday card. *Maybe there's some money inside?* There was no money. The card read:

'To Lee,

Happy birthday

From

The Family.'

No love, no names, no nothing. Lee was close to tears, but he refused to let either of them see him cry. He began to walk away from the table when Louvaine remarked, "Isn't there something you've forgotten to say?"

"Thank you," he said, and then proceeded to walk away to the sound of Louvaine chiding him for how ungrateful he was. He went back upstairs and stayed in his room until it was time to go to school. What was written in the card remained in his head for most of the day. If he didn't know before, he now knew his place within the family. *Even dogs get treated better*. He was so quiet at school that his teacher asked him if he was OK, but Lee said nothing. He didn't want anyone to know it was his birthday.

* * *

The following Saturday, Laura stayed in to watch television whilst Lee knocked for his friends. May 21st was the cup final weekend and a win for Liverpool against Man U would give them the double – having just won the league title. They went to the park to play football and exuberantly talked through all of the possible outcomes of the day as they ran around their make-believe pitch. His friends had all been given a time to go home for lunch, but Lee had not. If he hadn't been given a time by his mum, it usually meant that there wouldn't be any food prepared for him, or that Jon and his mum would be out shopping. When Lee's friends all went off back to their respective homes, Lee just said he'd meet them back at the park in an hour. At home, Laura was bored and her mum was working on some self-assembly drawers upstairs.

"Laura, can you go and find Lee? We're going out this afternoon."

It was getting towards the end of Multi-Coloured Swap Shop anyway.

"OK," she answered, and headed out the door. Her first port of call was the park, as that's where he said he was going. She walked around the park but couldn't see him. *Not unusual*, she thought. *I'll make sure Mum knows about this again.*

She headed up towards the top end of the park where there were a couple of shops. She was just coming out of the main entrance when she saw him. She stayed back to watch. He'd just come out of the grocer's shop and was walking in her direction when he pulled something out of his pocket. It looked like a six-pack of Clubs, but Laura couldn't really see from where she was. Lee opened the packet and began eating one of the brick-shaped chocolate biscuits. Laura timed her move to perfection. She walked out of the entrance just as Lee had taken a bite. When he saw her in the distance, he was shocked and immediately threw the rest of the packet over the wall of a nearby front garden. Laura acted like she hadn't seen this and continued to walk towards him until she got within 10 yards.

"Mum wants you home now. We're going out."

Lee couldn't really answer with a mouthful of chocolate.

"OK," he mumbled.

"What are you eating?"

Lee swallowed what was left in his mouth, the sharp edges of the biscuit tearing at his oesophagus as he forced it downwards.

"Nothing!" he lied.

"You've been stealing, haven't you?"

"No! Search me if you like!" Lee said defensively. He barged past Laura and made his way back through to the park and towards home.

Laura walked slowly towards the park a distance behind Lee so that, when he looked back, he'd think she was also walking homewards. He turned to check that she was still walking in the same direction before he entered the park and lost sight of her. *So predictable*, she thought. Laura immediately headed back towards the house near the shop. She quickly sneaked inside the front gate and retrieved the open packet that had dropped between a small fern tree and the front wall. She thought about going straight home, but instead did an about-turn towards the grocery shop. She walked in and went right up to the person at the cash register.

"Excuse me, but did you sell these to a young boy about five minutes ago?" she enquired.

"Nope," the man replied. He seemed disinterested in her enquiry, focusing more on the horse racing on the transistor radio he was listening to in the background. Laura said thank you and walked out of the shop. She knew that Lee had got the biscuits from the shop because it had their price label on the front. She headed home. When Laura got in she went straight to the kitchen to her mother and explained what she'd seen, and where she'd found the biscuits. Lee was just eating his sandwich and shouted back, "She's lying. I didn't steal anything. She probably stole them to get me into trouble!"

"How dare you call your sister a liar! You're the only one that lies around here!" Mum shouted at him. "Get upstairs to your room!" Lee went to grab the rest of the sandwich he'd been eating, but it was taken off him before he left the kitchen. "There won't be any television or tea for you either, so don't come downstairs again. I suggest you read that Bible I bought you!"

As Lee despondently made his way up the steps, knowing he wasn't going to be able to watch the final, Louvaine said to Laura, "Well done for bringing this to my attention."

* * *

On the Sunday afternoon, Louvaine and Jon invited a few of the neighbours round for a BBQ in the back garden. The weather was lovely, and it was a good chance for the adults to get to know one another and discuss the upcoming Silver Jubilee celebrations. Once the kids from all the families had eaten, they were all encouraged to go out the front and play. There were children of varying ages, from seven to twelve, and they had never really all played together before. The first game they played was chase, which was fun but had put the younger kids at a disadvantage. The only game they could all really agree on as being fair was hide 'n seek. Whoever was 'it' had to count to one hundred, which gave everybody enough time to hide.

On the round when Laura was 'it' Lee had a really good idea. He hid himself in the front driver's seat of Jon's car, which was parked outside the house on the short hill. Jon never bothered to lock the door because there wasn't anything inside worth stealing, and there was a real knack to getting it started. If anyone did try to steal it, he knew he could probably be out there by the time they could start the damn thing. Laura had managed to find everyone else and enlisted all of the other kids to help locate Lee. As she walked past the passenger side of Jon's car, she saw him poke his head up from behind the wheel. She opened the door and shouted at Lee for being out of bounds.

"I'm going to tell Dad!"

Lee leant over the seat to grab her, hitting his knee on the handbrake as he did so. Laura dodged out of the way and closed the door, just as Jon's car began to slowly move forwards. Laura rushed off to tell her parents, leaving Lee to his fate. The other children watched in disbelief as the car began moving in slow motion. Lee grabbed the steering wheel and tried to steer the car away from an impending crash into the pavement at the dead end at the bottom of the hill. He didn't know what the pedals did, or that the handbrake had gone off. As the car gained momentum, he could only hang on to the steering wheel, awaiting the impending doom. The car crashed up the pavement with a bang and carried on over into the field, until the mud eventually brought it to a halt. Laura went rushing into the back garden. "Dad, Dad! Lee's driving your car!"

Jon rushed out of his seat and ran down the driveway. Whilst Jon ran out into the road, Louvaine and Laura cast a glance towards each other before following the rest of the parents to see what was happening. Although he didn't see it, Jon heard the bang when the car mounted the pavement. When he arrived at the scene, Lee was out of the car at the front, trying desperately to push it back up the muddy field. He had no way of knowing how heavy a car really was or that there was no way a seven-year-old would ever have got the thing moving; the car was stuck and wouldn't budge an inch. Jon was livid. He grabbed Lee by the neck and dragged him back towards the pavement, shouting at him as he did so.

"What the hell have you done to my car, you piece of sh*t?" Jon wasn't looking for an answer. Instead, he kicked Lee up the backside, which almost launched him up in the air, and punched him in the rear of the head, which sent Lee to the ground, grazing his face. As the red mist retreated, Jon could see that he had an audience – the parents, the children, Lou and Laura. Unsure of what to do, he shouted at Lou, "Take the little b*stard inside whilst I sort this mess out, will you?" Jon dragged Lee onto his feet again and kicked him in the direction of his wife-to-be.

Everyone else was silent. Eventually one of the other dads offered to tow Jon's car out of the field. In the end, there wasn't too much damage to the Imp, except a misalignment of the front wheels. But for Jon, it was another problem with the car he didn't need. Lee's punishment didn't end there. After having the car towed out and everything checked over, Jon went back inside the house where Lee was already confined to his bedroom. Jon was on a mission. He went straight upstairs, removing his thick black leather belt as he did so. The poor seven-year-old never stood a chance. From downstairs Louvaine and Laura could hear the thuds and screams emanating from Lee's room. Neither said anything.

* * *

Anne had been driving back home from another case when she'd passed near the address of Louvaine Walker. She was surprised to have not received a call back from the woman in response to the rejection letter she'd sent out. She wondered if the letter had been received, given the current postal strikes, and decided to use this as an opportunity to knock on the door and discreetly see how things were going with the family. Anne knocked but was surprised by who answered. A black woman with a huge afro opened the door. Anne could smell the cooking spices immediately as they escaped the opening.

"I'm sorry to bother you, but is Louvaine Walker home?" The lady looked confused.

"That's a weird name. You sure you've got the right place?"

"Yes, this is the place. Do you mind if I ask how long you've lived here?"

"Not that long," the woman said. "We moved in a couple of weeks ago. You're not from TV Licensing, are you?"

"No," Anne chuckled. 'I'm from Social Services. My name is Anne. I just wanted to see how the two children were getting on from when I last visited, that's all."

"I don't suppose their names were Lee and Laura, were they?" the woman asked.

"Yes, they were. How did you know?" Anne said in amazement.

"Hold on." The woman went back into the house. When she came back to the front door, she handed Anne two parcels. "There was no return address, and we were going to open them soon to see if there was any contact information inside. But seeing as you're here, it's probably best for you to have them. As you can see, they're kids' birthday presents."

"That's very decent and honest of you. I'm assuming you don't have a forwarding address, then?" Anne asked.

"'Fraid not. Even if we did, there's no way we'd be able to afford the postage. You might want to try the landlord… see if he has it?" The woman went into the house and came back out again with an address written on a scrap of notepad paper.

"Thank you. I really appreciate your help," Anne said.

"No problem," the woman replied, as she closed the door.

Anne went back to her car. The next morning she needed to do some digging.

* * *

CHAPTER 8

AN UNEXPECTED CALL

Anne Dawkins had drawn a blank with the landlord. She was pretty certain that he knew where the Walker family had moved to, but no matter how she asked he wouldn't budge an inch. Even when she said that the situation could become a police matter, he still said no. *Maybe the mother had told him not to say anything?* she mused. After ending the call curtly, she rang down to the administrators and asked them to locate the Lee Walker case file for her. It was on her desk by the afternoon. She flipped through the file, located what she was looking for and called the number.

"Hello?" the lady at the other end answered.

"Oh, hello. I'm wondering if I could speak to David Walker, please?"

"I'm sorry, but David doesn't live here. I'm his mother, though. Can I help at all?"

"Well, it's really David I should speak with; do you have a telephone number for him?" From the well-spoken nature of her voice, Nancy

Walker could tell that the woman was calling in a professional capacity; she had an intuition for these things.

"I can't give you his number I'm afraid, but I could pass a message on to him if you let me just get a pen and paper." *God, it's like trying to get past the medical secretary at the doctors,* Anne thought, frustrated.

"Yes, that will be fine," she said. Nancy always had a pen and paper by the side of the phone. She made the sound of putting the receiver down and held her breath. She was listening for any tell-tale background noise that might be of use.

"Here we go. I have it now," she said.

"My name is Anne Dawkins. Could you ask him to call me? My number is 0732 533688."

"Is this your work number?" Nancy probed, but she already knew the answer from the background chatter and telephones ringing.

"Yes, it is."

"Can I ask what it's about? Only, David is at work from early in the morning and doesn't get back home till seven-ish." Anne didn't initially want to discuss too much about what she'd found out with anyone other than David; but as she came to the feeling that his mother seemed to administer his life, she really didn't have much choice.

"It's about Lee, and I can visit out of hours if that's more helpful?" Anne suggested.

"You have me worried now, Miss Dawkins. Is Lee alright? If not, then David and I both need to know. He's been going through a lot lately!" Anne was surprised that the woman had called her 'Miss' rather than 'Mrs.' Normally, people went the other way and got it wrong.

"How about I meet with you both and I can explain more in person? Would tomorrow evening at 7 o'clock be OK?" Nancy was pensive about the woman's caginess.

"That will be fine," she said. "You can come to my home. David's just got a small flat at the moment and it's barely large enough to swing a cat in."

"Are you at number 7 Woodland Rise?" Anne enquired. Nancy paused. Only people she knew had her telephone number, and even fewer had her address. She bristled but kept her emotions in check.

"That's correct."

"Thank you Mrs... Walker? … I'll see you then." Anne let Nancy's surname hang for just a moment. There was no correction before she put the phone down. Immediately, Nancy made two additional calls.

"I'd like a trace on the following number, please. 0-7-3-2-5-3-3-6-8-8."

"Should be with you in two hours," said the assistant on the other end.

The next call she made was to David at work. She told him about the call and that he should come round a little earlier tomorrow, if possible. David was just as worried as his mother now.

"I'll do my best to make sure I'm there. You could've just given her my work number, you know," he said.

"I know. But Lee's my grandson too, and it's important we both know if there's a problem. I don't mean this to sound harsh, but with the amount of hours you're putting in at the factory, coupled with night-school, you barely have enough hours to sleep at the moment." As he put the receiver down, David sighed. He felt guilty about having to cover more than his own job because of the pay strikes. When he added on the additional study for his Diploma, he knew deep down that he had neglected his family. *If only that bitch wife of mine had had more patience,* he thought.

Just over an hour later Nancy received a call about the trace.

"That number is listed under a range for Kent County Council. I did some more digging and it's within their Social Services department. Hope that helps?" There were no extended pleasantries – just a thank you from Nancy before the call was closed.

* * *

Woodland Rise was a private road, and Anne had to get out of her car twice to lift and replace the barrier just to enter. This was definitely an exclusive area and, as she drove further up the road, she could see why. All of the houses she passed were huge. They were all bordered with tall walls and large trees that allowed her only the briefest peek at what lay beyond. Every house was set quite far back from the road, so she drove slowly to take it all in – she also didn't want to drive past her destination. Number 7 was one of the smallest houses Anne had seen from the road, but that was relatively speaking; it was still three times the size of her own home. The road itself was too narrow to park on, and all the homes had at least two cars parked on their long driveways. At seven sharp, Anne turned into the woman's driveway, taking in the 1950s brickwork features as she got out of the car and rang the doorbell. Nancy opened the door and immediately adjusted her glance upwards to meet the tall, slender woman.

"Hello, you must be Anne?"

"Hello, Mrs. Walker. Yes, and pleased to meet you."

"Come on in. David is waiting inside. And please, call me Nancy!"

Nancy was completely different from what Anne had imagined over the phone, and in fact reminded her of a film actress from way back – she just couldn't put her finger on whom. She could see that the house went back quite a way and would've loved to have a tour but was instead ushered into one of the front reception rooms that branched off the main hallway. David stood to greet her, and as they shook hands he couldn't help being reminded of the artist sketches he'd sometimes seen of models in the fashion magazines left on the doctor's waiting room table.

"This is Anne Dawkins, David. Would I be right in saying that you're from Social Services?" Nancy enquired.

"Err, yes, that's correct. Pleased to meet you, David." Anne had been knocked off balance slightly by Nancy's correct assumption. David was keen to get straight to the point.

"What's wrong with Lee? Why have you made contact?"

"David, let the poor woman sit down for just a second! Would you like a coffee or tea, dear?" Nancy enquired.

"A coffee would be nice, thank you."

"David?"

"The same for me, Mum, thanks."

Having been admonished, David really didn't know what to say to the woman sitting across the room from him. He always seemed to feel this way around his mother, which was one of the contributing reasons he'd hastily moved out and married Louvaine within six months of meeting her back in '67. Nancy had constantly made her feelings about Louvaine and her intentions clear to David, but he'd had enough of his mother ruling his life and he wanted to make his own decisions. But the decisions he'd made, in spite of his mother's advice, had all now come home to roost; which was why he was in the situation he now found himself in.

Anne felt a little awkward but passed the time by scanning around the room at a mixture of old and new family pictures. She could at least now see a picture of Lee that hadn't been hidden away. It was a colour school picture of him sitting on a bench with his sister, both smiling like Cheshire cats. She wondered how recent the picture was; the last time she saw the boy he seemed to have lost a little weight by comparison. There were pictures of David at various ages and a couple of black and white pictures of Nancy and a man she assumed was her husband. It was clear that David was the son of the two people in the pictures. Nancy's husband didn't seem to be in the house, and she wondered to herself where he was.

Nancy arrived with the two coffees for her guests and sat them on the coffee table.

"So, Anne, I think we're both very alarmed and intrigued. Could you tell us why you got in contact?"

"Of course. I just have a couple of quick questions first for David, if I may?" She turned to David. "The information I have is that you and Louvaine Walker are divorced and that she has full custody of your children. Is this correct? And could you talk me through what happened from your perspective, including the last time you saw or spoke to Louvaine or the children?"

"I thought this was about Lee?" David said defensively. Nancy spoke before Anne could explain the question.

"I get the feeling that Miss Dawkins is trying to make sure she has all the supplementary facts, so let's all be as helpful as we can," she said. Anne nodded.

"Your mother's right, David. But please, call me Anne." David inwardly sighed before answering the question. He was a little embarrassed at having to repeat his mistakes again in front of his mother, but it would be good for someone else to see what kind of woman Louvaine really was. As David talked to Anne about the letter, subsequent investigation and having not seen his children in months, Nancy's mind whirred away, trying her best to work out why Kent Social Services were in her front room. After listening to David's version of events, Anne now had a much better picture of what had happened. She reached into her bag for an A4 manila folder and read from a summarised front sheet to aid her memory. "Were you aware that Louvaine contacted Social Services this year about having Lee removed from the home?" She watched as David and Nancy both looked at each other in shock. "I'm guessing not, judging by your responses?"

"You're damn right!" David said angrily.

"Please, continue." Nancy said, raising a hand towards David with a look that urged him to calm down. Anne started at the top of her list.

"On 10th February, the office received a call from Louvaine Walker enquiring about how to have her son removed from the family home. The case came to me and, honestly, I had to double check. I've seen a lot in my twenty-odd years, but this was an unusual request. I called Louvaine and went round to the house in Central Avenue a week later to make an assessment. I can tell you now that it was one of the strangest meetings I've had. She was very particular about what time I had to be in and out by amongst other things, which naturally spiked my antennae. The inside of the house had clearly been cleaned and tidied before my arrival to make a good impression, which again, is not something we would usually expect in families where there are problems." Anne took a hand-held Dictaphone from her bag. "With her permission, I then recorded the interview. Normally I would keep this confidential, but in the current circumstances I think it's something you should listen to." Anne turned the volume dial to its highest setting on the little device and suggested that Nancy and David come in a little closer as they all listened intently.

When the interview neared the end, she pressed pause on the Dictaphone. "How would you describe the relationship between Lee and Laura?" Anne asked David. He sighed, so Nancy cut in.

"I think Laura has always been resentful of Lee for some reason. I don't know why but it started to manifest itself a few years back and has been prevalent ever since. She's three years older than Lee and probably has a reading age well above thirteen by now, which makes a big difference. Lee's not an angel by any stretch but she's been known to create situations that set him up for trouble. I nip it in the bud when they're round here, but as David said – we haven't seen them in months; Christ knows what's been going on in that time." Anne nodded sympathetically and fast-forwarded the tape to the point she was looking for. "There's just one more thing I'd like you to hear, if I may." Anne found the place she wanted in the recording.

"So, in your own words, what do you think should happen to Lee?" she asked. Louvaine paused as if reluctantly revealing a heavy sadness.

"I just don't think he's suited to this family." Anne switched off the machine as David and Nancy looked at each other but said nothing.

"Like I said, I've seen a lot over the years, but her reply was cold. I decided not to pursue the conversation any further and wrapped things up. After taking a quick tour of the house I noted the following. There were no visible pictures around the home of David, which I expected, but there were none of Lee either. Lee's room wasn't as clean and well-kept as the rest of the home. It's as though he was being treated as a second-class citizen. And if I was a betting person, I'd say that Louvaine was trying to hide a pregnancy."

"Shit!" David muttered under his breath.

Having been a little cold to begin with, Nancy had now definitely warmed to Anne's insight and professionalism. But her years of training also made her more wary of any potentially damaging disclosures. Anne went back to her summary list and continued.

"On 23rd February I sent a decision letter back Mrs. Walker. We never take things lightly and the outcomes are based on the evidence and a number of other factors." She pulled out a carbon copy of the typed letter she'd sent to Louvaine for David and Nancy to read. David looked relieved that Lee hadn't been taken into care, but Nancy was a little perplexed.

"I'm not sure where all this is going Anne, if you don't mind me saying." Anne ignored Nancy briefly and focussed on David.

"David, can you tell me when you last visited the property?" It almost sounded like an episode of Columbo; but as far as he was concerned, he'd done nothing wrong.

"I dropped off a birthday present in April for Laura and one for Lee a couple of weeks ago. Why do you ask?"

"Did you notice anything different when you were there?" Anne asked.

"Not really. It was early in the morning both times so that no-one would see me, and it wouldn't cause any trouble." Anne returned her attention to include Nancy.

"David, I'm sorry to have to say this, but they no longer live in Central Avenue; they've moved away."

David shot up from his chair and began pacing the room, cussing under his breath. Nancy wanted to say something to him, but she knew her son better than he knew himself and didn't want the situation to escalate in front of someone like Miss Dawkins. She was absolutely as angry and concerned as he was, but her life experience had been far different and, even though she retired four years ago, keeping her emotions in check was still second nature.

"So how did you find this out, Anne?" Nancy asked.

"I happened to be near the area on another case a few days back. We're now at the tail-end of May and I was surprised to have not received a call back from Mrs. Walker in response to the rejection letter. So I used the opportunity to go and knock on the door and see how things were going with the family. But there's another family living there now who moved in at the beginning of April. They were kind enough to give me the telephone number of the landlord so that I could find out if a forwarding address had been left, but he wouldn't give me anything. If I was to hazard a guess, and I'm just speculating here, it wouldn't surprise me if he has been paid to not provide the address."

"I don't think it's such a great leap, Anne," Nancy said supportively.

"Even when I said that this might lead to a police investigation, he still wouldn't budge."

David was still pacing around the room, not really being any help. Anne wondered what he might do, but she was sure Nancy would have control of the situation; they seemed so different.

"So that's why I came to you. I'm going to put a memo out to my colleagues and the surrounding councils, but there's only so much I can do in this job if a crime hasn't been committed. At the end of the day, I only want what's best for you and your children, David." Nancy thanked her for both of them.

"I'm sure David has it somewhere, but would you be kind enough write down the landlord's contact details for me?" Nancy asked.

"Already done!" Anne pulled out a sheet of paper from the file.

"We appreciate your coming to us with this, and also your discretion, Anne. You may be right that we may need to get the police involved, but we'll try speaking to this landlord first." Anne knew it was time for her to leave them both; there was clearly a great deal for them to discuss. But there was still something in the back of her mind she needed to ask.

"I should get going, but there is one thing I'm curious about," she said to David. "If Louvaine was trying to remove Lee from the home, why would she not just let you take care of him?" David looked at his mother, who stood with a look ten times harder and sharper than her son's. They both knew why but there was no way they would reveal the truth to the woman. David let his mother answer, which didn't surprise Anne.

"I disapproved of David's marriage from the beginning but always loved having the children round. Louvaine knew that, and so after she was caught having the affair she went out of her way to try and hurt me and my son as much as she could. She's a twisted and bitter person, Anne, and if Lee isn't falling into line with her plans this may just be another way to lash out at us." Anne had seen the look between Nancy and David. She knew there was something else going on; perhaps if David had been on his own, she could've extracted more, but Nancy was clearly a formidable person and she knew not to push further.

"Thank you, Nancy ... David," she said, shaking their hands in turn. "Will you let me know if you find them first, for my records?" she asked, tapping her file.

"I think that's only fair," Nancy said.

"Before I go, I have something in the boot of my car for you." Anne went to the car and brought back the two unopened presents.

"The new residents were decent people," Anne said.

Nancy saw Anne out and watched her leave, and then went back into the house to talk to her son.

"David, this is very serious. I know you're as concerned for Lee as I am, but we have to do something. What's your relationship like with your old landlord?"

David had managed to pull himself together. "I never really spoke that much to him to be honest. If we ever needed anything, it was always Lou that contacted him." Nancy wanted her son to feel included in a plan of action; he needed the confidence boost.

"OK, here's what I think we should do. Can you call the landlord in the morning? Do whatever you can to get the information from him. Call me here by 10 o'clock to let me know either way. If you don't get the address, I'll go to the neighbours and see if anyone saw anything that could lead us to them. If none of this works, we'll go to the police. Agreed?"

It was a good plan and David was happy to be a part of it. It was nearly 9 o'clock when he left to go home. Nancy wasn't expecting David to be successful and dialled a number on the phone.

"Tom? It's Nancy. I'm sorry for the late call."

Chief Inspector Tom Barnes and Nancy went back a long way and had been there professionally for each other on a number of occasions.

He'd received his last promotion as a direct result of a tip-off she'd provided to him, which had subsequently led to the high-profile arrest of a serial killer - Patrick Mackay. Their relationship had been nothing but fruitful over the years. Nancy gave a short summary of the situation she was facing and the help she was looking for. She wasn't asking for a huge favour; all she needed was an inspector and a constable for a couple of hours. Tom had no problem with the arrangement and didn't ask any intrusive questions.

"When do you need them?"

"Tomorrow morning from about 11 o'clock."

"No problem. Anything else?"

"No, that's all. Thank you, Tom."

"I'll see you in the morning."

* * *

CHAPTER 9

RETRIBUTION

Don't wait

David called his mother somewhat sheepishly the next morning. He'd spoken to the landlord, who still wouldn't provide the forwarding address. Nancy thanked him for trying and chose to remain positive.

"Let me do some digging around today, and I'll call you later tonight if I have any new information. Is that OK?"

"Thanks, Mum. You know I appreciate what you're doing."

"It's family, son," she said, and clicked off the call. It was a beautifully sunny day and, after driving into town to see Tom, Nancy briefed the two police officers on what she wanted. Inspector Gray and Constable Jones could see it was to be a simple operation where a little intimidation would be the key to success. Nancy had briefed them well and she'd acquired the information she wanted within ten minutes of entering the premises. The landlord had an office that doubled as an estate agency and the inspector and constable had gone in first to clear the shop of a couple who were discussing a house viewing. Nancy walked in behind and went straight towards the office in the back – a pokey little place that hosted a Pirelli calendar on the wall and stunk of cigarette smoke.

The constable locked the shop door, turned the sign to 'Closed' and then escorted the man into the back office. Nancy politely spelt out what she wanted. Before he could object in any way, it was explained to him that he had no continuing loyalty to Louvaine Walker; further, the two fine officers with her would conduct an inventory of all tenants currently under contract and each would be contacted and convinced, if necessary, to invoke their new rights for 'Fair Rent' to be registered and thus affect future income for the business; finally, it was also made clear that the police may uncover certain irregularities during their investigations which may require the cessation of trading until everything was resolved.

When explained this way, the landlord became very compliant, providing Nancy with the information she needed. The family had moved out on the twelfth of March to an address in Bracknell. Nancy knew there wouldn't be a forwarding telephone number, so didn't labour the point.

"One last thing," she said. "Do not write or seek to contact Louvaine Walker in any way. I'll find out if you do, and you really don't want to see us again!" The landlord just nodded, after which he was left in peace. In the inspector's car, both he and the constable looked at each other.

"That was nice work back there. I wish it was all as clean at that!" Gray smiled.

"I've been doing this an awfully long time, Inspector. Coercion is easy when you know where pressure is best exerted," she said with a straight face.

Back at the police station Nancy asked for one additional favour from Tom.

"I need you to call the local authority for this address and find out which school or schools Lee and Laura Walker are registered at, please."

"Leave it with me. We'll get something for you in the next half an hour."

It was now approaching 12:30pm and Nancy had all the information she needed. There was enough time to drive to Bracknell by 3 o'clock. As she arrived with plenty of time to spare, Nancy decided to complete a quick reconnoitre of the family home. It was difficult to park somewhere where she wouldn't be noticed in the cul-de-sac, but she did the best she could. From the outside the house looked much nicer than the previous one, although the new estate itself was a complete mess, with half-made muddy roads and construction noise. There were no real comings or goings other than construction vehicles, so she headed to her primary target and found a good vantage point to watch the main school gate.

Just after 3 o'clock, children began to pour out from the school. She saw Lee playing and joking with a couple of friends but held back for a minute to see if Laura would also appear. As she didn't, Nancy started her engine.

Laura was just finishing up some additional work she had been given by the teacher, which took her a couple more minutes past the school bell. By the time she'd finished, everyone else in the class had left. She packed her books and left the class as usual.

Nancy wound down her passenger window and drove towards Lee. She gave him a quick beep of the horn as she pulled alongside. Lee instantly recognised her red car, got straight into the passenger seat and gave his nan a really big hug.

"Oh, I've missed you, my little man. You're changing so much, and you look so handsome in your school uniform!" Nancy enthused. But in truth, Lee was thinner than when she'd last seen him, which was confirmed when she put her arms around him and surreptitiously felt around his torso. "I'm just going to wait for Laura; I assume she won't be long." Lee felt hurt inside. He loved the times alone with his nan so much; they always had loads more fun than when his sister was around - she always needed to be the centre of attention.

"She always stays late on Tuesdays, Nan," Lee said calmly. It was a lie, but he knew it was exactly what his sister would do if the situations were reversed. Lee didn't like lying to his nan, or to anybody for that matter – but it seemed to be the only thing he could employ to counter the things his sister said about him at home, at school and in front of his friends.

"How long does she usually stay for?" Nancy asked.

"An hour on Tuesdays and an hour or so on Thursdays," Lee added, his heart racing a little. The worst thing that could happen now was for Laura to turn up. He crossed his fingers under his leg and hoped his nan would believe him. Nancy smiled. She knew but said nothing.

"I guess it'll just be me and my little detective then," she said as she clicked the indicator. Lee glanced back through the door mirror with a wry smile as Nancy pulled away from the side of the road. It was a close call and a rare win.

As Laura exited the school gates and walked towards home, she saw Lee get into a car she recognised. Her heart skipped a beat as she ran towards it, but it pulled away before she could get close enough to be seen. She shouted out, but it was too late. Her heart sank because she'd wanted to see her grandmother, too. On the way home her thoughts turned to anger and how she could make Lee pay in some way.

"How would you like to get a nice thick milkshake?" Nancy proposed.

"Won't I be in trouble if I'm late home?"

"You let me worry about that!" Nancy said sternly.

"Yes, please," Lee said. He smiled in satisfaction, knowing that whatever time he got with his Nan today would be worth all the pain he'd have to suffer when she wasn't around. They hunted around the main part of town for a bit before settling on a small café that promised they could make the required milkshake. Nancy also ordered a drink for herself and a jam scone for each of them. She had been thinking how best to tackle having a conversation with Lee on her drive to the school. She needed to find out what was going on but didn't want to put him under pressure or in a compromised position. In the café, she focused on making him comfortable and talking about all the things she'd missed, and about David. She figured that Lee would come out of his shell if she was forthcoming with information first. Lee always enjoyed listening to his nan, but he was concerned for his dad and a tear welled up in each eye.

"I'm sorry about what I said to Dad on the phone, Nan. I didn't want to but Mum... made me." Lee bowed his head, ashamed as Nancy touched the top of his head lightly.

"What was said was said, and there's no consolation for the past. Your father and I know who the real problem is." Lee looked up with a half-smile. He wished the rest of the family understood him like his nan. "We've been trying to find you, and it was only today that we managed to get your location with the help of the police. So, I came straight away to see for myself, as I'm afraid your dad's at work."

Always at work, Lee thought.

"I miss coming round," he said, being careful how he responded back.

"Can you tell me what's happened over the last few months?" Nancy asked.

"That man moved in, and mum wants me to call him Dad, but I don't. Jon King's not my dad!"

Nancy gave Lee a smile and a signal to continue on.

"Mum's got a baby inside her," he said. "I don't know how that happened?" Lee said inquisitively, hoping his Nan might enlighten him. But Nancy just raised her eyebrows in a casual manner.

"How do you know that your mum's pregnant?" she enquired.

"They told us on Laura's birthday," Lee responded – his mind wandered back to one of the most painful events of his life.

"And what about Laura? How is she?" Lee wasn't really interested and made no attempt to hide his contempt of her.

"She's doing alright for herself," was his only utterance.

"Hmmm, she can be a little madam sometimes," Nancy agreed, careful to keep Lee on-side. Whilst she had previously complimented him on how big he was getting, now he was seated opposite her she could see more of the changes in the boy's complexion and demeanour. She needed to probe a little further.

"How are they treating you?" she said as softly as she could. Lee froze briefly. His eyes began to water again, which he tried his best to suppress. He wanted to tell her everything, the lies his sister told to get him in trouble and the subsequent beatings, but the lump he now had in his throat wouldn't let him talk. He instead gave her the visual cues for *help* and *fear!* That was all Nancy needed to know now. She probed no further and wiped Lee's eyes with a napkin. She kept the conversation light as they finished up their drinks and headed off back to Lee's home.

"I'm not sure where the house is. Would you be able to give me some directions?" she asked. Lee was happy to. It gave him a chance to forget about the conversation they'd just had. Nancy admired his tenacity, his intelligence and his toughness. She expected they'd come in very useful one day.

* * *

After missing the chance to see her nan, Laura had a plan. She ran the last 200 yards home to make sure she was out of breath. Seeing her gasping as she walked in through the front door, Louvaine asked what the matter was. Laura explained that she'd seen Lee get into a stranger's car and that it had driven off before she could do anything. Louvaine paced for a minute or so to think things through whilst Laura confirmed what she'd seen. *Lee was a pain in the backside compared to Laura. Had he decided to get in the car to run away? Was he trying to get some attention?* She called the police to report that her son had been kidnapped and gave them all the details she knew over the phone. Within forty-five minutes a police sergeant and female constable arrived at the home with their marked car parked directly outside. As Louvaine invited them in, she could detect the curtains twitching from other houses in the road. Laura was now quite anxious, but it wasn't for Lee's safety. Her mother instructed her to tell the police what she saw. Whilst Laura had been quite used to lying about Lee to her mother, she had never lied to an authority before. She began to shake to the point where the constable sat and comforted her. She was really worried that her lie could really get her in trouble if she wasn't careful. Laura felt it prudent to be quite vague about the car make and could only really give the colour and rough shape. To the police officers, the reaction of both women seemed quite normal given the situation.

When Nancy rounded the bend to Lee's home, they both saw the police car parked outside. Lee's heart sank. *What have I done now?* he thought. Nancy had a feeling this could become very interesting. Lee didn't have a front door key, so they both walked up the driveway towards the rear of the house, with Lee running ahead.

The two officers were still in the living room talking with Louvaine and Laura when Lee burst in through the back door. He ran excitedly into the living room to give the good news about Nan when Louvaine shouted.

"Where the hell have you been? Why did you get into a stranger's car?"

Louvaine knew it wouldn't be a good idea to hit the boy in front of the police – that could wait for later – but Laura nearly voided her bowels there and then. Nancy deliberately held back to hear what the reaction was going to be to Lee being late home. There was no relief, just anger. Lee was about to answer when Nancy walked into the room behind him, using the chance to look the woman up and down as she did so.

"Hello, Louvaine," she said in a calm, almost sinister voice.

Louvaine froze for a split second, but that was all.

"What are you doing in my house? You're not welcome here! Get out!"

The situation started to become tense as Lee explained to his mother that Nan had picked him up from school.

"You don't have permission to do that," she said to Nancy. "Can you two get her out of my house?" she said sharply to the police officers. Before either officer could respond, Nancy took control of the situation.

"I won't be going anywhere, Louvaine." She then directed her attention to the police. "Would you mind both coming outside with me alone, please?" It was not meant to be a request. Louvaine was about to protest when the male officer placed his hand up. He wasn't too happy with the way she'd spoken to them, or the fact that they'd probably been misled. At least the old lady had said 'please.'

"Let us deal with this, Ms. Walker."

Nancy walked out to the back door and the officers duly followed. She then showed the two officers her ID. Even though she was officially retired, they were both stunned into silence. Neither of them had ever encountered someone like this before.

"I'm going to be brief. The woman inside has a habit of over-exaggerating and grossly misleading authority. I am the children's grandmother and Louvaine Walker has deliberately moved all the way from Kent to mislead and evade me, whilst extorting money from her ex-husband – my son. From a police perspective, I think this is a trivial use of your time; but I suspect that somebody may have lied to you about the boy getting into a stranger's car."

The two officers agreed.

"How do you want us to handle this?" the sergeant asked.

"I'm not going to tell you how to do your jobs, officers, but you did not see me in an official capacity, and you did not see what I've just shown you." The officers both nodded to each other as they all headed back inside the house. Back in the living room, the sergeant directed a question to Laura.

"Laura, did you see Lee get into a stranger's car or was it in fact your nan's car you saw him get into?" Laura was cornered. Louvaine could see what was happening and tried to do her best to protect her daughter.

"You don't need to answer that, Laura," she said defiantly. The sergeant ignored the woman and maintained his focus on Laura.

"Well?" he pressed. Laura's heart rate had more than doubled and she didn't want to lie to authority. But she also knew what the consequence of betraying her mother would be. She cried her eyes out and buried her head in a cushion. Neither of the uniforms comforted her this time.

"I think we have our answer, Sarge," the female officer said, completely absent of sympathy. Louvaine was angry now.

"What are you talking about, woman? She didn't say anything!" It was now time for the sergeant to read the riot act to the women who'd wasted their time.

"Ms. Walker, in light of this new information I am issuing you a verbal warning. If you lie to the police or waste police time again, we will arrest you – do you understand?" he said.

"What pack of lies did *she* tell you?" she seethed, pointing at Nancy.

"Would you like to be arrested right now, Madam?" he countered back. Louvaine was beaten, and in front of the kids too.

"No!" she said with as much bluster as she dared.

"We'll be making a report about the incident when we get back to the station." They thanked Nancy as they left via the front door. Louvaine looked at Laura, clearly vexed. Laura was seriously worried for herself. Nancy asked nicely if the children wouldn't mind going upstairs whilst she and their mother had a talk. Laura couldn't get up fast enough, and Lee glared at his mother as he went. Nancy explained to Louvaine what was going to happen from then on. She would be letting David have access to both children twice a month. David would dictate what time the children would be collected and dropped off, and the poisoning of the children towards their father would cease.

"Failure to comply with any of these conditions and I'll have the police back here in no time... is that understood?" Louvaine just wanted to hit the old bat there and then, but she knew she'd have a tough time explaining that one away to the police who'd just been there.

"Fine!" was the only response she gave. Nancy went upstairs to talk to the children and let them know about the new arrangement. They'd both listened intently to the conversation downstairs, so they pretty much knew it anyway.

"Ultimately," she said, "it'll be up to you if you want to see your dad, but it would be lovely to see you both again regularly."

Lee looked physically relieved, but Laura looked a little more pensive. Nancy comforted her and gave them both a big hug before heading towards the stairs.

"Oh, just one quick thing, Lee. Here are my car keys. Would you mind fetching the two parcels that are in the boot? One's for you and the other is for your sister. They were the birthday presents your dad was unable to give you both." As the two of them made their way downstairs, Lee scampered out the front door whilst Nancy walked over to the telephone. She made a note of the number that was printed on the centre of the dialler and wrote it down.

She looked in Louvaine's direction. "Don't think about changing your number now, will you?" Nancy didn't need an answer; she just walked calmly out through the open front door. "We'll be seeing you soon… enjoy your presents," she said to Lee as she passed him on his way back in. Lee gave her another big hug and went back into the house. After closing the door, he went straight upstairs without looking at his mother. He certainly didn't want to provoke her. He did, however, accidentally stamp on Laura's parcel and kick it at her door. "There you go, Snitch!" he said loudly, as took his own much larger present to his room and shut the door.

For slightly different reasons, both children stayed in their rooms until they were called downstairs for dinner. Both knew that being around their mother that evening would be a bad idea. Dinnertime was a very sombre occasion with barely a word said by anyone. Laura began to understand what Lee must go through sometimes. The tension was so unbearable that Lee nearly burst out laughing. Seeing the females in such discomfort was really quite amusing; he was actually quietly happy for once. Today he'd seen his nan, had a lovely milkshake treat, witnessed his mother being told off by the police and actually saw her angry with Laura for a change. And now he had a Matchbox Superfast Track Set with some cars to add to his collection. *Yes, today was a good day!* he thought to himself.

Laura got upset when she opened her present. It wasn't the gift itself; it was the notion that she may never be able to get to use the beautiful ballet shoes. She hung them by the ribbons in her wardrobe out of sight and sat quietly on her bed – listening to the sounds of Lee playing next door.

* * *

Jon had had a really bad day at work and didn't get home until long after the children had gone to bed. His already unreliable car had sheered a front wheel hub on the way to work, causing him to be late once too often during his probation. The company had really not been happy with him being two hours late this time and after his third warning they'd taken the decision to his terminate his employment with a month's notice. It was all Lee's fault, as far as Jon was concerned.

Jon had conveniently forgotten about all the other reasons he'd been late for work, such as the car overheating and a number of non-starts; but it kept his blood simmering all day. He not only needed to make up the two lost hours, but then find a way to get the car back home. It would be buses to work for a bit.

Louvaine was somewhat distant that evening and didn't think her day could get worse until Jon told her the bad news – she now had the worry about what they'd do about money and the house. It was a bad news day all round when she told him about David now having access to the children once again. She sat in Jon's arms for a while, contemplating what they should do next whilst caressing the bump now beginning to show below her chest. Ever resourceful, Louvaine began to plan.

"We're not going to let this defeat us, Jon. How does this sound? One, we're going ahead with the registry office wedding, but whilst we're there we'll all have our surnames changed to 'King.' It'll be just you, me and our parents; we can tell the children later. Two, you're to look for another job. I don't care where it is, but you've proved you can do it before, right?" Jon nodded. "And three, we need to get a more reliable car. Can we do that?" Jon sat and thought for a while. He really didn't have anything else up his sleeve and there would be no more embarrassment about the difference in surnames or the car breaking down. He smiled.

"OK, let's do it."

* * *

CHAPTER 10

NOT AGAIN

A month or so into the 'new arrangement,' both David and Nancy were so pleased that they at least got to see Lee every other week. Laura had chosen to stay away because she received more attention from her mother, and Jon especially, when Lee wasn't around. She wouldn't come to the door when David arrived to pick Lee up, so not knowing why she wouldn't come made him and Nancy wonder what they'd done wrong to deserve her not wanting to have anything more to do with them. After the bruising he'd received during the divorce proceedings, David had come to the conclusion that he'd been right when he originally confronted his ex-wife. She was a manipulative whore and he contented himself with that reason alone. Of course, his mother had been right all along; in his mind, David resolved to take on board more of his mother's advice in future.

When Nancy had nudged Lee about why Laura didn't want to come anymore, she just got the same determined answer each time: "She's disloyal." He said it with such a steely edge that she could only feel admiration. She'd tried to probe him more about what the message of '*help* and *fear*' meant in the café, but Lee had clammed up about it. Nancy also noticed small behavioural changes in him that she didn't like the look of. She knew something was going on and couldn't understand why he wouldn't talk to her. Lee, on the other hand, knew exactly what his nan was doing. As much as he hated his life at home, he was still conflicted by some sense of family loyalty that meant he couldn't allow himself to buckle under interrogation. The one thing he did know was that every time he said something, it seemed to end up with him or his dad being punished in some way.

Nancy and David both made sure Lee enjoyed himself during the short time that they had together. Nancy played her part in taking some of the pressure away from the father-son one-on-one situation. She found that treating Lee now and then and making him feel special worked wonders for his self-esteem. She also asked him what he wanted to eat at mealtimes, rather than dictate what he should have. Lee always chose a Pot Noodle or Crispy Pancakes for lunch, jam sandwiches for tea that he had to make himself, and digestive biscuits topped with real butter for supper. Seeing his eyes light up each time at the prospect was reward enough for her. Lee would play out with a friend from a few doors down and David often took him out somewhere in the afternoons; more often than not it was to a football match or the cinema.

Jon found another job working for Marconi in St. Albans, which meant he needed a reliable means of travel. He took out a small loan to buy a second-hand Ford Cortina Mk III. It was more reliable and definitely had more room inside for everyone, what with the baby coming and all. Instead of just blindly moving to another location this time, Jon scouted around different locations when he could during lunch breaks and evenings, whilst the family still remained in Bracknell. One of his priorities now was to find an area that was affordable and not too far from a grammar school for Laura. On the weekends that Lee had gone to David, the rest of the family went to house viewings in and around the city. It didn't take them too long to find somewhere that they liked, but this would be a big step for them. Louvaine and Jon now wanted to buy their first home. With some deposit money their parents had jointly provided, and a lot of searching around to find a lender, a mortgage had been agreed in principle. They'd shown the decree absolute to the bank manager, but the stipulation he'd put on the mortgage was that it would only be granted once the couple were actually married.

Louvaine had done a lot of phoning around to find a registry office with an opening in the time they needed it. The irony was that it would be back in their hometown of Tonbridge, Kent. She made sure to tell both their parents that she wanted to be close to them for the wedding. A midweek date was set and Louvaine provided all of the family's birth certificates ahead of time to make sure they could tie everything up on the day. The couple both bought new attire for the ceremony, but at nearly seven months term, Louvaine had only just managed to find a white sleeveless halter-neck style maternity dress that would double as a wedding dress. Jon had opted for a dark navy suit that he could easily reuse in the future. The ceremony itself wasn't particularly inspiring and they both realised that their parents had been less than impressed. "We'll do a proper church wedding when we can afford it," they both promised.

During the ceremony Louvaine officially became a 'King.' Additionally, both Laura and Lee also became Kings, but had yet to find this out.

Nobody at the registry office really batted an eyelid about it; it was just viewed as the norm. To make up for the lack of a church wedding, the couple took their parents out for a meal at one of the better restaurants in town. On the way home, and finally on their own, they discussed their future plans. Everything was falling into place, but they still needed to be careful. Louvaine would deal with the new local authority for the schools, applying for new bank accounts in their new names and working with the mortgage advisor for getting the purchase in place for the new house under their new name. Jon's sole responsibility was to make sure he kept his nose clean at work.

* * *

After David returned him back home one Sunday night in July, Lee walked into the house and instantly recognised the signs. Everything downstairs was packed in boxes. Lee was summarily told to go upstairs and pack up all of his belongings before bedtime. He didn't dare say anything, but down in the pit of his stomach he knew he may not get to see his dad again for quite some time. Laura had already finished her packing during the day, so now had time to annoy him by trying to be as distracting as possible. Every time Lee had things packed in a box, Laura would either move something or take it out of the box altogether. Their mum had said that anything that wasn't packed would be left there, so Laura did her best to unpack the things she knew Lee liked the best. Even when he shouted downstairs, his complaints fell on deaf ears and he was just told to shut up. Laura always seemed to know which buttons to press, and she finally riled him up so much that a switch finally flipped inside of him. She'd taken his Action Man and was busy disrobing the figure when Lee snatched it back out of her hand and hit her round the head three times with it. This initially shocked her. He then pushed her aside and walked into Laura's bedroom and turned over as many of her well-packed boxes as he had time to. Laura went to grab him, but he'd seen what she was about to do and grabbed her lead hand. Lee twisted it and Laura fell over onto her back. He then followed up with another whack over her head with the Action Man.

"Don't ever touch my stuff again or you'll really get hurt!" Even though Laura was taller than him standing up, he'd learned from his fights at school that everyone was the same size on the floor. Lee was heading back to his room when he saw Laura looking at the fingers on her left hand. Two of them were somehow facing a slightly different direction than the others. To Lee it looked as though she was performing a Vulcan greeting from Star Trek – but he knew it wasn't good. Jon heard the commotion from downstairs and was part the way up the stairs when he heard and saw Laura begin screaming out about her hand. As she held it up in front of her face, he could see what she was screaming about and instantly grabbed Lee by the back of the neck and threw him down the stairs.

With the momentum, Lee only hit about 4 or 5 steps on the way down. But he hit each one with such a velocity that all of the wind was knocked out of him. Jon steamed down the steps after him and pulled Lee up to a standing position. Not having any breath within his lungs, Lee fell again. Jon quickly pulled off his belt and proceeded to hit Lee more times than he could count with the buckle end. Jon didn't care where the buckle hit; the fact that each strike landed was good enough. All the boy could do was try to defend himself from the attacks with his arms, hands and legs. Lee managed to catch the belt at one point and tried to kick out at Jon, but the man was still too strong and wrestled the belt away again. Jon eventually stopped with the punishment, but only because Louvaine had said that they should probably attend to Laura. He dragged Lee back up the stairs and threw him back into his room, leaving him there whilst they took Laura to the hospital to get her fingers seen to. Now alone and trying to recover, every movement hurt; but now at least he had the room to himself to pack his things in peace and quiet. Whilst packing he had an idea. All the family did was hurt him and he hated them all anyway. Keeping one ear out for Jon's car, he gingerly went downstairs to the telephone and dialled his nan's number. There was no answer on the first or second time of trying. Foiled, Lee went back upstairs and lay on his bed trying to breathe through the pain in his ribs.

Later that evening the villain, as Lee now thought of him, and his wife returned home with Laura. Two fingers had been dislocated, so they were now bandaged with the other two on her hand. Lee was in the bathroom washing when Laura burst in. She knew he was there, but just couldn't wait to wave her fingers at him and gloat about the punishment he'd had for it. She stopped what she was about to say when she saw the marks all over Lee's shivering body. There were purple and red bruises in the shape of Jon's buckle all the way up his ribs and arms, where blood had pooled under the surface of his skin. There was dried blood still around the corners of Lee's nostrils, and he had a black eye and a swollen cheek.

"Get out!" he shouted at her in a voice she'd never heard before.

For once, Laura just did what she was told, sheepishly walking away and pulling the door to. Lee had seen her fingers; and the only silver lining for him was that she wouldn't be playing the guitar for a little while. But with the pain he was in, laughing wasn't a helpful option.

Laura went in her room and began picking up her things with one hand and placing them back into the boxes. She thought about the bruises she'd seen all over Lee's body and contemplated her role in what had happened briefly, before taking a look at her bandaged fingers and worrying about how she was going to cope.

On Monday morning neither of the children went to school; instead, they were asked to help pack things into the removal truck. The drive to the new house wasn't as long as it had been the last time, but Lee wondered to himself just how often this was going to happen. On the way Louvaine announced that they'd been married and showed off her new ring to both of the children. She then broke the news that all their surnames had legally been changed to 'King.'

"Jon King, Louvaine King, Laura King and Lee King," she declared. Laura sniggered to herself when Lee's new name was announced. She now had a wonderful new pet name for him and began thinking of all the little insults she could jab at him: 'Your bucket's got a hole,' 'You've wet yourself,' and 'Lee King Bum' were just a few she came up with in her head. When Lee finally cottoned on to what she was laughing at, he turned away and just looked out of the window. *My life's bad enough already!* he thought. Lee decided that whenever anyone asked him his name, he would still use 'Walker' rather than Jon's name. It would be his defiance to being called something he didn't want to be associated with.

Louvaine also announced that they would both be going to separate schools. She made a big deal to say that the one Laura was going to was for the very clever children and a feeder to the nearby grammar school. But the reality was that the local authority had only one spare place in this school at the time. Lee had been placed in a Church of England school that also had a good reputation, so he was to behave himself when he arrived.

Lee heard all of this but paid little attention. He had no control of his own life and the only people that controlled it didn't really give a damn anyway. He was reminded of this when the car went over a bump in the road and jolted his bruised ribs. He zoned out and thought about the regrets he had now. He wished he hadn't been so loyal to the family and told his nan about what was going on so that he could stay with her and not have to go home.

The house Lou and Jon had purchased was only about ten years old and on an estate that was now quite established. It had four bedrooms and an integrated garage; the downside being that it was in a staggered terrace. The previous owners had not looked after it very well, which was why it had been in the price bracket they could afford. But Lou liked the idea of the challenge and putting her stamp on things. As was becoming customary, Laura got first choice of the three remaining bedrooms. None of them looked particularly fresh; she of course took the largest, but Lou promised to get nice wallpaper and carpets once the downstairs was done. Lee wasn't quite so lucky. He wasn't even given a choice and was just told that he was getting the box room next to the bathroom. The new baby was getting the next biggest room. *Just another way of punishing me*, he sighed. The rest of the day for most of the family was spent unpacking boxes and moving things around; except for Laura, who couldn't possibly lift anything with her damaged fingers. Louvaine worked hard but was told by Jon to rest when things got too much for her. Lee was in excruciating pain every time he was asked to help move anything heavy like a bed or table but complaining was not an option.

The next day Jon went to work and Louvaine walked both children to their respective schools to go through the enrolment process again. Laura was taken to her school first. It was an old building that appeared almost medieval. They met with the headmistress, who extolled the school's values, achievements and behaviour expectations for some time. Her enrolment took over an hour, after which she was taken to her new class. Louvaine then walked Lee to his new school. It was only five minutes' walk away and in stark contrast to the one they'd just been to. It had red bricks, looked newer and had larger windows so you could see the children in their classes. The headmistress went through much of the same steps as the one in the previous school. Lee decided he was going to be brave. He knew that the woman would be able to see the marks on his face, so when she asked his mother to confirm his name, Lee corrected her and said 'Walker' when she said 'King.' Inside Louvaine fumed. She knew she couldn't swipe him round the side of the head there and then, so just put on her best actress face and smiled.

"No, Lee, it's King like we discussed." Louvaine handed the birth certificate to the headmistress and said, "I've only recently been remarried, so I think he's a little confused." Lee didn't push his luck anymore. He'd made his point to both women. After he was eventually escorted to his new class and Louvaine had left, the headmistress made a few notes on Lee's school file. *Child arrived with bruises/marks around his left eye and cheek. Mother very controlling. Boy required approval to speak, except to highlight his previous surname of Walker. May be worth discussing further with Lee to see if there are any problems at home.*

Over the next couple of weeks, Lee began to settle into his class. Unbeknownst to him, the headmistress had had a private chat with his teacher about her observations and asked her to keep an eye on him. The standards of work and behaviour required in the school were very high, which served to keep Lee's mind occupied in the classroom. He managed to make a couple of friends but was unable to get away from the grief his new name now gave him. He rebelled against this by crossing out King wherever he could and replacing it with Walker, such as in exercise books and his class drawer. But he couldn't change the register or how the teachers addressed him, so the other kids in the school began to make fun of him during break times. The pain and punishments Lee had endured at the hands of Jon had set him up to be totally undaunted when bigger children began bullying him. Lee just hit them as savagely as he had been by the villain at home. This had an equalising effect. He got in trouble with the teachers for fighting, but the fighting diminished when the other kids knew what would happen if they said anything out of line. More than anything else, Lee just wanted to be left alone with his friends.

Laura hadn't gone unscathed at her school either. When word had got around that it was a seven-year-old that had damaged her fingers, she'd been derided as weak. Kids had also said she could only count to six because she didn't have enough to count to ten. She'd tried to take on the 'I'm more mature than you' persona, but this only caused the other children to ignore her completely. In class she could manage the work and was still able to produce excellent marks in tests, but she was no longer top girl; that distinction went to Lisa Marsh who was just brighter than she was. Laura initially tried to make friends with her, but her overtures were rejected out of hand. Not only was the girl bright, she was also popular – especially with the boys in the school. Laura could see she had much to learn and set about analysing the reasons for the girl's popularity.

* * *

Two weekends after the move, David made the now usual drive to collect Lee. He knocked on the door and waited. There was no answer. He knocked again twice, but the door was still unanswered. He began to get angry. *How could they go out on his day?* He tried to look through the front widow to see whether anyone was home, but the curtains were drawn and there was no car in the driveway. He went around the back to see if anyone was in the garden, but there was no-one there either. He jumped over the fence to see if he could see anything through the back window. The house just looked bare. There were a couple of bits of furniture, but the place looked lifeless. David had a sinking feeling. He headed back to the car and was just about to get in when he caught the eye of a neighbour in their driveway. David introduced himself to the man, who said that he hadn't seen any activity from the house in the last week or so.

"Let's ask my missus. She'd have a better idea than me," he said, beckoning his wife to come outside.

"I'm really sorry to bother you both, but I'm the children's real dad. I don't get to see them much and this family have disappeared before."

"There was a big van outside a couple of weeks back. We didn't see anything more from them after that." David was rocked. "I'm really sorry," the wife said, as she and her husband looked at each other, feeling sorry for the stranger. "They were a strange couple, and that boy was forever in trouble," the wife said. "His dad… sorry, stepdad… really gave him a hiding about that car incident, didn't he?" she said to her husband. David thanked them and gave them his telephone number in case they remembered anything that may be helpful in trying to locate them. It was a long drive home that day. He had a hard time keeping it together when he had to explain to Nancy what had happened. Nancy was seething. She wasn't angry at her son; he'd done nothing wrong – it was that bitch ex-wife of his. She suggested that they both should go back the next day and canvas the surrounding houses together to see if anyone saw anything that could help them find the family.

The next day bore no major fruit; the only things they did find out were that the boy was possibly being mistreated, and that the van they'd used to help them move had no logo or name on it. The family now had a red Cortina, but no-one could provide the registration.

The first part of the journey home was pretty silent. It was only when Nancy suggested getting the investigator involved again that David reacted angrily.

"She's expensive and look where it got me last time!" he said.

"Kim didn't create any of the problems we're now encountering, David; she just uncovered them," Nancy responded. Once David calmed down and conceded the truth, he agreed with his mother. He couldn't think of any other way to find Lee.

* * *

CHAPTER 11

SAY GOODBYE

Say Goodbye

Now that she had her own house to do up, Louvaine wanted the children out of the way as often as possible so that she could concentrate on the DIY jobs. She especially liked to make sure they were out on weekends when Jon was at home. It was on a Sunday during the summer holidays when the incident happened that would have dire consequences. Lee and Laura were both doing their morning chores in the kitchen before being allowed to go out to play. Laura took the easy task of washing-up whilst Lee, as usual, ended up doing the wiping-up. This always allowed Laura to finish first so that she could get out before him or choose what programme to watch on television first.

As Laura was gloating about how good her school was compared to his, Lee noticed one of the breakfast knives hadn't been washed up properly. He looked at it as he picked it up from the draining board and gave it back to her blade first saying, "You have to do this again."

Laura went rushing upstairs as if she'd just seen a ghost. Lee just thought it was her usual acting-up again, so he put the knife back in the sink and continued to finish what was left.

"Mum, Dad, Lee just threatened me with a knife!" Laura shouted.

Jon went thundering downstairs and straight into the kitchen. A heavily pregnant Louvaine followed at a slower pace.

"Did you just threaten her with a knife?"

Lee was confused and about to say something when the first blow hit him. Neither Jon nor his mother waited for the answer. The ferocity of what happened next stunned Laura. Both of her parents kicked, smacked and punched Lee around the house to such an extent that he was dazed and unable to block the attacks after a while. Laura knew that this was one lie that had gone too far – but she didn't intervene.

Lee was just about conscious when Jon dragged him upstairs and threw him into his room. Louvaine followed. As they were about to shut the door Lee shouted, "I hate you!" with a ferociousness that he'd never shown before.

"That's all I wanted to hear!" his mum shouted back, as she slammed the door shut. Lee was perplexed. *What did she mean? Why did she say that?*

Downstairs, Jon put his arm around Laura and comforted her in the back room. Louvaine had had enough and began making phone calls in the front hallway. Laura listened to what was being said and began to shake. Jon thought that this was the shock at being threatened by Lee, but it was really due to what was being said by her mother. She was now actually worried for her brother.

Lee hadn't been allowed out of his room for hours and no-one had been in to see him either. He looked at himself in the mirror. There were red marks all over his face and neck, finger gouges by his nose and jaw. He removed his jumper. The marks continued down his body; he didn't dare look any further. He lay back on his bed; it was the least painful thing he could do. At various times throughout the rest of the day, Lee heard traces of his mother speaking on the phone – his name was mentioned time and time again. He was hungry and hadn't been allowed any food, which didn't help his anxiety.

* * *

Lynn Franks had drawn the short straw on the rota to work that weekend at Hertfordshire Social Services, which generally consisted of manning the phones and taking enquiries. She'd been with the department for nearly eight years, having moved down from Berwickshire in late 1969. Whilst working weekends wasn't much fun for any of the staff, it did allow her to catch up on her somewhat overburdened caseload. There had been nothing to disturb her all weekend and so she had managed to finish her last report on Sunday morning. She was about to start reading her Woman's Own magazine when the phone rang. *Damn*, she thought. *Nearly made it all the way through!*

The call was from St. Albans Police Station, so she sat up and made sure she had a pen and paper ready. They'd had a call from a woman who had a young child that was a serious risk to their daughter, and the mother had stated that the family couldn't look after him anymore. The officer gave Lynn the mother's name, address, telephone number and a few case details before thanking her and ending the call. This wasn't the first call of this type Lynn had dealt with, so she was reasonably prepared for what process to follow. She called the number.

"Hello, can I speak to Mrs. King, please?"

"This is Mrs. King," Louvaine said sharply.

"My name is Lynn Franks from Hertfordshire Social Services. I've just received your details and been asked to speak with you regarding Lee?" Louvaine lowered her voice slightly.

"Yes, that's correct. I need someone to come and collect him immediately so that he can be permanently removed from my family." This seemed slightly odd to Lynn. The woman was so decisive on the action required.

"Why's that?" Lynn probed. Louvaine had found the rejection letter she'd kept from Anne Dawkins of Kent Social Services and decided to repeat two of the lines she'd cited as considerations for removal.

"Because Lee is '*a serious risk to my daughter*' and '*we are no longer able to take care of him anymore.*'"

Lynn kept further comments to herself and instead asked Louvaine for details of why Lee was a danger. Louvaine cited a car theft, stealing from shops, breaking his sister's fingers and threatening her with a knife that day. Lynn agreed that these were all very serious, but initially suggested that perhaps some counselling would be beneficial, which she could arrange. This angered Louvaine.

"Who's to know what he'll do next? I don't want him in the same house. He might kill her next time for all I know, and I have a baby on the way!" This put Lynn in a very difficult position. She needed not only to do what was best for the child but for the rest of the family as well. Lynn let out a deep breath. She had an idea in mind.

"OK, I'll need to take a set of details from you now about Lee and the family, please."

Now that she seemed to be getting her way, Louvaine provided all of the details Lynn wanted.

"I'll need to make a couple of phone calls, Mrs. King. This will not be the immediate solution you were asking for." Louvaine wanted to make one thing very clear to Lynn.

"I want him removed from this home within 24 hours; otherwise, we'll drop him off at the council offices for you to deal with!"

Lynn didn't particularly like the tone of the woman's voice and had already begun to dislike her.

"This is a serious matter, Mrs. King. Like I said, I will make some phone calls. Please do not go out today, and I will call back when I can. Oh, and just one more thing, Mrs. King. It's a criminal offence to abandon a child under the age of 16, so you would be ill-advised to take that course of action, especially seeing as I have all your details now." Without waiting for a response, Lynn put the receiver down.

Bitch! she thought. She took a few deep breaths and poured herself a glass of water before calling two of the children's homes she'd worked with in the county. She already knew the answers before picking up the receiver – they were both at full capacity. Her next call was to Fred. Fred was the manager of a children's home seventy miles away in Bury St. Edmunds who she'd met at a training conference about new housing regulations four years ago. To this day, Lynn had never understood why a woman would be called Fred, but that was one of the quirks she liked about her. Fred was certainly not expecting a rushed call from Lynn about work, on a Sunday of all days, but she always tried to accommodate whenever she could. Lynn was in luck because she had two spare rooms. Lynn gave her a condensed story of the call she'd had with the mother that day. Fred expressed a concern that the boy in question had threatened his family with a knife.

"Judging by the mother's tone on the call, I would've too!" Lynn admitted. Fred agreed to house Lee temporarily with a view to assessing him for the first couple of weeks. It was all that Lynn could ask for given the lateness of the call.

"I'm planning to pick him up at 10 o'clock tomorrow morning, so should be with you at about twelve-ish."

"No problem," Fred said. "I'll make sure a room's ready."

When Lynn put the receiver down, she prepared a short formal file based on the information she had been provided by Mrs. King. That gave her time to calm down before having to speak to the vile woman again. As she completed the report, she cursed herself for not giving Fred the boy's age. *I'll iron that out tomorrow*, she thought.

Lynn called Mrs. King back, who was a little more contrite than she was expecting.

"I've pulled a few strings and managed to find Lee a place in a suitable home. Would you like to know the address?"

"No, thank you," Louvaine said to Lynn's surprise.

"Oh… OK. Well, I'll be at your home for 10am sharp. Please ensure that you have all of his belongings ready and that you provide me with his birth certificate and any other documentation you have." Even though Louvaine had been polite on the call, it didn't matter; Lynn still didn't like the woman after she'd put the receiver down.

Later that afternoon, Lee heard somebody scraping around in the loft. Minutes later, Louvaine opened the door and entered his room. He thought she was going to let him come downstairs for some food, but he was wrong. He'd never been so wrong in his short life. She threw a tatty, small brown leather suitcase onto the floor by his bed.

"Pack the things you need – you're leaving." Lee's heart sank as far as it could go. He pled with her to let him stay, but she pushed him away and just coldly said, "You've got till the morning. Be ready by 9 o'clock." Just as she was about to shut the door on her way out, she added one last twist to the knife. "And by the way... you weren't my baby!" she stated, looking at him without any emotion before closing the door.

Lee stumbled back to his bed and sat there for a few minutes, contemplating what had just happened. He laid down, put his head in his pillow and sobbed to himself. Two minutes later, Louvaine stormed back into his room.

"I don't hear you packing!" she shouted and stormed back out again. Dutifully, Lee started packing the suitcase. It wasn't that big, so he really needed to think hard about what he might need, even though he didn't know where he was going and didn't really know what to include. Eventually, he settled on some essential clothes (pants, socks and t-shirts), some small toys and a pair of shoes. He also remembered to pack his sterling silver duck moneybox. Although there wasn't much in it, he thought it could be worth something if he had to sell it. Throughout the time he spent packing, what his mother had said swirled around inside his head. '*You weren't my baby'... what did she mean by that?* Eventually Lee put himself to bed, but he could barely sleep due to the anxiety and hunger.

Laura remained very quiet that night. In bed, she thought about going into Lee's room to say sorry or something, but her courage, or lack of, let her down. Early the next morning, Louvaine gave Laura two pound notes and said that she could go to the shops and buy whatever she liked. She got the hint when her mother also said she'd see her at lunchtime. She now knew that everything was for real. She walked slowly down the road, guiltily contemplating what she'd done with the realisation that her mother was serious about the calls she'd made. It was her fault that he was going, and it was a difficult pill to swallow that even the prospect of buying the new single from Blondie couldn't alter.

Lee didn't dare come out of his room. At 9 o'clock Louvaine shouted up the stairs that he should get washed and dressed. He still hadn't had anything to eat by 10 o'clock when she opened his bedroom door and said, "It's time for you to come down now. Put your coat and shoes on and bring the suitcase."

As Lee walked painfully down the stairs, Louvaine said, "You have a phone call."

That's strange, Lee thought to himself. He picked up the receiver. It was Jon's voice.

"Lee? I'm sorry that the situation turned out this way. I hope you'll be OK in the future?" he said awkwardly.

Lee was angry now. *This horrible, gutless w*nker is trying to say sorry on a phone call to me now?* He wanted to say what he really thought of the man, but his mother was standing right over him and he decided the last thing he needed was another beating. Louvaine ended the call and opened the front door. Outside was a lady waiting by the passenger side of a car. She was about 5ft 2in with permed long blonde hair. Lee had never seen hair like it before. She had a natural smile and opened the car door, beckoning for him to get in. Lee looked back at his mother, but she was stone-faced. Louvaine gave him an envelope that contained a number of documents, including his birth certificate. "Give that to the lady," she said coldly.

As Lee walked towards the strange woman, she took the suitcase and envelope from him and in a soft voice said, "C'mon, it's time to go." Lee could barely hold back the tears, but he was brave and refused give anyone the satisfaction of seeing him cry. As he made his way gingerly into the front passenger seat, the front door of the house closed with a thud.

* * *

CHAPTER 12

DISPLACED

Lynn started the engine, shaking her head in disgust. She'd seen situations before where parents couldn't bear the emotional strain of giving a child away, but this wasn't the same. The woman she'd just seen was cold and so dispassionate. Lynn could see that the boy's head was bowed and marked, so she chose not to say anything right then.

As the stranger backed the car out of the driveway, Lee just sat there feeling numb. *They really did it to me!* he thought to himself over and again. Many thoughts swirled throughout his young mind. *Is this what happens to bad kids? Am I bad? Is this what happens to children who say they hate their parents? Why did I have to open my mouth? Would Richard's parents have ever done this?* He missed his best friend from Tonbridge. Lee never really understood why Richard's family were always so upbeat and generous, even though they'd had a real hard time of it during the strikes and could barely make ends meet. It was one of the reasons he liked to go round their house; Richard's mum was always welcoming and would often give Lee a little hug, a little ruffle of the hair, or a [illegible]ing rub on the shoulder. He'd always shrug it off of course, but it still made him feel relaxed and wanted. It was different at home; it was tense, as though he was always in the way.

Lee's thoughts were transported back to the present. *Who is this lady? And where are we going?* Lee snapped out of his self-questioning and decided to concentrate on memorising where the woman was taking him. He chose not to speak and focussed on the route and road signs. This was serious now and the observation quizzes he used to play with his nan came in very useful. But after they'd been driving for a while, there was only had so much he could retain.

Having seen Lee's head perk up a little, Lynn decided to break the silence.

"My name's Lynn," she said. "How are you feeling, Lee? Are you OK?"

Of course I'm not OK! he thought to himself.

Lynn put her left hand out to take a hold of his hand, but Lee withdrew. She continued,

"I'm from Social Services and we've been asked to take you away from your home." She paused, wanting to see his reaction. Lee finally spoke.

"Where are we going?"

"I have a friend who has a home and helps me out from time to time. You'll see... it won't be too long." She paused again, before gently asking Lee a sensitive question. "Can I ask how you came to get all of those marks on your face?" Given the story she'd been told on the phone and the coldness of the mother, Lynn had a pretty good idea. But she wanted to test how forthcoming the boy would be. Lee said nothing and continued to stare out of the window, constantly checking road signs to gauge where they were heading.

"Would you like something to eat?"

Lee nodded. He hadn't eaten for a day, but he'd become accustomed to the feeling of hunger. Being sent to his room without dinner or tea if he didn't fall into line had been a common practice since before he could remember, so stealing food or sweets from shops had become a necessity.

"There's some Wine Gums in the glove compartment. Can you pass me some, too?" she said with a smile. For each one Lynn pulled from the bag, Lee took two. He tried to disguise it as much as he could, but Lynn chuckled at him. "I can see you're hungry, son. Take as many as you like."

Who is she to call me 'son'? She's not my mother! That thought brought Lee straight back to what his mother had said. '*You weren't my baby*' ... *what did that actually mean?* Lee took the sweets anyway - self-preservation was the key now.

* * *

Louvaine was glad to see the back of Lee. *He was never one of us*, she thought to herself. *The whole adoption thing was David's idea anyway... idiot!* She called his school to tell them Lee wouldn't be going anymore and spent the rest of the morning packing up what was left of Lee's things into boxes.

We might be able to get some good money for some of this stuff, especially the car track, she mused to herself. When she'd completed the job, she stood by the door.

"Ideal room for all the decorating stuff," she said quietly.

* * *

The drive took longer than Lee expected, not that he really knew what to expect. But the woman had definitely exaggerated when she said it wouldn't take long. When they finally did arrive, Lee saw that this was a much bigger house than the one he'd just left.

"Come on, young man. We're here now," Lynn encouraged. They both got out of the car. She gave Lee his bag and walked him down the long path towards the dark blue front door. By the side of the door a sign read, 'Alexandra House for Children.' Lee had heard of children's homes before and knew what this would mean – he was going to be like the misfits at school that no-one associated with. Before they got to the front door, Lynn diverted their direction to the side of the house and knocked on the side entrance door.

The door was opened by a rather large lady with medium-length and wavy grey hair. To Lee's eyes, she looked about seventy. She wore frumpy old clothes with tights that showed her dark, hairy legs.

"Hello, Lynn, and welcome, young man! You must be Lee?" she said in an over-friendly way to mask her surprise at his age.

Lee just said, "Hello." He wasn't sure what else to say.

"My name is Fred," she said, as she invited them to step inside what was a boot room attached to the kitchen.

Lee frowned. He wondered why she had a man's name and made a mental note to ask her later. There was no need.

"Funny name, I know... it was an old nickname I had at school," she said quirkily.

They all stood in the kitchen for a minute whilst the two women talked briefly about what had happened.

"I didn't realise he was so young," Fred said, eyebrows raised at Lynn.

"I'm so sorry, but in the rush I forgot to include that in our conversation," Lynn said apologetically.

"So, Lee... I suspect you're wondering what you're doing in this strange place and how everything works here?" Fred didn't need a response. "I think we can answer all that in a little while. For now, why don't we take you to the room I've prepared for you so that you can settle in?"

"OK," he said quietly.

Lee noticed she smelled funny when he walked behind her. And by funny, what he really thought was that she smelled of poo. As they made their way through the house, there were uncomfortable glances and stares from a couple of other children and teenagers. When they reached what would now be Lee's room, Fred asked, "Is that all you've got?" glancing at Lee, then Lynn. Lee nodded.

"We'll have to look into that," she remarked brightly as she ushered him into the room. "Why don't you spend a little time unpacking and making yourself comfortable? You can pop back down to the kitchen when you're done."

Before Lee could respond back, Lynn asked, "Lee, there's something we both need to check out before we go downstairs. Can you take off your jumper and t-shirt, please?"

Lee was reticent about doing this and his face showed his displeasure.

"There are just some things we need to check, my darling," Fred added. "Don't worry, we're not going to ask you to take off your trousers."

Lee turned his back and reluctantly removed the items of clothing. They both approached for a closer inspection. Lee began to shiver slightly. Lynn crouched down on one knee and gently manoeuvred him round in a 360-degree rotation. It wasn't the worst the two women had seen, but it wasn't pleasant. They gave each other a knowing glance.

There were bruises all over his front, sides and back. Lynn caressed her hands across Lee's ribs that were beginning to protrude, to see if there was anything broken. She felt bad about taking sweets from the packet on the way there; clearly the boy had needed them more than her. Lynn stroked Lee's bare back.

"Thank you, Lee. We'll let you get dressed now," she said in a soft tone.

The two ladies pulled the door to and went back downstairs to the kitchen. Lee put his t-shirt and jumper back on and opened his suitcase. His mind wandered, briefly, in the glow of the soft touch of the social workers' hands. He had no recollection of a time when anyone in his family had ever touched him in such a caring fashion. He sat for a while contemplating the last twenty-four hours and wondered what was going to happen to him, and whether life could get any worse. He looked around the sparse room; it was larger than the bedroom he'd left behind, and at least had a decent view out the front of the house.

Downstairs in the kitchen, the two women discussed their assessment of the case and what they'd been able to observe during their brief interaction with the boy.

"He looks a bit malnourished?" Fred questioned. "Nothing a few good meals wouldn't take care of, wouldn't you agree?"

Fred was peppered a couple of times with curious questions from the children who had seen Lee arrive. But she'd told them off in a kind way, saying she would introduce him in a while. Rather than potentially cause a commotion if Lee was reluctant to stay, Lynn elected to leave before he came back down from his room. It was harsh, but always better that way. The women both agreed that this would be an assessment and that Fred would keep a special eye on the boy. They also agreed to weekly updates, and Lynn said she'd try to come back in four weeks or so if things went well.

Upstairs, Lee didn't unpack very much; instead, he chose to store his suitcase in the wardrobe and live directly from that. *I'll need to be ready for when they come back for me, he thought*. Lee heard a car start up outside and jumped on to his bed to see Lynn's car reverse out of the driveway. He was on his own now. With not much else to do, he headed downstairs to find Fred. On the way down, he spotted an older girl looking at him. They caught each other's eye and she smiled faintly. Lee smiled awkwardly as she went back to reading her book. He was heading to the kitchen just as Fred was coming out.

"Ah, just the young man I'm looking for. Come on, we'll do a tour of the place and I'll introduce you to some of the other children."

Lee didn't want to hold her hand when she offered it, but Fred didn't take this sort of thing personally. It often took a while for new children to adapt and trust the people and their new surroundings.

"It's a big house, and there'll be more children to meet when they get home from playing out," she said. As he was introduced to the ones that were there, he couldn't help thinking there was something wrong with all of them; some had speech problems and some were clearly backwards, whilst others had physical problems. They didn't appear to be bad kids from first meeting, just defective. Lee didn't feel like he belonged in the same house as them. They were getting closer to meeting the girl who'd smiled, and he could see that she was a lot older than him. *She's got boobies,* he thought to himself. When he was introduced to Angela, they both smiled. Angela was thirteen years old and well developed for her age. She had long black hair, and when she smiled her cheeks dimpled in very odd places. She'd been at the home for most of her life and was now quite the matriarch. She was a thalidomide baby and Lee noticed one of her arms from the elbow down was malformed, ending in only three fingers. Lee had never seen anything like this before, and Angela recognised the look on his face.

"It's a claw for tickling little boys," she giggled. Lee smiled back. He had already forgotten the names of the other children he'd just been introduced to. On the way round the home, Fred also talked Lee through the house rules and the do's and don'ts. She saw the same level of despondency expressed on Lee's face as all the new arrivals at Alexandra, but she knew this would ebb away over time. Lee turned to Fred and opened up for the first time.

"What's the real reason for your name, Fred?" he said, his eyes boring deep into hers.

Well, well, she thought. *We have a perceptive one here!* Everyone else, including Lynn, had always taken her explanation at face value. She deliberated for a brief second.

"A very good question, young man, so you deserve an honest answer. Way back, hundreds of years ago, men always wanted their first-born child to be a boy. Only boys could continue the family name, and the inheritance was always passed to the eldest son. My father was of that belief, and when he realised that I was a girl he named me Fred anyway. As a child I was brought up as boy until I eventually left home. It's what's actually still on my birth certificate!"

"Are you saying you're hundreds of years old then?"

"It sometimes feels that way," Fred responded back. Lee smiled. He could tell by her face she'd been honest. "Why don't you head back out to where the other children are for a bit whilst I make you some beans on toast? Two slices?"

"Yes, please," he said. He could really feel the hunger now. Lee didn't feel that comfortable with any of the other children, so he went over to the toy box to see what was inside. There wasn't much. After devouring the beans on toast, Lee went back upstairs to his room. He was tired and needed to lie down and rest his body. Later that day, Fred popped up to see if he was up for meeting more of the other children. She brought him downstairs again. It seemed like slim pickings, but there were two twin boys who were of a similar age that he could maybe see himself getting on with.

* * *

Laura arrived home in a sombre mood. Her mother seemed quite perky, which didn't help. On her way upstairs she saw Lee's belongings all boxed up. The finality of it gave an impression of death that made her shiver. She went to her own room and stayed there to play the Blondie record and read the magazine bought using the money she'd been bribed with to stay out of the house while Lee left.

When Jon got home from work, he was a little downcast too. He knew what he'd been part of was something unpleasant, but Louvaine convinced him that everything was for the best. They had a moment to themselves in the kitchen before she said, "Everything will be better when the baby comes, you'll see." She brushed her hand over the very conspicuous bump that sat in front of her.

Listening to music and reading had temporarily taken Laura's mind off the day's events. She heard her parents talking in the kitchen and knew it would be time for tea soon. Laura began to get changed and was down to her knickers when Jon popped into her room without knocking and sat on her bed, half-watching her. A pleasurable pulse ran through her body that she didn't understand. She thought about covering up, but Jon gave her a smile so she continued. Since moving in and becoming the new head of the family, they'd both hit it off really well, especially when her mum and Lee weren't around. Now dressed, Jon motioned for her to sit on the bed next to him to talk through what had happened. Laura decided to ask him the question she didn't dare ask her mother.

"Where's Lee?" she asked.

Jon had very little to respond with because he didn't actually know. "He's been taken away, and honestly we weren't told where he was taken."

Despite all of her participation in the events, Laura was upset. They sat and cuddled for a good ten minutes while Laura wept into his jumper. She felt secure with his big hands around her. At teatime there was a muted atmosphere at the table. Louvaine was the only one to initiate any conversation and it was not about Lee. It seemed there was now an unspoken rule that Lee would not be mentioned again from this point onwards.

Over the next few weeks, Laura received questions from the local friends Lee had made. She found it hard explaining away his disappearance. She initially just said that he was away, not honestly knowing if he would be coming back. In the end she decided to tell anyone who asked that he'd gone away to live with an uncle and he was never coming back.

Louvaine eventually gave birth to a new boy of 6lbs 3oz in September. It was unfortunate for Jon that he couldn't be there for the birth, but they'd agreed that keeping his job was the priority. Upon first sight of his new son, Jon was completely euphoric and emotional. It took a couple of days to decide on a name and Lou suggested naming the child Jonathan Jr. after his father. They both smiled.

* * *

During this time, Lee, as always, began to adjust to his new environment. He hadn't been trusted to go out on his own just yet, so he set his mind to working out exit routes if he needed to get away from the home. He hadn't come fully out of his shell, but he spoke a little more and was friendly with Fred and the twin boys. He especially liked it when Angela spoke to him now and then. Fred was an old hand and noticed the little friendship she'd made with the boy. Rather than question Lee directly, she felt that an indirect route might be more productive and so she asked Angela if she wouldn't mind spending a little more time with Lee to get to know him a little better.

"I think he could do with a kind friend right now," she said. Angela agreed. He was a breath of fresh air around the place anyway.

Lee preferred to play football outside in the garden rather than socialise, but Fred felt that he must be lonely playing on his own. She tried getting some of the other children to play, but Lee just got frustrated at their lack of ability. The twins weren't very good at football either and the older kids didn't really socialise down the age ranks. In his room, she noticed that he still hadn't unpacked his case. When she asked him about it, he simply answered, "It's just in case they come back for me." She really didn't know quite how to break the news to him, so chose not to. Time had a way of working these things out.

* * *

CHAPTER 13

IMPATIENCE

Kim Montrall was back on the case. Nancy had called again after Miss Dawkins' visit, but even she was surprised at how the situation had escalated since her last involvement. Both Nancy and David provided her with as much new information as they could, including the pregnancy, but Kim warned that there really wasn't that much to go on. Nancy suggested that initially the best lead might be to see if Kim could trace the removal firm used, if they indeed used one. Other than that, the trail had gone pretty cold. They agreed that Nancy would be the lead contact for Kim and that updates should be every two days, at a minimum. David was worried about the costs because he felt that this could go on indefinitely.

"I'll help you with the costs," Nancy said. "You can use Louvaine's maintenance money, and I'll cover the rest. Anyway, you've got your final exams coming up soon, so you need to pass those."

Kim's first actions were to go to Bracknell and do a little house-to-house investigating around the cul-de-sac. She wanted to uncover something more than David and Nancy had. But other than what she already knew, the only things she really heard were additional speculations about how they treated the boy, and that nobody liked the mother. She also contacted the local police to see if there had been any more incidents since the alleged kidnapping, but there had been nothing. There was nothing about them on the electoral register, and the local authority weren't helpful at all. Whilst they couldn't give specific details, they did say that the mother had made a complaint that David was violent and a threat to her family.

"This woman was really covering her tracks this time," Kim thought. She did manage to trace the new landlord, but he didn't have any more information except that they'd scarpered owing him a month's rent. Some digging around local removal companies brought no more leads either, and even trying local van hire companies drew a blank. Not one solid lead had been generated, and she didn't know what to tell her clients.

* * *

Lee was now enrolled into the local school and Fred had been shopping with him for some uniform, shoes, a coat and a school bag. By the end of his first day, he could tell that it wasn't the best school in the world and his view hadn't really changed much over the next few weeks. To him, the teacher was thick because she asked stupid questions. He could get his work done long before the others, which gave him time to muck around afterwards. He felt like he lived in a home full of rejects and now felt he had to spend the day with kids who weren't a lot better. He needed more stimulation. The headmaster had reported the disruption back to Fred after a couple of weeks. He had no complaints about Lee's work, just the attitude.

"I'm thinking of trying him in the year above. Would that be OK with you?" he asked.

"Based on my observations, the more stimulation and work you give him the better he'll be. I think he needs his mind taken off the past," Fred replied. The headmaster agreed to get the ball rolling.

At the home, Fred kept a discreet watch over the boy. One evening during a conversation with Angela in the kitchen, Fred asked what the girl made of Lee now that she'd had the time to get to know him a little.

"He's pretty sweet, clever and quite the tinker sometimes. He's a good kid."

"Do you think you could find out what happened to him over the last year before he arrived here?" Fred explained that Lee had been brought there as a very quick favour. In order to help him, it would be useful if Fred knew more about his background.

"Why don't you just ask him yourself?"

"I don't think he trusts adults," Fred explained sympathetically. "Lee will just clam up if I start probing. I've tried and he's very defensive. Would an extra £1 pocket money a week swing it for you?" Angela agreed with a smile, but in truth she wanted to get to know him a little better anyway, so the £1 was easy money.

"Make sure you're subtle about it and let the conversations flow naturally. I don't want him spooked." Angela understood the request. She'd been at the home longer than anyone else, often acted as Fred's second in command, and had welcomed countless other children in her time.

At the home Lee had integrated only with the children he wanted to associate with. That wasn't very many, and all the others were surplus to requirements unless he needed something from them. He wasn't horrible or nasty to them like his sister would have been; he just didn't feel like he had anything in common to talk about. There was one boy, though, that started to cause him a problem because of his friendliness towards Angela. Gordon was twice Lee's age at 14. He was taller, very thin and seemed to have a head disproportionately larger than his neck should've been able to support. In a comedic way, Lee sort of felt sorry for him; ginger hair and a face full of freckles topped off with such a big head was never going to be a winning combination. The longer Lee spent with Angela, the more annoyed Gordon would get. Lee could tell he had the hots for her. So just for fun, Lee always made sure he and Angela would smile and laugh a lot when they were together.

Their friendship was good. The mental stimulation Angela attained with Lee was like nothing else she received at the home. His ability to pick things up and his quick wit were a welcome change. For fun, they often talked about really difficult, strange or improbable scenarios using 'what would you do if…?' questions. They'd write the answers down and compare notes. She would often laugh at Lee's responses; not in an unkind way, but because he often came up with the most bizarre solutions. He also liked to test her too by asking random funny questions, like 'Which is faster - fire or water?' Angela quite liked the attention of Lee's rather obvious crush. He was cute, but of course the large age difference ruled out any prospect of a deeper, more romantic relationship as far as she was concerned. When Gordon was around, she tempered her friendliness towards Lee. It wasn't meant to be unkind, but she was just giving Lee the hint that she wanted to be with someone else. From Lee's perspective, it was the price he paid for her popularity.

Lee had been given various chores to do on the same rota as the other children – no-one escaped the rota. The job he hated the most was the making of tea. The smell and build-up of soaking wet teabags by the side of the sink disgusted him. From that time on, Lee decided he'd never drink the stuff.

Fred seemed OK, although she did seem to watch him a lot out of the corner of her eye. She'd try to be subtle, but Lee knew full well what she was doing. Having earned her trust, he'd been allowed to play out the front of the house and even slightly further afield. Lee used the time wisely to get to know his surroundings in more detail. He ventured further and in different directions each time, looking for possible places to run to if needed. Lee wanted to call his nan, but the telephone at the home was out of bounds for all the children and the rumour was that Fred received an itemised bill each month to check any usage. During their conversations, Angela had confirmed the rumour to be true, as well as the draconian punishment for anyone caught using it without permission – two months of not being allowed out and no pocket money. Lee didn't get pocket money anyway because the family hadn't provided it. Access to the phone would be problematic; it was in the kitchen where Fred spent most of her time and, even when she wasn't there, there was never enough time to use it without being seen. With some money he'd scrounged from his wheeler-dealing with kids at school, he tried calling a couple of times from a phone box when he'd been out exploring, but nobody had picked up.

As promised, Lynn kept in touch to check on Lee's progress and Fred had updated her about his enrolment into the local school. As was customary, Fred had discussed Lee's background and her own observations, which wasn't much, with the headmaster. She'd enrolled more children into this school than she cared to remember and, with an open dialogue and a little work, they generally turned out OK. Lynn felt that now Lee had been enrolled into the school she could be confident that he would be able to remain at Alexandra House. Besides,

Fred was always happy to receive the cheques from Hertfordshire County Council.

Although Alexandra House was well out of her jurisdiction, Lynn was able to make a visit to see Lee on one weekend. Four weeks since she'd last seen him, she could see right away that he had improved drastically. He was cleaner, had put on a little more weight and was coming out of his shell. She'd been told by Fred not to sugar-coat anything with the boy. "He'll see right through it," she warned.

Lynn sat Lee down and told him that she needed more detail for the report she had to compile. He had been quite open when talking about the routines of seeing his father and nan, but really clammed up when asked about home life with his mother. He didn't want to give too much away, just in case they wanted him back. She was surprised at the detailed recall he provided in some of his answers, so when he was vague or uncooperative she could tell that he just didn't want to talk about that particular subject. There were two things he was adamant about – finding his father and understanding when he would be leaving Alexandra to go back home. For the former, Lee said that he didn't have his father's current address, but he did write down his nan's name, address and telephone number for her. On the matter of leaving Alexandra, Lynn found this sort of thing difficult to break to a child. Heeding Fred's advice, she said tentatively, "I'm sorry, but I can't guarantee that you'll be going home, Lee. But I can look into the address you've given me and see what I can do." Lee wasn't too impressed by this non-committal response, but it was the best he could get for now.

* * *

CHAPTER 14

BETRAYAL

David finally received the Diploma in Management that he'd been working so hard for over the last two years. In the subsequent three months, as a reward for the hard work he had put in, and for going above and beyond during the strikes, he was given the promotion he so desperately desired. Nancy was extremely proud of him, given the strain he'd been under for the last year or so. By way of celebration, she took him to the Savoy restaurant, just off the Strand in London. This was all they'd had to celebrate as Kim hadn't got too far in her investigation. Cold cases were always difficult to get started, so she'd looked for leads at hospitals for women with the name Louvaine who'd recently given birth. This had brought no luck, and she was finding it difficult to think of new ways to get the case going. Nancy was not impressed.

"You need to step up your game! Is civilian life making you go soft, Kim?" Nancy questioned. That really irked Kim, but she decided to bite her tongue for now. "Go back over what you have and find something!" Nancy barked. Kim acquiesced and said she'd be back in contact when and if she found something. "Let's assume that's a 'when,' if you want me to try to get you back into the good graces at HQ, that is." Nancy put down the receiver abruptly, not requiring a response.

With much of her time in the early months spent nursing and devoting herself to looking after the new child, Louvaine had too many opportunities to think. The problems caused by David's money stopping, coupled with post-natal depression, made her angry and bitter – more bitter than usual anyway. Jon had always been as helpful as he could, which she appreciated, but Laura and her extracurricular activities had had to take a back seat for now. What angered her most was that she'd played herself into a corner. She couldn't go to David, Nancy or the courts to demand money without giving away their location. She was pretty sure they'd have a field day with her anyway if she did. She was now trapped and isolated and her moodiness spilled over on to Laura, who had begun to physically develop and was going through some hormonal changes which sometimes led to clashes between them. They were all pleased that she'd passed her 11+ and been offered a place at a good grammar school – but that required a great deal of capital investment, something they didn't have right now. Louvaine said that they would have to think about an alternative, which devastated Laura; so the drama would run on. With Louvaine's money drying up, Jon tried his best to work longer hours to try to make up the shortfall. When he arrived home now, he was often as white as a ghost and his eyes were permanently bloodshot. He barely got time with the new baby because Jon Jr. was generally asleep. He'd spend time with Laura before she went to bed, so by the time he got to Lou she'd be in bed asleep. Laura seemed to be the only person who really gave him any attention.

On the evening Jon arrived home, after Laura had clashed with her mother about the alternative to grammar school, he'd found her in floods of tears. To Laura, her whole future was crumbling right before her eyes again. Jon said that they might be able to apply for a grant or something, which helped soothe her tears. As good as his word, the next day during his lunchtime, he popped into the local council offices and, after a number of enquiries, got the correct forms to complete. In the evening, Laura had been the one to complete the information and Jon dutifully hand-delivered it to the council the next day with a self-addressed envelope. From then after, it was a waiting game.

Laura was a nervous wreck for weeks, but finally the decision letter arrived in the post which Jon gave to her to open and read. The decision had been in her favour and Laura was so relieved that Jon had come through for her that she gave him the biggest hug she could muster. Jon returned the gesture, his hand briefly sliding down to cradle her bottom. The same pulse she'd felt before discharged throughout her body once again. She still didn't understand the feeling, but she couldn't ignore it.

* * *

As promised, Lynn looked into the phone number and address details that Lee had provided. She assumed Lee had given her the wrong number, because an unobtainable tone was all she heard each time she called. She had a heavy caseload and let things ruminate around her subconscious for a couple of weeks. As Nancy's address was in Sevenoaks, Lynn opted to call Kent Social Services. She enquired to see if there had been any activity relating to Lee, or anyone from the address he'd given her. Whilst she didn't get through to anyone with specific knowledge, the person on the other end made some notes and promised to send out a memo to all case workers. Lynn gave her contact details but didn't hold out much hope. Her next plan was to go directly to the address unannounced, though this would have to wait until she could find time in her schedule.

* * *

Anne Dawkins had not had any further dealings with Lee's case since her meeting with Nancy and David. Although she'd asked to be informed of any updates, nothing had been forthcoming. So, with a higher caseload than usual, Lee Walker had fallen off her radar. A slew of messages and unopened mail sat on her desk, and so one particular afternoon she resolved to clear her backlog and informed everyone that she was not to be disturbed. Partway through the pile she found a memo bulletin to all case workers. It asked:

To all case workers:

If you recognise the following names, please contact Lynn Franks on 0727 533633 ASAP:

- *Lee King*
- *Louvaine King*
- *Nancy Walker*

She immediately connected the dots between Lee, Nancy and Louvaine and picked up the phone. Unfortunately, Lynn wasn't around to take the call, so Anne left an urgent call-back message. Two hours later, she received the call that she was waiting for and was astonished at what she heard. They both traded stories as Anne confirmed that the father and grandmother had been looking for Lee. This looked like the same modus operandi she'd seen before, but before making any rash moves Anne needed to be sure this was the right Lee they were talking about.

"From recollection, we have a photograph of Lee on file," Anne said. "I'm going to mail you a copy. Could you call me back to confirm that we're talking about the same boy, please?" Three days later, Lynn called and Anne had her confirmation. The family had moved address again, but this time with different surnames. Cross-border cases were always tricky but, as this was Anne's case originally, Lynn asked her how she would like to proceed.

"It's good that we can now account for everyone's whereabouts, and that you have Lee safely in care. I'm going to ask you to not say anything to the boy or family for a bit whilst I make contact with the father. I'll be in contact with you soon."

"OK," Lynn said. "I shall make my notes and put the case as pending for a week."

This had been a stroke of luck for Anne. With it being out of jurisdiction, a less experienced case worker could have just put this information on file and not bothered to investigate it further.

* * *

The headmaster called Lee to his office. As always, Lee wondered what he'd done wrong this time, but he was actually being given some good news for a change. He was being placed into a class one year above what he should normally be. This had been quite a nice stroke to his ego. Getting up to speed with older kids kept him more occupied now and this in turn resulted in less disruption to the class. The teacher seemed to have a lot more control over his pupils than the previous one, and when Lee did act out it was mostly the other children that put him in his place.

He'd settled in as much as he was going to settle into the home and exhibited more patience with the other less fortunate inhabitants. Angela's suitor was getting on his nerves, though. He felt that acting menacingly towards Lee would put him in his place, but he was nothing to Lee. Yes, he was bigger, but Lee wasn't scared of anyone. Lee didn't even flinch when Gordon simulated throwing a punch towards him, which perplexed the older boy. But as the weeks went by, Lee became disillusioned. He hadn't heard anything from Lynn, and so he just assumed that she hadn't been able to do anything. It certainly didn't look like she was coming back. Lee needed a way out. He needed to do something; otherwise, he'd just rot in the place. He made his mind up to write a letter to his mum and Jon, borrowing some writing paper from Angela. Lee took the time to write the letter in his best handwriting.

Alexandra House Children's Home
268 Risbygate Street
Bury St. Edmunds
Suffolk

Dear Mum & Jon,

It's been two months since I was sent away from home and I have had time to think about what I've done. I promise that I didn't threaten Laura with a knife. I was just washing a knife up when we were talking. Please don't think of me as bad, I would never do that. I am sorry for all of the things I've done and I'm sorry that I broke Jon's car. Please take me back. I'll be good for you I promise, you won't be sorry.

Please please. I hope to see you before Christmas

Love from

Lee

Happy with the spelling and confident that there were no mistakes, Lee posted the letter on the way to school.

Angela hadn't spent quite so much time with him as weeks went by, as Gordon had stepped up his game for her attention. But in the time they had spent together, she'd allowed Lee into her room; not even Gordon was allowed there yet. Lee had opened up a little to her when she'd asked about his past. He told her that his parents split up, that he had a sister who had been nothing but cruel and had told a lot of lies about him. When Angela asked what sort of lies, he told her that he was there because she'd said he threatened her with a knife. Lee told her it was something he'd never do. Angela reciprocated by telling Lee a little bit about her situation, how long she'd been at the home and that she didn't remember much about her parents. Her parents had just dropped her off at the home when she was four years old and never came back. Lee wondered how Angela really felt. She'd put on a brave face but it was a sad story, nonetheless. They both agreed that neither would say anything to anyone about their conversations and shook hands. They kept shaking hands until they were both laughing and swinging all around the room.

The next day Fred caught Angela on the stairs and asked how she'd been getting on with Lee. They moved to a nearby room and Angela spoke of what she had gleaned to date and that what was said was said in confidence. Fred chose not to let on that she already knew of the knife-threatening incident. Instead, she simply said, "Thanks, Angela. Keep up the good work and 'Mum's the word.'"

* * *

PART 4

(December 1977 - February 1978)

CHAPTER 15

RUNAWAY

One December afternoon after returning home from school, Lee found a letter had been posted under his bedroom door. He recognised it instantly as the one he'd sent to his mother. It had been opened, and 'RETURN TO SENDER' was written in big letters across the front. The family address had been crossed out, with his new one written above in his mother's handwriting. There was nothing inside other than his original note. *She must have read it*, he thought, as '*You weren't my baby,*' reverberated around Lee's mind again. Ever since his mother had made him leave, that statement had been at the forefront of Lee's thoughts before he went to sleep, and when he awoke each morning. Lee knew now for sure that he was stuck in the home. No-one was coming for him. He'd given Nancy's address and phone number to Lynn weeks ago, but not even his nan or his dad had come to take him away.

His friendship with Angela had also taken a slightly different turn. She used to be fun to be with, but now she seemed to keep asking questions about his past. Lee became wary of her. Angela and Gordon had now become an official item, so Gordon made sure that Lee knew he was on the outside. Lee believed there was nobody he could really trust and felt just as unwanted as when he was at home. Upset, he sat on his bed for a while and thought about his options.

Lee headed off downstairs to the main room to see if the twins were around. Along the corridor walking towards him were the new couple. Emboldened by his new status as a boyfriend, he'd recently caught Lee off guard a couple of times whilst he was disadvantaged carrying plates or cups. Now more resolute, Lee had decided that a disadvantage wouldn't stop him next time. *Screw the consequences!* As Lee tried to walk past this time, Gordon shoulder-barged him into the wall. Lee turned and leapt at the fourteen-year-old, squarely hitting him in the face. Instead of just stopping and running, Lee kept on hitting him, unconcerned for his own safety. Fred heard the commotion and came bounding in to break the two up. She pushed Lee away and grabbed Gordon by the ear. As she dragged him away, she said, "You better watch it, lad. He knows how to use a knife, you know!"

What followed was like a slow-motion realisation for Lee. *How did she know that?* he thought. As he turned to look at Angela, her look said all he needed to know. After Fred told him off, he walked off back to his room. A few minutes later Angela came upstairs and knocked on his door.

"Lee, it's me. Can I come in?"

"Get lost!" he said with hostility. Remorseful, Angela went back downstairs.

In his mind he'd been betrayed again by another female. Lee made his decision there and then; he was going to run away. He packed up his warmest clothes and the little money he had into his suitcase, along with his toothbrush and what toothpaste he had left. His silver moneybox would be dead weight, so Lee left it with the few toys he'd brought with him on the shelf. He then had an idea. Whilst Gordon was being given extra jobs in the kitchen, Lee sneaked into his room and stole any money he could find. He also snapped the suspension on a model motorbike that sat on a shelf. *That'll teach him,* he said to himself, smiling. He then went into Angela's room and stole her money, too.

In Lee's mind, everything was ready to go. He carried on as usual for the rest of the evening, contributing to putting up Christmas decorations with the other children. Fred had managed to have a real tree delivered, and it was much bigger than the artificial one his parents had dragged out from the loft the year before. Lee looked around and pondered. So many of the children were excited about Christmas, but he couldn't understand why. They'd all been thrown away just like him, so how could they be so happy? *Maybe they just had each other*. Right then, he would have traded the big tree in all its splendour for just one gift under a bare-bones tree with someone who cared for him. He wouldn't even ask that they love him; to just care for him would be enough.

Lee snapped himself out of his thoughts and went back to putting baubles on the lower branches. The tree looked amazing with the fairy lights and tinsel, and after they'd all finished, he went to bed at the normal time. Lee knew what time Fred went to bed and that he needed to get as far away as possible in the time he would have. He'd watched news reports before of how the police searched the local area when someone went missing. He knew that the night-time was going to be his best chance to get where he needed to go before someone raised the alarm.

At 11:30pm Lee's alarm clock went off under his pillow. He put on the clothes he'd left out that would make the least noise and grabbed his pre-packed case. He crept downstairs, dodging the known creaks in the floorboards and walked through the kitchen. He needed food, so he took two packets of biscuits from the larder on his way out through the back door. It was nerve-wracking but surprisingly easy to escape. Lee headed for a truck stop he'd explored previously along the A14. He didn't know what the distance was, only that it would be about one and a half hour's walk from the home. The weather was chilly and so Lee alternated between jogging and walking. He couldn't risk having somebody see him and possibly report him to the police, so he stuck to the fields and paths that ran alongside the main roads, knowing that he would eventually find his destination. At about 1:30am, Lee reached the truck stop. It was quite a noisy place, even in the early hours. He kept a very low profile and began moving around the truck cabs to see if any were empty and open. Lee moved quietly between the cabs and had checked six before he found one that was open.

This is it, Lee. Do this or go back to the home! he told himself. He knew the answer. *No going back!* He took the chance and got into the empty cab, closing the door behind him as quietly as he could. He'd never been in a lorry before and figured that the best place to hide would be in the back behind the driver's seat. There was a blanket, so he got comfortable and covered his body and head. A minute later, Lee realised that he needed to go to toilet. He got back up, checked outside for any movement and quickly got out of the cab for a wee underneath the trailer. Relieved but cold, he quickly got back in again and resumed his previous position. Lying there apprehensively, he thought to himself *this could be the beginning of something new.* Lee tried to stay awake and alert, but eventually fell asleep at about 3am.

The owner of the truck had relaxed with his evening meal in the truck stop café before he walked to the Bed & Breakfast next door; an arrangement that he'd been accustomed to whenever he was delivering to this part of the country. Arnauld Wouters was originally from Belgium and had been a driver for 20 years – his first and only job after inheriting his first truck from his father back in 1957. Where most drivers would have put on significant weight during that time, due to diet and lack of exercise, nothing had stuck to him. He was a taller version of a fly-weight boxer, with black hair that receded at the temples. He smoked now and then, but not habitually. He was well known at the B&B, and for him it was one of the little luxuries he permitted himself on his regular excursions to England.

The next morning he woke up early and went downstairs for the superb complimentary breakfast. Now set up for the day ahead, he walked next door to his truck which sat amongst a sea of others. Arnauld took his keys out of his pocket and went to unlock the driver's side door. He knew the lock didn't work properly, but he didn't need anyone else knowing that. He stepped in, past the cheeky sign that said 'Veuillez retirer les chaussures et le slip avant d'entrer' (*Please remove shoes and knickers before entry*), started the motor and drove off. He had no idea that he now had a stowaway. Lee woke when the driver got into the cab and started the engine.

All good so far. He hadn't been noticed and just kept quiet; no coughing or sneezing allowed. As the lorry began rolling, Arnauld headed south to Dover. Lee had no idea where he would be by the evening. *Hopefully in another country*, he thought and went back to sleep. The one thing Lee hadn't really thought through was that his money would be useless in another country, but he mulled it over as he went to sleep. The next time Lee was awoken was by a bump and a crashing sound as the lorry clattered over what sounded like metal. The driver pulled to a stop and got out of the cab, 'locking' the door behind him and heading straight up to the bar for a beer. Lee waited for a while before peeking out from under the blanket. He was starting to feel cold when he felt a jolt. As the truck then began to sway, he looked out into the darkness to see lots of other cars and lorries at close quarters. Lee realised he was on a ferry. This was exciting! He needed the toilet again and took his toothbrush and paste from his case. He quietly exited the truck, making sure to leave the door unlocked, not knowing the lock was faulty. Lee saw the signs for a WC and headed for it, making sure to avoid any human contact where possible. When he'd finished, he headed straight back to the truck, nestling into the back compartment again. Lee wasn't sure when he'd next eat again, so he ate two biscuits and put the packet back in his case. He knew he could go days without food if he needed to, so a couple of biscuits would get him by for a while. He tried to keep as warm as possible and went back to sleep.

An hour or so later, the message came through the Tannoy system for vehicle passengers to go down to the vehicle deck to get ready for disembarkation. Lee woke again, as butterflies fluttered across his stomach when the driver got back into the cab. Under the blanket, he listened intently to what was happening. The truck eventually lurched into motion, and he felt the same bump and crash as it drove off the ferry. Arnauld drove through Calais customs without having to stop and headed south towards his next destination. Lee's anxiety subsided as the truck's tyres droned consistently along the tarmac; feeling more relaxed, his eyes closed. Arnauld's next job was to complete a drop-off and pick-up just on the outskirts of Nantes in France. After three hours en route, he had to stop; the beer needed to follow its natural course. He pulled into the nearest Relais Routiers, parked up and switched off the ignition. He got out of his seat and moved into the rear of the cab to get his coat.

It's here somewhere. He pulled back the blanket and was completely startled when he saw something move. Not knowing what it was, his split-second reaction was to hit out at it. Crack! The movement stopped. Arnauld cautiously pulled back the blanket fully to reveal a small boy. Without realising it, the driver had punched Lee fully in the side of the temple, knocking him unconscious.

Arnauld was worried now. "D'où venait-il?" (*Where did he come from?*) he said quietly. His next thoughts were "Pourquoi est-ce que je l'ai frappé?" (*Why did I hit him?*) and "Qu'est-ce que je vais faire maintenant?" (*What am I going to do now?*). He checked that the child was breathing and gently agitated him a little. Lee eventually came to. His surroundings were all still the same, but he felt groggy and sick. Arnauld was immensely relieved to see the boy come round. As the boy looked up at him, he said, "Qui êtes tu?" "D'où êtes-tu?" Lee frowned and looked blankly as he began to shiver.

"Who are you?" "Where are you from?" Arnauld rephrased in English, trying his best not to be too intimidating.

"England," Lee said, and nothing else.

The back of his cab had entertained the odd woman in its time, but never a stowaway. This was a whole new experience to the driver. Not too sure what to do next, Arnauld apologised to the boy for hitting him and said that he didn't mean to hurt him. The kid looked a little groggy but seemed OK, so Arnauld sat him up. He saw that the boy had a small suitcase and put the puzzle together. Feeling bad for punching a child, Arnauld asked if he would like a drink and pointed to the café. Lee looked up and nodded in agreement.

"Do you think you're going to be OK to walk?" he asked.

Lee nodded again. As they walked over to the café entrance, Arnaud put his hand on Lee's shoulder for a second and said, "Let me do the talking."

When they entered, Arnauld told the boy to go find an empty table and sit down whilst he ordered some food and a drink. "Hot chocolate?" he asked.

Lee nodded.

This kid doesn't say much! Arnauld thought to himself.

Lee found a table and looked at the menu. There was nothing in English, which made him feel quite buoyant. Arnauld ordered some food and sat down opposite the boy. So far he'd only introduced himself with a fist, so it was only reasonable that he should break the ice.

"My name is Arnauld. What's yours?"

"Lee," he said with a slight smile. He could smell cooked food and his tummy began to rumble. They began to talk. Arnauld's English was very good.

"Where are you from?" he enquired. Lee was guarded.

"England," he said again, with a slight glint in his eye.

Arnauld pulled a comically frustrated face.

"You told me that already. Come on, I'm just trying to help. Whereabouts in England?"

Lee wasn't unfriendly; he just shook his head as if to say, '*That's on a need-to-know basis.*'

"OK, fine," Arnauld said. "At least tell me why you've run away. You're so young!" Lee was brutally concise with his answer.

"Apart from one person, everyone I've known has been uncaring, nasty or a liar."

"Surely not everyone?" But Lee just nodded. Arnauld chose not to dig any deeper on that subject.

"So how old are you and what are your plans?" Lee just shrugged. With a steely look in his eyes he said, "I'll work it out." He didn't reveal his age. From their brief time talking, Lee felt that the man seemed decent enough. He hadn't kicked him out of the truck straight away like he could have, and there was genuine concern on his face.

An assistant brought their food over and smiled at them both. As a special little treat, she gave Lee a little iced bun that Arnauld hadn't ordered. Lee was about to say 'thank you,' but Arnauld cut in and said "Merci" on his behalf. He watched Lee wrap the bun in a serviette and put it in his pocket. *Smart kid*, he thought. They finished their food and Arnauld looked at his watch.

"I have to head off now. Do you need the toilet?" They both went, and Lee followed Arnauld as he headed back to the truck.

Before opening the door, Arnauld said, "I should really take you back to England, you know. There must be people there looking for you?"

Lee was adamant about not going back. In a polite but forceful way he said, "Thank you for the food. But if you give me my case, you can leave me here, please." Arnauld was a good and decent man. He didn't like the idea of just leaving a small boy at a truck stop. How bad would that be?

"I'm heading to Nantes; it's south-west of here. You can come with me there?" Arnauld offered. Lee accepted and they both got into the truck, this time with Lee promoted to the front passenger seat. As he would be returning back to England via a detour home afterwards, Arnauld was hoping that he could convince Lee to go back with him over the coming hours.

* * *

Still feeling bad about the incident from the day before, Angela knocked on Lee's door the next morning to apologise again for what had happened. As there was no response, she tentatively opened the door. Lee's bed was made and neither he nor his coat were there, so she headed downstairs for breakfast. There was nothing unusual to her and she just assumed Lee had already left for school.

Fred walked into the breakfast room at the usual time of the morning. It was always the same; the children were all at different stages of their morning routines. They ran on pretty self-regulated shifts, with some eating earlier than others. Fred always thought it akin to King's Cross Station, where the trains just came in and departed to their timetable. Angela and Gordon were both at the breakfast table and stopped talking to each other when they saw her. There was an atmosphere between the three of them. Seeing that Lee wasn't there, Fred said to Gordon, "You should go up and apologise to Lee." He reluctantly started to get out of his seat when Angela said, "I already went to apologise but he's already left for school."

"Thank you," Fred said. "You'll need to apologise to Lee when he gets home, though," she told Gordon. Nothing more was said and all three carried on about their business as usual. Fred had a number of errands and grocery shopping to complete that day. When she arrived back in the early afternoon, there was a message for her to call the junior school. This was not an unusual occurrence for the children's home, so she put the shopping away first before making the call. When she called back, the secretary told her that Lee hadn't been at school and asked Fred if he was ill. Fred was put on the spot a little.

"No, he's not ill as far as I know. Hmm, he's a bit young to be skipping school. Can I call you back? There's something I need to check," Fred asked. She went upstairs to Lee's room and looked around. There hadn't been much there to begin with, and it looked neat and sparse like it always did. She looked into his cupboards. His toys and moneybox were there but his suitcase was gone and some of the clothes were missing. His toothbrush and paste were also gone. Fred shook the moneybox, and the silence confirmed her suspicions.

"Damn!" she hissed under breath. In one of the drawers, she also found the letter that had been returned back to him from St. Albans. She immediately called the local police station to report the boy's disappearance. They said they'd send someone round to complete the Missing Person's Report later. She then called the school back to inform them of the situation.

* * *

Anne was finally able to make contact with Nancy after she had also had difficulty getting through. Nancy apologised because the phone company had apparently been completing some upgrades to the line, which had been very inconvenient. When the social worker informed her about the chance information she'd been given about Lee, Nancy was over the moon. This was just the break she needed, and she couldn't thank Anne enough for getting in touch. Anne gave her Lynn's contact details and said that, because the boy's current location was out of her jurisdiction, Lynn would be the best person to liaise with.

"I'm going to call Lynn now and ask her to work with you on this one, Nancy. She's a dedicated woman," Anne said.

"Thank you, Anne. I'll give it an hour and then I'll get in touch." Nancy put down the receiver. Exactly one hour later, she called Lynn, who then filled her in on the details she had encountered about the case.

"Lee was very clear that he wanted to see you and his dad again," Lynn said. "But because of the nature in which this case came about, I needed to be sure that was in his best interests. That's why I contacted your local Social Services first. I'm sorry, Nancy, but it was important to establish what you and his father were like before making contact with you directly. We were lucky that Anne received the message!"

"You did the right thing," Nancy responded. "Both David and I have been given the run-around by the vicious woman he once called a wife. Ultimately, we just want the boy back and for him to be happy again. But I notice that you have not provided Lee's current whereabouts – is that something you can give me?"

"Well, I can tell you that he is in a children's home and is safer there than when he was at home. I'm going to make a suggestion. I was planning to visit him next week anyway. Why don't you come with me? I think he'll enjoy the surprise." Nancy thought that was a wonderful idea, and Lynn gave her the meeting time and her office location. Nancy kept this information from David, but she did call Kim to tell her of the possible break in the case. Kim hadn't had much luck at her end, although she had just acquired a possible lead at Watford Maternity Hospital of a woman with the same first name giving birth.

"What surname did you have?" Nancy enquired.

"It was King," Kim said.

"No need to follow up with that one, Kim. Lee's surname was changed to King," Nancy affirmed. "Stand down for now. I will be seeing him next week with a social worker from Hertfordshire. Maybe we can get him back with us before Christmas."

"What about the rest of the family?" Kim enquired.

"I'm hoping the social worker will provide that information for me. Sorry, Kim, we just need to save costs."

"No problem, and good luck next week," Kim replied as they ended the call.

* * *

It was a two-hour drive for Nancy to get to St. Albans. After meeting Lynn, they agreed to drive to the home together in Lynn's car. En route Nancy could tell it was going to be another long drive when, ten minutes in, Lynn said that they would be heading to Bury St. Edmunds. Nancy contemplated the great lengths that Louvaine had gone to create distance from her son.

"There's something you need to know, Nancy. Something I didn't disclose on the phone."

"What's that?" Nancy enquired.

"When I brought Lee to the home, the manager and I looked over his body briefly. He was covered in marks and bruises. He wouldn't shed any light on them, but I would say from my experience that it wasn't the first time he'd been mistreated. Some of the marks were older."

Nancy thought for a few seconds. *Help, Fear. That's what he was talking about!* She felt bad that she hadn't done anything more about it the last time she saw the boy. Nancy's lack of physical reaction surprised Lynn. Normally she would have expected a family member to be in shock, but Nancy seemed to take it in her stride. Lynn began to feel a little uneasy about the situation but decided to be bold and tackle her feeling head-on.

"You don't seem shocked, Nancy?" she probed.

"I'm sorry, Lynn. I was more ashamed of myself. Self-recrimination, I guess."

"How so?" Lynn questioned.

"I'd found Lee once at a previous address. This isn't the first time Louvaine has pulled the relocation trick. Lee had given me a coded message that I should have acted on more decisively. That's why."

They both sat there not saying anything for a short time. Nancy stared straight ahead, whilst Lynn focused on the driving. Nancy spoke first, but this time her voice was much more commanding.

"I'm going to need the family address from where you collected Lee from, please."

"It's not that I don't want to, Nancy. I'm just not allowed to divulge that information."

"There's another child potentially at risk, an older sister. It would be in the family's best interest if I had the information." Lynn was still reticent. Nancy reached into her left breast pocket, took out her ID and passed it over to Lynn. Lynn took two to three glances whilst keeping the car on the road. She was astounded at what she saw.

"There's a case file in the bag behind my seat. You should probably take a look at it," Lynn said. Nancy read through the file and took out a pen and notebook from her handbag. She made some notes, including the address, and put the file back.

"I would appreciate it if you do not divulge anything about this to anyone, and that nothing is referenced in any of your reports, Lynn."

"I didn't tell you the address, did I?" Lynn said.

"Exactly!" Nancy smiled.

They arrived at the home and Lynn led the way round to the side entrance. She knocked on the door, which was opened by Fred with a gasp. The last person she was expecting to see was Lynn and, for once, she was not happy to see her. Lynn introduced Nancy and Fred to each other, and Fred invited them into the kitchen.

"I've brought Nancy here as a surprise for Lee – is he around?" Lynn asked. She hadn't quite read Fred's shock correctly, but Nancy had.

"I'm so sorry. I wished you'd called ahead, Lynn. I could've saved you a long trip. There's been a problem. Lee ran away three days ago. I know I should have informed you, but I was hoping that the police would've found him by now." Fred was apologetically nervous. Not wishing to sound completely incompetent in front of the boy's relative, she added, "We filed a Missing Person's Report with the local police, but I don't think they have a clue to his whereabouts currently."

Nancy was a simmering pot of anger but did her best not to shout at the home manager. She needed a willing participant, and if the manager took a defensive posture she could potentially withhold vital information.

"Which police station is that?" she asked.

"It's just in the high street," Fred responded. Both she and Lynn felt like a couple of shamed schoolgirls in the presence of the headmistress.

"I'd like to see Lee's room, please," Nancy said in a stern voice. Lynn said nothing but cast an irate glance in Fred's direction as the woman directed them out of the kitchen. They endured stares from all the children as Fred escorted them both through the house and up to Lee's room.

"Has anyone moved or taken anything from this room?" Nancy asked.

"It's as I found it," Fred said. "His case, some clothes, toothbrush and toothpaste are gone. There's a letter in that top drawer as well."

Nancy had begun her own search of the room. "Thank you," she said, without making eye contact. Lee running away seemed the most likely conclusion to her, too. Angela came to the door whilst they were in the room.

"I'll speak to you later, Angela," Fred said dismissively.

"I just want to let you know that *someone* stole my money – and Gordon's," she said in a matter-of-fact tone. Fred looked sheepishly at Nancy.

"There'd been a misunderstanding before he ran away," she explained. Nancy read the letter and looked up at the three others.

"Lee was definitely angry at someone!" she said. With nothing else to see at the home, Nancy asked Lynn if she wouldn't mind taking her to the police station. Lynn nodded in agreement. When they arrived at the police station, Nancy asked Lynn to stay in the car. Inside, she went straight to the front desk and asked to see the chief inspector. She was told that there wasn't a C.I. because it was only a small station.

"Do you have an inspector I could see, then?" she enquired. Nancy was beginning to run out of patience and finding Lee alive was going to be harder as time evaporated. When the inspector came out, Nancy identified herself and asked him to give her all the information they had about Lee's case. The inspector blushed in embarrassment. They currently had nothing other than the original report and that he'd left between the hours of 8pm and 7am. Nancy knew that missing persons were not a high priority for local policing at Christmas time, and was not particularly surprised by the answer. She gave the officer her telephone number and said that he was to inform her personally of any new information they received.

When they left, Nancy asked Lynn if she wouldn't mind undertaking one last favour by driving her around the local area. Lynn gladly obliged. There was a bus and train station in the main part of town, both within one mile, but she couldn't rule out Lee trying to hitch-hike. There wasn't much else to see in the market town, so they agreed to head back to Lynn's office. As they were both hungry and in need of the ladies room, Lynn stopped at a rest area about five miles out of town on the A14 that doubled as a truck stop. After using the washroom, they both purchased a sandwich and cup of tea and sat for a while. Nancy looked around the place, deep in thought. When they eventually got back to her office, Lynn apologised to Nancy for the way things had unfolded that day. Nancy appreciated the sentiment, but it wasn't really the woman's fault.

"Actually, I need one more favour. Do you have a private phone I could use?"

"Of course." Lynn escorted Nancy to a small office and waited outside. Nancy called Kim and updated her on what had happened that day. Kim's mission was about to change dramatically.

"We do now have some vital information," she said. "We know where the family lives, and that there's a probability that Lee used the bus or train, as neither were a great distance away. But I also want you to check out the Risby's truck stop five miles out on the south section of the A14. He could have gone there."

"I'll get right on it in the morning," Kim said.

"No, Kim, you'll get right on it now, please," Nancy insisted.

When Nancy had finished her call, Lynn asked if there was anything she could do to help.

"Please call me directly if you get any further information," Nancy replied. As the old lady drove her car away from Hertfordshire Social Services, Lynn couldn't help but be surprised that someone so unsuspecting could be a government agent. *You learn something every day.* As soon as she was back at her desk, she called Fred; there was a piece of her mind that she needed to give her.

* * *

CHAPTER 16

BIG CITY, SMALL TOWN

Lee was quite enjoying the lorry ride; being so high up and able to see everything on the road gave him a more privileged perspective on the other traffic. He remembered having to sit in the back of Jon's old car with Laura, so close to the engine and petrol fumes. *This is the life.* He also thought it was weird how the French drove on the opposite side of the road. Arnauld tried to find a balance between being conversational, but not overly chatty. He showed Lee the route they were taking and how to read the map, something Lee showed an aptitude for. As tactfully as he could, Arnauld attempted to persuade Lee to go back to England with him once he'd made a stop in Belgium.

Lee understood why Arnauld felt he needed to return him to his home, but he was adamant about testing his mettle and living under his own survival skills. Arnauld pondered how bad the boy's life must have been at home to make him so determined to run away. The best way he thought he could help would be to teach the boy a few essential

French phrases such as: merci – (*thank you*), pardon – (*sorry*), s'il vous plait – (please) and emmène-moi à – (*take me to*). Arnauld had used a repeat, repeat, repeat method to teach Lee the words until the boy said, "Arrêt... s'il vous plait!" (*Stop... please*). Lee had seen the new word on a couple of dual language road signs along the journey. The phrases Arnauld had taught him were memorised now, so repeating them just became annoying. Seeing the surprise on Arnauld's face, Lee pointed to a stop sign on the road as they passed it. The man smiled in admiration.

Lee sat back; it wasn't the first time he'd been looked at in this way. Nan always seemed to have a smile for him, and his dad had been super proud when he learned to ride a bike at the same time as Laura. He was five and she was eight but while Laura remained cautious and shaky, Lee always wanted to learn more. Wheelies, skids, jumps or speeding round corners with Richard, it didn't matter to him; it was always about finding out where the limits were – which often meant trips over the handlebars, teeth hitting concrete, grazed skin and holes in his shoes. As the memories flickered across his mind like a home movie, he realised that Laura had no sense of adventure at all. She might be clever, but she was boring as hell and just did her best to stop him having any fun. *Perhaps that was her idea of fun?*

Arnauld continued just south of the city Nantes to a distribution centre.

"I have to drop-off this consignment and pick up a new one," he said. "You wait here. It will probably be about an hour." Lee motioned to get his suitcase, but Arnauld put his hand up. "I won't say anything. There's a truck stop at La Grassiniere. We'll stop there afterwards, and you can get off there if you want." Arnauld felt bad the moment the words left his mouth. Lee sat forward in the seat and watched Arnauld through the huge mirrors as he left the cab and walked to the rear of the lorry. He fetched his case anyway and put his coat on so that he'd be ready for a quick escape if the man had lied. The coat was a good idea because the cab soon became cold once the engine was switched off. It was actually nearly two hours before they had completed loading his truck and Arnauld was back in the driver's seat. Lee asked him a question and watched the man intently as he answered.

"Did you tell anyone?"

"I promised I wouldn't," Arnauld said. Technically, that didn't answer the question, but Lee didn't think the man had lied, and so put his case back in the rear compartment. He'd been looking at the map whilst the lorry was being loaded and was glad that La Grassiniere truck stop was only a short hop away – he was desperate for the toilet again. When they arrived, they both got out to stretch their legs and Lee ran quickly to the toilets. Arnauld stayed to fill the lorry up with diesel. After he'd finished, and feeling much relieved, Lee decided to take a quick look around the place to get his bearings. It was a bleak place and there wasn't much space for trucks to park overnight. He mulled over whether he should hang around to see if he could hitch a lift somewhere else or start walking back towards the city on foot. He walked back to Arnauld's lorry, keeping his hands in his coat pockets for warmth.

"I'm going to rest here for the night. You're welcome to stay in the cab again, if you like?" offered Arnauld.

"Yes, please." Lee thanked him.

Arnauld went to pay for the fuel, so Lee hung around the cab thinking to himself. He knew that to sleep one more night in the cab would just be putting off the inevitable. Winter was the wrong time of year to run away, and the realisation that he really hadn't thought this through was becoming more obvious as doubts tried to take hold. He snapped himself out of the swirling negativity. He was here now and there was no going back, so he needed to tough it out. When Arnauld got back, he said, "You should go and get a shower over there. It might be the last chance you get for a while." He gave Lee a token and pointed to the side of the building in front of them.

The next morning, Arnauld offered Lee one last meal and one last chance to go back to England with him, but Lee stubbornly stuck to his position. Arnauld really wasn't happy about leaving such a young boy alone.

"You have to let me do this. I'll be OK," Lee promised. The man shook his head but didn't see how he could stop him without causing a huge scene and even a possible arrest. They finished the rest of their breakfast in silence. Arnauld seemed to have lost his appetite, but Lee ate every scrap of food in front of him. When they went back to the lorry to get Lee's suitcase, Lee had a question.

"I'm sorry to ask this, but do you have any spare French money I could have? I could swap you some English?" With a wry smile, the driver gave the boy 200 francs from his pocket and Lee offered him some of the pound notes he had in return. Arnauld politely refused the money and said that the 200 francs was worth about £20, which should last him a while. Lee asked for the best directions into the city. Arnauld pointed in the northerly direction. "Just follow that road there and you'll see the city." He wished Lee well with a shake of the hand, and then got into the cab and drove off towards the west. Arnauld took one last look in his rear-view mirror and waved out of the window. On top of feeling guilty, he was going to miss the company. Lee watched the lorry pull away and started his new journey towards the route he'd been shown.

After three miles, Lee began to have regrets. It was hard work; his shoes were old and were almost worn-out, his case was beginning to get heavy, and he wasn't sure whether to try and hitch-hike or not. The only thing he could think of to take his mind off the walking was to try and make vapour patterns with his breath. He eventually made it to the south-eastern quarter of the city. His feet hurt and all the walking had made him hungry. Along the main thoroughfare, he found a busy supermarket. He walked in and scoped the place out. Nobody really took any notice of him, so it was time to go to work. He pulled the drawstrings of his coat around his midriff and tied them as tight as possible. With only so much room, Lee took a large round country loaf, a bottle of fizzy orange, toothpaste, another toothbrush, some soap, some pens and a map, and stuffed them all inside.

To his relief, Lee got out of the shop without any issue, but he couldn't completely relax until he was well away from the area. He then put all of his stash in the case and loosened the ties in his coat. One of the top priorities for the next few days would definitely be to find some sturdy sneakers. Just like when the family had moved, Lee walked around for a while to get a feel for the place, but his feet were really hurting now and he had to find somewhere to rest up where he could potentially remain for the night.

From a sign he'd spotted, Lee was heading towards what he assumed was a river called '*La Loire*.' He got the odd look from one or two passers-by which he tried to ignore, but no-one really bothered him. The one thing he did know was that he would need to get out of sight; this area of the city was too heavily populated. Lee made sure to memorise as many road signs as he could on the way to a T-junction where the road ran left to right, parallel to the river. He crossed over the road and stood at a stone wall that was the only barrier between the road and the riverbank. He turned right and walked for a little while, looking for places he could pitch up for the night. There was a spot that wasn't too overgrown, so he hopped over the wall when there was a break in the traffic.

Placing his coat down on the ground, Lee opened his suitcase. He pulled out a jumper and put that on first. Next, he took off his shoes and socks, neither of which were in a good state. He then pulled out the map. He knew he'd come from the south somewhere, and that he was by the river, but it still took him ten minutes to trace the journey from La Grassiniere. He marked his current location with a pen and thought about what his options might be for the next morning as he ate some of the food and drink. He changed his socks, put his shoes back on, and tried to settle. He eventually fell asleep, but without anything soft for a pillow, he didn't sleep well that night. The ground was hard and cold and the noise of the cars passing by was closer than he had ever been used to. In the morning, Lee stretched himself out. His back hurt from the awkward sleeping position, and he was cold and stiff. He made a mental list of the things he needed to do: get some new padded sneakers, find something better for sleeping on, and find places for food and to wash.

Lee foraged north of the river for the next few days, always making sure to keep his bearings with the map. He spent time looking for places he could potentially rely on for food. He realised that some shops threw away their leftovers in the evenings when they closed, and marked these places on the map. It had been too risky to steal a pair of sneakers, so Lee had actually gone into a shop and bought a pair of 'PF Flyer' boots that had a thick rubber sole and heel. This proved difficult because Lee didn't understand what the assistant was saying and, secondly, the woman seemed quite dismissive until he showed her that he had money. What Lee hadn't realised was that he was beginning to smell, and the woman simply didn't want to serve him. He ended up buying a pair that was one size too big for him so they would last longer, but they were still a big improvement over his old ones. As a punishment to the unpleasant shop assistant, Lee wore the new boots out and left his old shoes by the counter for the woman to deal with. He had used up almost half of the money Arnauld had given him but walked out of the shop with a new spring in his step.

As he traipsed around the city, the hardest things to find were places to get clean. Small drinking fountains proved very useful, but he'd only come across one large fountain in the city where he could submerge himself. Lee resorted to washing there in the early hours of every other morning with his stolen bar of soap. He not only had to wash himself, but also his clothes too. With no way of drying them, he became borderline pneumonic and shivered and shook for hours afterwards. For the most part, Lee regretted everything he'd done and realised that maybe life wouldn't have been so bad in the children's home; his clothes would've been dry at least.

* * *

Kim Montrall checked out the bus and rail stations first, as they were the closest and most obvious places for the boy to travel from. Her looks had just about managed to get her into the nightclub when she'd first been assigned the case to follow Louvaine, but there was no such luck this time and she had to bribe a night watchman at the train station to let her look through hours of grainy CCTV footage. There was nothing so advanced at the bus depot and after all her efforts she had no new information. Kim drove to the truck stop to see what that would unearth. This was going to be difficult and time-consuming. The truck stop manager said that most drivers didn't pop in every day, only once, twice, or maybe three times in a month. He was very helpful, though, and agreed that she could question any of the drivers she wanted. He also suggested that she should try the B&B next door to see if there were any drivers there, which she duly did. The B&B owners agreed to ask each driver to make contact with her over at the truck stop if they thought of anything. Kim spent three days and nights camped out, either in the café or her car. Each night she would check in with Nancy, but nothing else had surfaced from the stations or even from the police. Nothing had been seen of the boy, who could be anywhere by now. She always carried spare clothes in a holdall for remote work, but even those were beginning to run out. Kim and Nancy agreed that she would wait it out for another four days before trying to pursue other, as yet undetermined, avenues.

* * *

Although running away to a foreign city might have sounded exciting, finding things to do in Nantes each day was not particularly easy. For the most part, Lee spent his time milling around shops or hypermarkets or looking for places to stay that would be warm and dry in the evenings. With the shops decorated in Christmas themes, his thoughts often drifted back to England; he wondered what the family would be doing and whether they'd miss him at this time of year. Lee even wondered what Christmas would be like at the children's home. But even though it was probably a better option to be there instead of walking the streets, he wasn't going to give up... not yet anyway.

By now, Lee had had a couple of close calls when attempting to steal food, and his instincts told him to get out of the city before his luck ran out. The south seemed a lot quieter than the main city, so he headed back to where he'd first found the river. Instead of sleeping by the riverbank, he found a spot in a small, wooded area across the road that was a little more sheltered from the elements and the traffic noise. His chances of being disturbed here were a lot less than in the industrial areas or shop fronts he'd used north of the river. The next morning, he decided to try his hand at hitch-hiking. He'd walked at least two miles and many cars had passed by the time a little red Renault 5 finally stopped by the side of the road for him.

"Merci!" Lee said more confidently than he actually felt.

That morning, Servane Fortier had driven into Nantes to shop for groceries ready for when her daughter arrived home. As she drove along the Côte Saint-Sébastien, she spotted what looked like a very young child walking along the right-hand side of the road. He was carrying a suitcase in one hand and clearly trying to thumb a lift with the other. Concerned that this was not normal, she pulled over to offer help.

From the moment he spoke, she knew he wasn't French. Lee pointed to a place on the map further along the river. "Emmène-moi à, s'il vous plaît?" (*Please take me to*) he said as best he could. Servane smiled.

"Ma maison est à Saint-Julien-de-Concelles?" (*My house is in Saint-Julien-de-Concelles?*) and shrugged. Lee shrugged too, not knowing how to respond. They both smiled. Servane unlocked the passenger side door and Lee got in. The fan heater was warm, and the velour seat so comfortable, that he instantly relaxed. Servane turned back onto the road and carried on her journey. Taking a chance, she asked him what his name was in English and where he came from. He looked at her with a polite smile.

"My name is Lee, and I'm from England." Servane's English wasn't completely fluent, but she did the best she could. *He's clearly a runaway*, she thought, *but why so young, and all the way from England?*

"My name is Servane," she said. "My house is in Saint-Julien-de-Concelles. About 20 minutes from here." Lee smiled back again, not really knowing how best to respond; he just wanted to get away from the city. Servane was just as nervous as she spoke a little more on the journey. Lee wasn't rude and spoke whenever she asked a question. Servane's voice was soft and loving. She seemed genuinely concerned for him and didn't just interrogate him like others did. When they arrived at her home, her immediate concern was to give him some rest and food. "You can stay for a while if you like? I'm currently here on my own and would be glad of the company."

"Thank you for the lift, but I have to go," Lee said, reluctantly.

She could see the boy wrestled with the decision. *Perhaps it's a trust issue?* she thought.

"Are you sure?"

The answer still came back the same. She just wanted to cuddle him and take him inside but trying to force him would probably cause a scene; she didn't push any further.

"Wait!" she said. Servane wrote down her address and telephone number for him and said softly, "If you need anything..."

Lee thanked her and asked her which direction to the town. She pointed him the right way and watched him leave. For the rest of the morning, Servane considered what she should do. In the end she decided to call the local town police to tell them about the boy and the direction she thought he was heading to. *It will be for his own good in the end.* Racked with guilt, Servane jumped into her car and drove around to look for him herself. The town she lived in wasn't that big; but after thirty minutes with no sighting, she returned home, hoping that the police had found him.

A day later and Lee's luck took a turn for the worse. The weather had begun to deteriorate; it was cold, and the rain hadn't stopped all day. He was walking a street looking for some shelter when two older boys spotted him as they approached from the opposite direction. They knew he was vulnerable as they stopped and spoke to him in French. When Lee wouldn't respond, they tried stealing his suitcase and pushing him around. Lee used all his strength to whirl around and hit one with his case, knocking him over, and then ran as quickly as he could. The other boy chased him, caught him up and tripped Lee's trailing leg, causing him to tumble and fall. The fall was severe enough to graze Lee's face and rip his coat. They tussled, but Lee put up a fight. By scratching, biting and clawing, he eventually fought his way free and just ran, as far away as he could. He was now injured, as well as soaked through and hungry. As the night drew in his options were limited. He hated this life and realised that he not only needed shelter, but help. So Lee retraced his route back to Servane's home.

Servane was a kind woman of forty-two and had been a widow for many years. Her husband had died in a car accident, and she had brought up their daughter alone ever since. She was lucky that her husband had had insurance, which now enabled her to maintain a modest way of life and send their daughter away to university. She was in the back room, where the open fire was still popping, when she thought she heard a knock at the door. When she opened it, there was Lee, soaked through and looking thoroughly miserable. She immediately ushered him in.

"I'm sorry," he said tearfully. He looked broken.

Servane almost choked with tears herself. She quickly removed his coat and outer clothes, stood him in front of the fire and got him some towels. She saw the new scrapes and bruises. She could tell that he needed a bath to warm him through, so she went upstairs to run the water. She kept him wrapped in towels and fed him some soup until the water was ready, keeping her arms around him to keep him warm. Lee loved the smell of the woman. He'd noticed before when he'd got in her car, but now he was closer the smell took on a dream-like scent. Servane allowed him to have a bath in privacy. He had almost forgotten how wonderful a warm bath truly was; he didn't want to get out, but eventually the water began to cool. Servane knocked on the door and left some fresh clothing just inside. When he got out of the bath and put the clothes on, Lee couldn't help but chuckle to himself. Not only were these girl's clothes, but they were way too big for him. *Still, beggars can't be choosers!* he thought.

When he was all done in the bathroom, Servane put some antiseptic cream and plasters on a couple of his grazes and showed him to a room that had a very feminine decor. She smiled and said, "You're welcome here for now. It's my daughter's room and she'll be home in a couple of days, so you can meet her?" She put his suitcase on the side and watched him climb into bed before closing the door and heading to her own room. Thinking about it, Servane wasn't quite sure what she would do about the boy once her daughter was home, but she was sure they'd work something out. She decided she wouldn't inform the local police of his whereabouts for now. Besides, the station would be closed anyway.

In the room next door, Lee thought about what the woman had said. *You're welcome here for now. It's my daughter's room and she'll be home in a couple of days.* The house was small, and it didn't look like there was another room to sleep in. Servane seemed very kind, but her daughter was bound to want her room to herself. Although he would have loved to, he knew he couldn't settle here; he would have to leave soon.

* * *

It was day five at the truck stop when Kim got lucky. Arnauld had pulled in and headed for the café as usual. The manager gave a nod in Kim's direction and told him why she was there. Arnauld collected his food and drink and nervously headed over towards her table. She gave him a warning look when he sat down. In the four days she'd been sitting there, at least seven drivers had tried their luck propositioning her.

"Do you have a picture of the boy you're looking for?" Arnauld asked as he sat down opposite. Kim showed him the picture she had. He sighed and confirmed it was the same boy he'd unwittingly taken to France. He told her everything that had happened, with Kim interrupting the story to ask for extra information as he went along.

"How could you have just left a small boy alone in France, for Christ's sake? What were you thinking?" Kim asked when he'd finished the story. Arnauld clearly felt bad and was put on the defensive by the accusatory question.

"I took care of the boy as best I could, and I tried to convince him to come back a few times. If I'd have tried to force him back, he would've just run away again. He was of that mindset. And anyway, before you start criticising me, you should get your own house in order first! Why was he running away in the first place?"

Kim wouldn't furnish the man with any more information, so he just picked up his food tray and walked off to another table.

The guy had a point! she had to admit to herself. Kim was much happier now that she had a solid lead. She had the driver's details. She knew where he'd dropped Lee off and in which direction the boy had headed first. She called Nancy straight away with the news.

"I need to head home first and get some money and repack for a longer haul. I'll then drive down to Nantes," she said. They knew the situation had become even more serious with Lee now being on foreign soil; the French authorities could be obstructive at the best of times.

"Whilst you're en route, I'll drop into HQ and see if we are able to mobilise some personnel in France. When you get to Nantes, you should liaise with the head of the City Police. Any further information I have I will make sure is available to you there. And one more thing..." Nancy added before she clicked off the receiver, "...well done!"

Nancy made some phone calls and then caught a train into London to make a rare visit to Century House. When she arrived, she was immediately met by 'The Chief' and his assistant and escorted to a meeting room. The layout of the place had changed a lot since Nancy had last been there, and half of the faces she saw were also new. Nancy's former boss hadn't underestimated the earnestness of the situation. Even though it was not a threat to national security, the least he could do was to help one of his own in a time of need.

Nancy told him that she had Kim assisting, and summarised what her next steps would be. The Chief outlined what was being put in place and what Kim needed to do when she arrived in Nantes. He had contacted and enlisted the help of the French police, who would be given a description of the boy once Nancy provided it to the assistant. They were also going to notify a couple of field agents about Lee once they had the description. Nancy gave the only pictures she had of Lee to the assistant to be copied and distributed. She suggested going to France herself, but they soon realised it wasn't a good idea. If Lee had got to France by himself he could just as easily return and he would need someone to come back to.

* * *

Nantes was a big city. After London had called, the Inspecteur Général instructed the station commandant to assist where he could. The police posted a few missing signs around the city, and some of the lower ranks asked about the boy during the course of their usual day. They had not uncovered any sightings, and no-one had come forward.

After the ferry crossing to Calais, Kim made sure to hire a car. She didn't want to put the mileage on her own and driving with French number plates would avoid arousing unnecessary attention. It was late in the afternoon when she eventually arrived in Nantes. She headed directly for the Central Police Station and, after some initial cooperation issues, was eventually met by Commandant Marchand. He escorted her to a side office and said he would be as helpful as he could. She needed to wait there whilst he collected the latest information they had about the boy. The wait was longer than expected, but Marchand was in good spirits when he came back.

"We have limited resources within such a large city, and no sightings have been recorded here. However, we have today just received information from a town nearby of a boy matching the description given. It's all we have and the information itself is a couple of days old, but it's better than nothing." Kim was very thankful to the man as he handed her a carbon copy file with the information they had. Just in case her French wasn't up to par, he pointed out some of the key information, including the details of the woman who'd made the initial report. He gave her his number and said that she should contact him directly if there was anything else she needed.

This was good work, she thought. She would question this woman called Servane in the morning. "Can I use your telephone to call my superiors in England?" Nancy was pleased to hear that there was already a lead and insisted that Kim update her with any developments, no matter what time of day it was. Kim left the station to find a bureau de change, where she exchanged £100 for 800 Francs. She purchased some supplies, including a map, and booked a room for the night in a small boutique hotel. It was a much-needed rest after spending so much time at the truck stop and on the road.

After closing the call with Kim, Nancy was both concerned and impressed with her seven-year-old grandson. *He's got the making of something good if he can be found alive*, she mused to herself.

The next day, Nancy undertook her own little side mission. She figured she had enough time to hire a car, pay a stealthy little visit to Louvaine's new address and be home before Kim called again. For her own peace of mind, she wanted to check for herself that the family still lived at the new address. When she arrived, Nancy could see that checking the place out would be more difficult because of the nature of terraced housing. But she had an old trick up her sleeve. She parked a long way down the street and grabbed a large handful of fake church leaflets from the bag she'd brought with her. Starting at one end of the street, she began posting leaflets through each letterbox. No-one would assume anything of an old lady posting leaflets – it was the perfect 'in plain sight' deception. When she got to No.24, she surreptitiously looked through the letter box. She could see Louvaine moving around in the back room. It was all she needed for now, and so she made her way back to the car. On the journey back home, Nancy contemplated what she would tell David.

* * *

David couldn't help but worry about the welfare of his two children. He also worried about the size the bill would be the longer it took Kim to find the family. With the money he'd been able to save by not paying maintenance to Louvaine, he'd moved to a nicer two-bedroom flat in a better part of town. He just wanted a spare room for Lee when he got to see him again. Work had been going well, and he was repaying the faith of his superiors for the promotion he'd been given. But the emotional scarring of the divorce had really taken its toll. It had been a while, but a couple of David's friends from work had encouraged him to go to the pub with them once a week. It was a brief respite from all the worries he couldn't really speak about.

When Nancy got back home, she called David at work and kept it brief. "I have some more information about Lee. Can you stop by after work, and I'll cook you some dinner?"

"Of course," he said, excitedly. "I'll see you about 6.30pm."

That evening Nancy revealed that Lee had been placed by Louvaine into a children's home near Bury St. Edmunds, that he had run away just before Christmas, and that Kim was currently searching for him. For now, Nancy left out his current location and how he'd got there, knowing how David would be affected by the news. She hoped that Kim would find Lee before forcing her hand to reveal more information. David asked what he could do to help with Lee, but Nancy just said that Kim was much better at this sort of thing and that he would probably be a hindrance. He continued to ask about Laura's well-being and Louvaine's new address, but last thing Nancy wanted right now was for David to take matters into his own hands and cause more complications.

"We can only afford the one investigator, David, and Kim's bill is going to be quite high when all is said and done. Right now, Lee is the priority. From what we've uncovered from the social workers, it is Kim's belief that Laura is alright for now. I think we should deal with Laura once we get Lee back, don't you?"

* * *

CHAPTER 17

BIG MISTAKE

Lee had tried to keep track of the days. He knew Christmas had been and gone, and it was definitely January now; but each day and night seemed to blend into the last. The one thing he did know was that this was his first night in a comfortable bed for a very long time, and so he allowed himself time to relax. He hadn't realised his bones and feet hurt quite so much until he pulled the blanket over his body. For the first time in weeks, he also slept the whole night through. It was light by the time he was woken by movement downstairs. Lee got out of bed and put the girl's oversized clothes back on. He still looked funny, but at least they were warm and his feet didn't have to touch the cold stone floors in the kitchen. That's where he saw Servane washing his clothes. Lee tensed.

"I hope you do not mind but, while you were sleeping, I took the clothes from your case. They really needed a wash," she said innocently. "They smelled... a lot," she said, putting a clothes peg on her nose for effect. Lee smiled and relaxed a little, which to Servane was a good sign. It was a good sign to Lee, too, that life wasn't quite as hopeless as he'd recently imagined. Servane pointed over to the table.

"I put any money from your pockets there," she said. "I will get some breakfast ready when I have finished this. Come, sit with me and keep me company." Lee shuffled over as she held him close and lifted him up on to the sideboard. Lee inhaled the sweet smell infused in her blouse. He couldn't remember the last time anyone who'd cared had held him in such a way, and so he allowed this fleeting moment to embed itself into his mind's *good place*.

"Are these the only clothes you have? There's not much here for winter?"

"I have to travel light. There's only so much I can carry," he said.

"I'm only asking out of concern, but what are you running away from? Please tell me - it must be awful if you have ended up all the way en France?

Lee clammed up initially, but she gave him a gentle little rub on the leg for encouragement. Lee looked at the woman who stood in front of him. His deep gaze seemed to look right through her, but Servane had nothing to hide and just smiled back in a way that conveyed her genuine feeling towards him. After being let down by so many women in the past, Lee had resolved to never trust a woman again when he left the children's home. He felt that if he became more like a Cyberman from Doctor Who on the TV – emotionless and robotic – he could override the conflicting emotions inside. But this actually went against what he really wanted; so much so, that his heart actually began to hurt. In truth, all Lee wanted was a mother's love and someone he could love back, so he made the decision to trust Servane. He told her about some of the things his sister and mother had done, and that he was no longer welcome anywhere. His father didn't fight to keep him and was too busy with work, so he really didn't feel that he'd had any other choice. Servane did her best to subdue the lump that had begun to build up in her throat. She wanted to reach out to hold and embrace the young boy who'd come so far, but she also worried about her own feelings as well as his.

"Do you know where you want to go?" Lee shook his head.

"I haven't quite worked that one out yet," he said. "Some place where I'm liked, but never back home... I'd rather be dead than home!"

Lee's eyes remained open, but his mind went back to a fantasy he'd played out over and over again – a woman who would pluck him from obscurity, hold him in her arms and truly love him. The face and figure of the woman who would save him had always been a blur, with nothing ever quite emerging into focus. But now, looking at Servane, he had the face to transplant onto the figure in his dreams. It was unfortunate that this kind woman who'd now come into focus had a daughter. Lee knew there would be no room for him; with only two bedrooms, he'd always be an outsider and would eventually have to leave.

After a much-needed breakfast, Lee helped Servane with some chores around the house. It was the least he could do for the bed, food and having his laundry done.

"Did you have Christmas decorations in your house?" he asked after a while. Servane gave a resigned smile.

"I used to put up a tree when my daughter was small, but after my husband died it was never the same. My daughter, Emilie, had also grown out of the notion of Père Noël, and so we just stopped." Lee saw that his question had made Servane sad, so he kept quiet and carried on with anything that she needed help with.

By the evening, Lee's clothes had dried and so he asked her if it was OK to take them upstairs to the room.

"Of course. Will you come with me to collect Emilie in the morning? She'll be coming into Nantes by train." Lee hated lying to the woman who'd shown him such kindness.

"Sure," he responded, but whilst upstairs he prepared his suitcase for a swift exit. Servane cooked them both the most amazing meal that evening. It was the best he'd had in his entire life, which just made it harder on Lee's heart to leave. At the dinner table, Lee started to develop a yawn or two. Servane said that if he was still tired, she didn't mind doing the washing up so he could go to bed early. He cleaned his teeth and went to the toilet. He found a pen in the daughter's room and took a 10 Franc note out from his case. On it he wrote Servane a long thank-you letter that took up both sides and left it by the side of the bed. Lee also left a fifty-pence piece so that hopefully she wouldn't forget 'the boy from England.'

At about 1am Lee woke up and got dressed in his own clothes. He looked out of the bedroom window – the weather outside was cold, but not wet. The house was silent... it was time to leave. With all of his belongings he quietly left the house as Servane slept. He looked back one last time and walked towards the town, this time taking a route nearer to the riverside. He made sure not to break cover and continued walking under the cover of darkness until he found a place to rest in the early morning. He rested when tired and continued walking when he wasn't. He just wanted to get to the next town on his map as soon as possible.

Servane woke the next morning only to find that Lee had gone. Although initially hurt that he had simply used her, she saw the note on the bedside table and began to read. Tears made tracks down her cheeks as she read his last sentences:

'One day of kindness from you is more than I've had in years. I wish you were my mum. I'd be a good son, but you already have Emilie and I have to go. There won't be room for me here when she comes home.'

Even though she'd barely got to know him, Servane knew she'd miss the little boy around the house. She hadn't said anything to Lee, but he had brought back strong memories of the still-born baby boy she'd given birth to a year after her daughter. Subconsciously, Lee would have filled that gap in her life and been a small reminder of her husband. She took the note and placed it by her bedside; she wanted to read it again before she went to bed that night.

* * *

Kim set off at 8 o'clock in the morning to Servane Fortier's home. Without knowing it, she passed the woman en-route as she drove in the opposite direction. She knocked on the door a few times, but there was no answer. This was a quiet little hamlet and Kim thought better of breaking in; she decided to return later instead. To do something constructive with her time, she went into Saint-Julien-de-Concelles to do some canvassing around. But after two hours and with no new information other than a possible sighting days ago, Kim headed back to Servane's home. The signs were good as there was now a car parked outside. Kim went to the front door and listened for a brief moment. There were voices inside, so she knocked on the door.

When a woman answered, Kim asked, "Puis-je parler avec Servane s'il vous plait?" (*Can I speak with Servane, please?*).

"Ça, c'est moi." (*That is me*).

"Parlez vous anglais?"

Servane nodded. "Oui."

Kim introduced herself and told Servane that she was there on behalf of Lee's grandmother. They'd been trying to find him for some time now. Servane gave a short sigh and invited Kim inside. She made her a coffee as they sat down in the kitchen. Servane told Kim everything she knew. She also went upstairs and retrieved the note Lee had left. She let Kim read it but wouldn't part with it; it was a memento and very personal. Kim could tell that the woman had treated him very well, but she was angry at herself for not taking the drive yesterday evening. To miss her target by less than a day was agonising. Nancy would not be happy either, but Kim at least now knew that Lee was alive that day and that he was in good shape. What she didn't know was the likely direction he took when he left. She thanked Servane for the information and gave her the telephone number of Commandant Marchand at Nantes Police Station.

"You must contact this man directly if you see him again, do you promise?"

"Oui," Servane said quietly.

Kim sat outside in her car for a while and studied her map. She had no real idea which direction Lee had taken, only that he had ended up east of the main city. The only direction she could think of was to continue east until another lead materialised. *Which would be the likely route you would take, Lee?* she muttered to herself. Kim folded the map into a square of what she thought Lee could cover on foot in one or two days and headed north-east towards a road that ran alongside the river.

* * *

Lee had indeed kept by the riverside for as long as he could, but he was now thirsty and hungry. There was no food in the suitcase, and he needed to replenish his stock with something if he could. There hadn't been any shops on the road for hours, but if his map was right there was a small town not far away to the south. Lee headed inland towards the centre of La Chapelle-Basse-Mer – a mistake that would forever change his life.

In his usual manner, Lee looked for a supermarket or some kind of grocery store to scope out. He much preferred shops to be busy so the person at the till would be preoccupied; but this was a small town and the shop was empty, which was never good. His instinct told him to walk away and perhaps come back later, but the shopkeeper had his nose buried in a newspaper and Lee thought that meant he wasn't paying attention. The shopkeeper looked up to acknowledge his presence and then went back to reading the paper. Whilst Lee thought the man couldn't see him, he quickly scooped a drink and some bread into his coat. It wasn't much, but it would be enough to get him by for a while. He zipped up and walked towards the door, but just as he was about to reach for the handle, the man pushed a bar by his seat that locked the exit. *Sh*t!* In a move so swift it caught him by surprise, the man jumped out and grabbed Lee by the neck – cursing at him in French. Lee tried to fight him off, but his coat was too tight to leverage his arms and the man was far too strong.

The shopkeeper pushed Lee down to the ground and jumped on him, smashing his left wrist on the ground. Lee yelped in agony, but the man didn't care. He turned Lee over and tied his hands with string he had in his pocket. Now reasonably secure, the man dragged Lee back behind the counter and held him down with his foot whilst he made a phone call. Lee couldn't really understand what was being said but there was one word he did hear... *POLICE!*

Before Lee knew it, he was in a police station sitting in a filthy cell. They peppered him with questions that he just didn't understand; they even tried roughing him up a little to intimidate him, but Lee remained silent. If they didn't know he was English, they couldn't send him back.

* * *

Kim took a slow drive in the direction of the riverside road Levée de la Divatte, maintaining a horizontal sweep along the way. The road itself was nothing special, but there were plenty of places on either side that could provide cover. Even though the road followed the river's curves for miles and miles, it was barely used. On the river side of the road was a continuous stone wall with trees along the bank, which Kim had to raise her head to the roof to see over. The other side of the road had a mix of small buildings and open farmland. *This definitely wouldn't have been allowed to happen in England; the area would have been developed into riverside holiday homes long ago*, she thought.

Kim adjusted her focal length so that her attention was concentrated on the farthest distance possible. She saw nothing. She did some light canvassing of the area, but no-one had seen anything. Had she got it wrong? After all, he hadn't taken the obvious travel options back in England. She headed into the next town on her map... La Chapelle-Basse-Mer.

* * *

It was hard to know how much time had passed as Lee's watch had been broken during the scuffle in the shop, and there was no clock on any wall that he could see. The one thing he did know was that the longer he was there the worse the situation was going to get for him. This wasn't like the punishments at home. They always seemed to follow the same routine: get sent to your room, lose a meal, possibly two depending on what time it was, and start again the next day. But new thoughts entered Lee's head. If they couldn't get anything out of him, maybe they might take him to an actual prison. Maybe they wouldn't let him go if he said nothing. They also had guns, which made them a lot more frightening than his mum and Jon.

From the first moment of his incarceration, Lee observed the comings and goings of the police, the cleaner and any other staff. There was one opportunity. When they took him out to go to the toilet, security was relaxed. *Probably because I'm a kid.* There was a set of keys on the wall that could be taken. *I'll have to create a diversion on the way back to the cell.*

Kim walked into the local police station at La Chapelle-Basse-Mer hoping that maybe there'd been a sighting – or something to help break the case. At the front desk she saw a young male officer. When she didn't have territorial jurisdiction, a little flirtation usually proved helpful for extracting information. But at nearly thirty-three years old, she wondered how long she could pull that little trick off for. Even though it was cold, she undid the top button of her blouse and approached the young officer.

Lee was escorted back from the toilet again by an old officer who really didn't pay much attention to him, like the other times. *This is it.* Lee turned around and walked backwards as if to say something to the man. At the same time he 'accidentally' kicked a cleaning bucket that was stationed at the side of the corridor. That sent it flying, releasing dirty water that sprayed up the wall and cascaded along the corridor floor. With the officer's attention momentarily diverted to retrieving the bucket and sidestepping the water, Lee jumped up, grabbed the keys from the wall and put them in his trouser pocket. The officer berated Lee in French after he'd picked up the bucket and nearly went to side-swipe him with the back of his hand.

"Pardon," Lee said, his only word to the police to date. The officer grabbed Lee by the shoulder and put him back in the holding cell.

As Kim and the young officer were talking at the front desk, their attention was diverted to the noise of a commotion at the back of the station. Five seconds later she saw a young boy being walked to a cell. He looked different from the picture she'd memorised, but she instinctively knew who it was. *What a break.* With eyes now firmly on the prize, she pointed in Lee's direction and told the officer that they had the boy she'd been looking for. The officer seemed immune to her request.

"Vous pouvez pas prendre le garcon. Il y a la question du vol et j'ai besoin de completer les formalités, madame" (*You cannot just take the boy. There's the issue of the theft and the paperwork to deal with, madam*). Kim was annoyed. So near and yet so far! *Do they really want to charge a small child?* The officer was typical of the people that annoyed her the most – so wrapped up in their own self-importance and authority. She just wanted to punch the guy in the face, but it was that type of reaction that had nearly killed her career in The Service before it'd even started. Kim took a deep breath to calm herself.

"Je dois appeler le Commandant Marchand de la police de Nantes. Puis-je utiliser votre telephone?" (*I need to call Commandant Marchand from Nantes Police. Can I use your telephone?*) she asked.

"Je ne connais pas cet homme. Vous devrez trouver un téléphone quelque part en ville, madame. Vous pouvez essayer la Chambre d'hôtes du Bois Fillaud" (*I do not know this man. You will have to find a telephone in town somewhere, madam. You could try the Chambre d'hôtes du Bois Fillaud*).

Kim's blood was beginning to boil. Not only was the little sh*t being uncooperative, but he'd called her 'Madame' twice now! Manners were clearly not his forte. She thought about grabbing him by the throat but realised that ending up in the cell next to Lee probably wouldn't help. Instead, she calmly asked, "Combien de temps allez-vous garder le garçon ici?" (*How long will the boy be kept here for?*).

The officer shrugged his shoulders and said, "Je ne sais pas" (*I don't know*).

Really helpful! she thought. Instead of punching him, she thanked him and left the station to try and locate a telephone. At least she knew where Lee was and that he was safe.

Over the course of the afternoon, Lee got up on occasion to walk around his cell. Each time he quietly did a quick test to see which key opened the cell door. He eventually established which one it was and memorised it.

Le Chambre d'hôtes du Bois Fillaud was a small bed and breakfast just outside the centre of town. It had taken a while for Kim to find, but the patrons were friendly enough. She gave them 10 Francs to use the phone in order to call Commandant Marchand; but when she called, she found that he wasn't at the station and had finished for the day. They wouldn't give out his personal number when she asked, but there was no harm in trying. It was going to be expensive, but Kim had to call Nancy. When she was eventually put through, she explained the current situation. Nancy was relieved that she'd at least seen the boy and he was alive. She instructed Kim to call her back first thing in the morning. In the meantime, she would try to smooth a pathway at her end to see if the French police would release Lee into Kim's custody tomorrow. With nothing else to do but sit tight, Kim asked the owners of the B&B if she could have a room for the night, which they greatly appreciated during the off-season.

When Nancy got off the phone, she immediately called HQ and asked The Chief if he could make arrangements with the French for an extraction. He was only too happy to help, and said he'd call her back as soon as he had something. Whilst she waited, Nancy called David at work to give him the good news. It lifted his spirits no end, but he asked if she could look after Lee when he arrived back because he had to go away for a week or so on business.

It was just after midnight when Nancy received the call back to say that Commandant Marchand would speak with the principal officer at La Chapelle-Basse-Mer first thing in the morning to allow Kim to take responsibility for the boy. It would be on the condition that she must bring him back to England straightaway, which was what they'd intended anyway. The Chief had also organised for the necessary immigration arrangements to be in place to allow them unencumbered passage out of France and into England.

* * *

At the same time, when the station was quiet, Lee saw his opportunity to escape. He slowly turned the key in his cell lock and quietly opened the door. He stepped out through the gap and decided it would be good fun to lock the door again. *That'll give them something to think about!* He chuckled inwardly. Lee walked towards a locked storeroom where he knew his bag was located. He found the key to the room and walked in, quickly locating the case. He didn't bother closing it when he exited for fear of making a noise. There were two officers on duty – one at the front of the station and one at the rear. The officer at the rear had dozed off and placed his firearm and belt on the table next to him. As Lee walked past him, he quietly took the belt containing the firearm. With the keys in hand, he found the one to the rear door and silently let himself out of the station's rear entrance.

It had not been the best time to escape weather-wise; Lee hadn't found his coat in the storeroom and heavy rain poured down, peppering his face like small pieces of gravel. He had to be strong and would rather be wet and free than dry and locked up. Lee opened his case and put the policeman's belt inside, which doubled the weight. He then ran as fast as he could to gain some distance away from the station, changing hands with the case whenever his arm felt fatigued. When he was happy he'd got far enough away, Lee decided to maintain a steady walking pace. Although he didn't know exactly where he was, he tried to find his way back towards the river route that had served him well so far. Even though it didn't necessarily offer him the shelter he needed, it would be much easier for him to spot, and hide from, danger. He remembered something he'd been taught by Richard's dad when they'd all gone walking in the woods last summer. He'd said that the sun rises in the east, so he knew that was the direction he needed to head towards. But it was dark and if he got the map out now it would soon be ruined. Besides, he wouldn't be able to see much anyway. Lee kept walking in the direction his instinct told him to. He'd try and find some shelter for the rest of the night and try to work out where he was when the sun came up.

When Kim spoke to Nancy in the morning, she told Kim what Commandant Marchand was going to do and suggested going to the station at La Chapelle-Basse-Mer at about 10 o'clock. This would allow Marchand time to straighten everything out with whoever was in charge. Once Lee was in Kim's custody, she was to call Commandant Marchand to confirm extraction details from France. Nancy hoped to hear good news soon - and maybe even Lee's voice, if Kim had the chance.

* * *

CHAPTER 18

QUESTIONS

That morning, the police at La Chapelle-Basse-Mer were in utter disarray. Not only had a child escaped their custody, but it looked as though he'd also taken an officer's firearm. This was going to be a real headache for the principal officer. He knew that their reputation would be in tatters with the other local forces and the local community if this got out. With so few staff at the station, they didn't have the capacity for a huge manhunt. The officer who'd lost the weapon was a laughingstock within the ranks, with the principal saying he could end up being dismissed for his gross error.

At just after 10, Kim walked into a police station that was clearly in chaos. She caught the attention of the young officer she'd spoken to before, who told her of the boy's escape.

"Qu'est ce qui se passe ici?" (*What the hell is going on here?*) she said loudly.

"S'il vous plaît, tranquilment, Madame" (*Please, keep your voice down, Madam*), he said in a sheepish voice.

There he goes again with the 'Madam'!

"Je suis ici pour voir l'officier responsible; il m'attend," (*I need the officer in charge; he's expecting me*) she said, exasperated with the stupid little man. Kim was taken to the principal's office, where they both introduced themselves and he awkwardly explained what had happened.

*F*ck!*

The plan that had been put in place was now in tatters. She offered her help with the manhunt, which was gratefully accepted. He insisted, however, that due to regulations she had to be assigned to one of the other officers at all times. Kim agreed to this but, unfortunately, the officer she was assigned to was the idiot she had already spoken to twice. The principal also told her that if anyone asked who they are looking for, it was a 28-year-old, dark-haired man with a 7-year-old accomplice. Kim initially looked quizzical before she understood the man's embarrassment and that he needed cover to hide the fact that a young child had managed to escape alone from his station. She nodded her agreement; the story made no difference to her anyway – it was the tail-end of a cold January, and her sole focus was finding Lee. Kim asked to use one of the station phones. She hated the idea of giving Nancy the bad news, but it had to be done. Nancy was furious, and Kim felt her ear burn with the tirade that came from the woman's mouth.

"You do realise that I've just arrived to find this pig's ear, don't you?" Kim said firmly. Nancy let out a sigh.

"You're right, Kim, and I'm not angry at you. I'm angry that grown policemen have locked-up a seven-year-old and allowed him to escape... with a gun! Jesus Christ! Do you realise how dangerous that is?" Kim knew all too well the danger Lee had now put himself in but wasting time talking about it wasn't going to help.

"I'm going to help out with the manhunt here... such as it is; I have a hunch which direction he'll be heading in. He's tenacious and very much alive." Kim added, trying her best to inject some positivity into the situation.

"Do whatever it takes and ensure the police don't get over-zealous."

"I'll do whatever I can," Kim promised.

Kim joined the young officer to begin their search for Lee. She asked him if they could take the river route, as that was where she thought the boy would be. But he said he had to follow orders and cover the main part of town first. He certainly didn't want to get in as much trouble as his colleague was in. By canvassing the main town first, they could cover the riverside in the late afternoon.

By the end of the day, they'd uncovered nothing but a big fat zero. When they got back to the station, nothing had been found by anyone else either. There was no choice – they'd have to broaden the search tomorrow. This would put the principal in the unenviable position of having to enlist the help of other local forces. Kim called Nancy again from the police station – there was no reason why she should have to pay out of pocket for their incompetence. The call was pretty short.

"I'm sorry, Nancy, but there is nothing to report. Tomorrow, I am going to ask the principal to put me in charge of the officer that I'm paired with."

"Sounds right," Nancy said in a clipped voice. *Should've done that today,* she thought. As she put the phone down, Nancy managed a wry smile before she caught herself. Although she wanted Lee safely back home, she realised she was rooting for him to see how far he could go. She hadn't seen this kind of spirit in a person for a very long time, especially one so young. But now came the tough part – she had to inform David about current developments but did so without mentioning the gun.

* * *

Lee was soaked through and in need of food and shelter. His breathing had become heavy and slightly wheezy. He remembered being laid up in bed last winter with what the doctor called bronchitis. His dad had put a miner's lamp by the side of his bed each night to burn off coal tar vapours and rubbed his chest with Vicks when he came home. The memory of the smells filled Lee's mind. He knew that he had to keep warm, and when the sun came up he walked towards it and finally found where he was on the map. He marked it with a pen and, once along the riverside again, continued to walk at a decent pace the five miles east towards the smaller town of Champtoceaux. Along the side of the twisting narrow road, he found a disused stone pathway that led up a hill towards a church. Not wanting to be seen during the day, Lee stayed out on the hillside behind the trees and bushes until dusk. It was a long time to be in one position and his wet clothes were extremely uncomfortable, creating irritation under his arms and in his groin. But he stayed there because it was ideal to see comings and goings near the church, as well as any cars passing along the road below. He hadn't seen any police cars go by above or below, so he thought that the church could be the ideal place to sleep overnight.

As dusk turned to darkness, Lee emerged from his hiding spot and walked towards the church. On the way, he noticed that it seemed to be surrounded on two sides by what looked like a campsite. As silently as he could, he moved around the church building to see if there was any way in. He was in luck; there was a small side entrance that only used a simple slide bolt for a lock. There was a house next door, and Lee made sure to open the door as slowly and quietly as possible. Inside were the usual pews, aisle and altar configuration. Lee walked around checking doors and any openings around the building, but there really wasn't anything interesting he could see.

Having done his reconnaissance, Lee exited the building the same way he entered to find food and clothing. There weren't that many shops around and the whole town seemed silent, with the exception of the odd dog barking in the distance. The one good thing in his favour was that the place was barely lit. *Apparently, street lamps aren't really needed around here?* he thought. Lee initially looked in a few bins, but there was nothing to be found that wasn't disgusting. He knew he was going to have to take a risk again; he'd have to break into a closed shop. It seemed that some people were more trusting than others, or perhaps more careless. At the rear of a bakery, he found a door just closed, not locked. He dipped in and out as quickly as possible, taking some bread and cakes. He wrapped them in a paper bag and put them in his case, his heart racing at the fear of being arrested again. Although he had got quite used to taking things from shops that were open, breaking and entering was really not something he'd ever saw himself resorting to.

He moved quietly around the streets, making his way further into the town. There seemed to be one clothes shop for adults which would have to do. He looked through the front window and started planning which items would be best to take. Lee looked around. The risk of getting caught was extremely high, due to the way that the shops and houses were packed together into the small streets, but he was desperate and simply had to find some dry clothing. He made his way around the back to see if there was another way in. The door was solid and securely locked. Lee went back around to the front, where the door had more conventional top-and-bottom window panes.

The only way in was for Lee to smash through the bottom glass of the shop door, and the only tool he had was the gun in his case. He pulled it out and held the gun by the back of the barrel. Remembering what he'd seen in an episode of The Rockford Files, Lee placed a pair of socks on the window to dull the sound and tapped at the bottom right-hand corner of the glass. Each tap was slightly harder until the glass splintered. He paused briefly, listening for any disturbance or alarm. *Nothing*. He put the gun back in the case and wrapped the socks around his hand. Lee then pushed sections of the glass inwards as quietly as possible, pausing each time to see if he had disturbed anyone. The hole was eventually large enough for him to clamber without cutting himself in the process. Lee snagged some clothes he thought would fit or could soon grow into. He didn't hang around and squeezed out of the small hole as quickly as possible. He got back to the church unscathed, his pulse still racing as he slid himself into the open doorway he'd explored before. He placed his case and the new clothes on a pew and started to go through everything. He'd taken a corduroy jacket that had fur lining, some socks, pants, t-shirts, gloves, trousers and a belt. He took a look around the church to see what else was around.

In a vestibule, he found some cassocks that were hung from an open closet. Lee decided to use these as towels and for bedding warmth. He changed into some of the new clothes and put the rest in his case. Lee then sat on the pew and ate through half the bread and cakes whilst he contemplated that stupid Bible his mum and Jon had bought for him. His breathing returned to normal, and he began to think more about what his mother had said to him: *You weren't my baby!* Many questions flowed through his mind, but any answers he could think of just led to more questions. *How am I not your baby? Was Laura your baby? If Laura was her baby and he wasn't, then how did it happen? If Mum was having another baby, that means that she was able to have children. Am I adopted? If so, why? Who is my real mother? Is Dad really my dad?* Lee just didn't understand any of it.

* * *

CHAPTER 19

WATER FALL

After a slightly more comfortable night, under shelter provided by God of all people, Lee awoke early the next morning. With the morning light refracting beautifully through the stained-glass windows, he revisited his map to confirm where he thought he was. He predicted that if he continued east along the road he'd come from for a while, he would find a path that spurred off to the left that would shadow the south side of the river. Lee gathered his things and put the cassocks back where he found them. The new trousers he'd put on were a bit big, so, using the prong from the buckle, he skewered a new hole in the belt to help keep them up. He then tucked the trouser legs into his socks and quietly snuck out of the musty-smelling church into the crisp fresh air.

Once back on the road below, Lee maintained a steady walking pace and carefully avoided traffic wherever possible. He wondered how long he'd survive just moving from town-to-town indefinitely. None of the outcomes he could envisage seemed sustainable, so Lee blocked those thoughts out as best he could. With his map in hand, he eventually found the path; he figured he didn't have to hide as much now. He passed the odd dog-walker along the way, but they just looked at him strangely and politely said '*bonjour.*' Lee recalled Arnauld's coaching, so just repeated the word back and kept walking. He knew his map-reading was correct when he saw the next town of Ancenis on the other side of the river. The only access was via a long steel and iron suspension bridge. Lee had been taught by Richard's dad to always walk on the side of oncoming traffic so that drivers could always see you. But he didn't want to be seen, or even noticed at all, so he entered the bridge on the right-hand side instead. Once across, he kept on the outskirts of the town and eventually stumbled upon a large supermarket. Lee was nervous about going in; but if he was going to survive this journey, wherever it may take him, he was going to have to be brave and stay tough. Looking at his battered suitcase, he realised he also had the gun if he needed it. Before going in, Lee made a mental note of what he wanted. After his brush with the law, he was apprehensive about shoplifting during daylight hours. In the supermarket he put the more expensive items inside his coat and pockets and, as a form of cover, put a few small cheap items in a shopping basket. He figured it would arouse less suspicion when he went through the tills. Lee's heart pounded and his legs shook a little as he came to pay. The only things in his basket were some bubble gum, some biscuits and the cheapest drink he could find. The woman at the till gave him a strange look but smiled anyway, so Lee smiled back and said nothing. *Est-ce qu'il porte les vêtements de son père?* (*Is he wearing his father's clothes?*) she wondered. She continued speaking as she typed the prices into the cash register and packed the items into a bag for him, but Lee really didn't understand anything she said.

"C'est trois francs et cinquante, s'il te plait" (*That's three francs and fifty, please*). The lady looked at him expectantly. Lee took out 10 francs from his pocket and gave it to the woman. He'd added up the prices of what he was buying beforehand and knew how much change he should be getting. As she opened the till, he looked around to see if anyone was watching him or making their way to the exit. The woman counted out the change in Lee's hand. "Merci bien."

"Merci," he replied, putting the money in his pocket. He took the bag and walked hastily towards the exit, which turned into a jog once he was out the door. Once at a distance he felt to be safe, Lee slowed to a steady walking pace. The muscles in his arms were burning from the sheer weight of his case as he ran, which triggered thoughts about what he'd just done. He cursed himself inwardly. *Just hide the case before you go in and walk out calmly next time!* He knew it would be much better to have his hands free if he needed to escape from an adult.

Now at the tail-end of January, the sun shone low, trying its best to peek through the grey haze, but it was still cold enough for Lee to see his own breath. He found a little ridge-top in a field about half a mile away from the supermarket and laid out his coat to rest on and take stock. The weight of the suitcase was tiring; he wondered whether anything could be got rid of, but the only item he could think of was the gun. He took the belt and placed it on his laid-out coat then lifted the suitcase again to see how much lighter it was. The difference was huge. Lee looked at his arms and flexed his biceps. It'd been over a month since he'd run away, and both his arms and shoulders seemed to be harder and more defined. *Maybe the weight is a good thing after all?*

He picked up the belt and took the gun out of its holster. It was a lot heavier than the toy cap guns he'd played with at home. As he moved the pistol around in his hand without touching the trigger, Lee thought it looked like the Walther PPK that James Bond always used – except this had MAB written on the grip. There were two different mechanisms behind the trigger, an up-and-down switch that didn't seem to do much and a push button that released the bullet magazine from the base of the grip. The magazine seemed to work like a PEZ dispenser as Lee slid the bullets out from the top with his thumb. *Eight bullets... I need to be careful*, he thought. Having never seen a real bullet before, he was surprised at how something so light and small could kill someone. Although it took a few goes to get it right, Lee slotted the bullets back into the magazine and pushed it back into the grip with a solid click. The big question was... how did it work?

After munching on a few biscuits and taking a well-earned drink, he packed up the case and fastened the gun belt diagonally across his right shoulder and torso before making his way towards a wooded area a hundred yards away. Having the belt across his shoulder was far less strenuous on his carrying arm, and also allowed him to unholster and holster the weapon quickly from under his coat.

Lee set his belongings down ten yards away from a group of trees, took the pistol out of the holster again and, with his right eye, aimed at the widest one. He was scared and apprehensive as he slowly applied pressure against the trigger with his forefinger. He wondered whether he was strong enough when the trigger wouldn't budge, but then realised that the other switch behind the trigger was in the upward position. He slid it downwards, braced himself again and slowly pulled the trigger.

BANG!

Lee fell backwards onto the dirt, his ears ringing in the aftermath of the small explosion. As he got up and dusted himself down, he walked over to the tree he was aiming at. *Nothing!* He looked around as he walked back to his spot. *No movement... OK, seven bullets left.* This time, Lee tried to visualise the police shoot-out scenes he'd seen on TV. He changed his feet to a ten-to-four stance and bent his knees and elbows slightly. He aimed at the tree once more and fired the pistol again with more conviction.

BANG!

This time he was still standing and felt a surge of pride when he saw the small puff of dust where the bullet hit the tree. *Six left.* Lee switched the safety back up and holstered the gun as he walked confidently towards the small hole that splintered the bark. He couldn't see it, but he knew the bullet was there somewhere, embedded in a small hole about three inches deep. He looked around again; although there were no real signs of any reactions to the gunshots, it was time to move on. As he walked its streets, Ancenis felt more like the city of Nantes than the small town he'd been to before. He contemplated which was harder to survive in; it was easier to find food in towns with higher populations, but more difficult to settle at night. *Maybe I'll get used to it?* His exploration of the town took him past a school where the boys in the playground were playing football. Lee couldn't understand why, but he actually missed school when the teacher was interesting; more than that, he missed playing football. His mind wandered back to last summer before all the problems with his parents began. One-on-one against Richard with the ball at his feet, he'd jinked the ball past him and put one in the top right-hand corner of the net past Richard's dad. It'd been the best goal of his make-believe career for Liverpool FC and left Richard's dad floored as he tripped and hit the ground with a thud, swallowing a mouthful of dust and dirt in the process. The two boys had both cracked up laughing until their stomachs hurt. When Lee's mind slowly brought him back to the present, a smile flashed across his face – he didn't have many good memories, but that was one of the best.

Walking around the streets for a while, Lee looked for places to settle down; but the place was too lively and there was nowhere sheltered enough to avoid being discovered by someone. Having decided the place wasn't suitable, Lee headed back towards the bridge to the south.

* * *

Kim and her dim-witted chaperone took a police car and drove to Champtoceaux, the next town over. When they arrived at the local police station, they discovered there had been a report of an overnight break-in at small clothing shop. Kim insisted that she wanted to go to the scene to check whether the two cases were connected; speaking with the shop owner, it was pretty clear they were. He had said that there were more expensive things that could've been stolen, but only a handful of items were actually missing – a jacket and some trousers; possibly some undergarments, but he couldn't be sure about those. He gave Kim a description of the jacket and trousers. This was good news; she was definitely on the right track. Back in the car, she asked the officer for a map. After tracing her finger along a couple of different routes, she said, "We need to go to Ancenis immediately." The officer was not pleased at being ordered around by a woman and said he needed to radio into HQ first to make sure it would be acceptable to the Ancenis Police. Ten minutes later, they had the green light to proceed.

It didn't take them long to reach the bridge that led directly into the heart of the town. They drove to the local police station to see if there'd been any sightings; there hadn't, but Kim hadn't been expecting any. By her reckoning, they were less than 12 hours behind the boy. They drove around for a while and canvassed a number of places in town; no-one they asked had seen anything at all. At just after 3 o'clock, Kim asked to be taken back to La Chapelle-Basse-Mer so she could collect her car. If Lee wasn't going to surface during the day, she would come back and resume the search on her own that evening. This obviously suited the officer perfectly; he gave his first smile of the day. This was all a waste of manpower as far as he was concerned anyway.

As they drove south across the bridge, Kim thought she saw a familiar silhouette ahead on the right. *There can't be too many kids lugging a suitcase around town,* she thought. As they passed, Kim turned in her seat to get a better look. *That's definitely him.* The officer saw him too, but with a lorry right behind he couldn't just stop the car. He got straight onto the radio and called for additional support to aid the capture of the boy. Back-up was a minute away.

Lee saw the police car as it passed him on the bridge; as it didn't stop, he carried on walking. After a couple of seconds, he stopped in his tracks. At the south end of the bridge, the car had pulled over and two people were heading in his direction – a police officer and a woman. Lee immediately reversed direction and began walking quickly the other way. He started to pick up the pace into a jog, but as he did so he saw two different police cars enter the bridge ahead of him – their sirens a constant drone. His exits were blocked. Lee looked back over his shoulder. Both sets of police were moving in on his position – he was trapped.

We've got him! Kim thought as she jogged alongside her French counterpart. But what happened next absolutely astounded everyone. With his suitcase, Lee managed to climb up onto an iron girder that was supported by one of many intertwined steel cables. He stood facing the road and shouted in both directions for everyone to leave him alone. He was just a kid, so they all continued walking towards him. Lee pulled out the weapon, which caught them all by surprise.

The two Ancenis officers pulled out their guns and pointed them at the boy. They were apprehensive; it wasn't normal to have to unholster their guns, especially to point them at a child. Horrified, Kim instinctively shouted, "LEE!"

Lee turned to face the woman and studied her briefly. Although she knew his name somehow, he didn't recognise her. He could see that they were all edging closer on his position, 30 yards... 25 yards... 20 yards. He turned around to face outwards towards the river and pointed the gun to his own head.

"Oh, my god!" Kim exclaimed in horror. "Lee! No!" But it was too late. Everyone stopped as a single shot rang out across the bridge and the boy fell forwards over the edge. The police officers weren't completely sure who'd fired the shot, but Kim saw the muzzle flash from the gun Lee was holding. They all hurried over to the side of the bridge and looked down to see the boy's body and case floating down the river to the west. The Ancenis Police and her chaperone just stood there and did nothing. Kim shouted at her officer, "Tu ne vas pas sauter dedans?" (*Aren't you going to jump in?*).

"Non, il fait trop froid. Nous devons aller en aval et essayer de récupérer le corps là-bas" (*No, it's too cold. We should head down river and try to retrieve the body there*), he replied.

"You gutless pr*ck!" she said in English. Kim had had enough of the incompetent idiot. The least she could do for Nancy was retrieve the body, although the thought of dragging Lee's corpse from the river made her shudder.

"Here, hold these." She took off her shoes and gave him her purse and jacket. She climbed the ironwork, just as Lee had, and jumped straight off into the river without hesitation. Kim tensed as she dropped through the on-rushing air, waiting for the inevitable pain to come. She kept her ankles together and hit the water feet first.

* * *

At the very last moment, Lee diverted the pistol barrel forward in front of his forehead before pulling the trigger. He didn't blow his brains out, but the muzzle flash singed his skin. The sound of the shot firing left a dull ringing sensation in his ear, which made the fall seem that much farther – the breeze brushed past his face as the dark rippled surface approached ever nearer. He let go of the suitcase and tried keeping his legs and arms together just before hitting the water, but the impact seriously hurt. Lee wasn't sure which hurt the most – the landing which winded him, or the temperature of the water, which was numbingly painful. Once he got his breath back, Lee put the gun back in the holster and fastened the small leather safety strap to stop it falling out. The river was fast-flowing and he struggled initially to stay afloat; swimming with clothes on seemed impossibly difficult, but it was a little easier once he'd managed to remove his coat while trying not to make any sudden movements that might give him away. He could see his suitcase was not too far in front of him and whenever Lee rolled face up to catch a breath, he gave a look back at the bridge to see what was happening. He saw the police head back to their vehicles and the woman who'd called his name jump into the river after him. *She's either brave or stupid,* he thought. *The men have just left her to it.*

The Ancenis Police began walking back towards their cars.

"Tu ne vas pas aider?" (*Aren't you going to help?*) the officer from La Chapelle-Basse-Mer called over.

"Ceci est votre désordre, vous devez le nettoyer!" (*This is your mess. You need to clean it up.*) and "Il rentre de toute façon à ta ville" (*He's floating back to your town anyway*), were the only responses he received as they got into their cars and drove back into town. The incompetent officer was left standing there, unsure what to do, with a woman's jacket, purse and shoes in his hand. Leaving a growing group of bystanders behind, he dashed back to his car and radioed in what had just happened. He offered to drive along the riverside, where that was possible, to see if he could catch the woman up. HQ said they'd try to commandeer a boat and set up a base at the Pont de Mauves Bridge a few miles down-river – they'd see if they could retrieve anyone if they went by.

Although the river had a fast flow, it wasn't choppy – which was probably the one thing that stopped Lee drowning. The ice-cold water seemed to make his muscles contract so much that it was hard to move. Lee started to kick a little to try and pick up speed and close the gap to his case. He stayed on his back to keep afloat, using his arms to help guide his direction as the river bent. He could just about see the woman in the water behind him, so he kicked harder.

Kim tried her best to catch up to the body, but with the strong flow she wasn't reeling it in as quickly as she'd hoped. *Did I just see it kicking?* she thought to herself. When the corpse changed direction and headed for the suitcase, her heart missed a beat. *He's alive! Jesus, how many lives has this kid got?* She psyched herself up for one last burst and pushed herself harder to catch up.

Lee caught up with the case as he rounded the bend just out of sight of his pursuer. He knew she was catching up, but he was cold and exhausted, and needed to get out of the river fast. He kept kicking towards the south bank, pushing his legs down at intervals to see if his feet would touch the bottom. He waded towards the bank once he eventually found the riverbed, stumbling twice as he tried to find his footing. As he crawled out of the river, the gun belt around his shoulder fell off onto the mud. He quickly wiped it clean, as best he could, and put it back in the case, which thankfully hadn't let in too much water. As Kim swam round the river bend, she saw Lee walking away on the left riverbank.

"Lee!" she shouted, but he continued to walk away from her. As she slogged her way out of the water and onto the sandbank herself, she called out to him again. "I was sent to take you home!"

"I'm not going back and I don't have a home," he protested.

"But your nan sent me to find you."

Lee stopped and turned around. He looked at the woman through questioning eyes. The woman was now fully out of the water and within 30 yards of him.

"What's my nan's name, and where does she live?" he asked. She gave Lee the correct response, and he relaxed a little. "Who are you?"

"My name is Kim, and your nan and dad hired me to bring you back; I'm a private investigator." Lee felt a heat radiate around his chest. *Dad didn't give up on me after all.* The journey from the home had hardened his resolve and he kept his emotions in check, even though he was secretly happy that his dad and nan had gone to this much trouble. He looked past the woman and just said, "We need to get out of here." Lee waited for Kim to catch up and they both helped each other climb the bank to the adjacent footpath. He turned back towards the direction of Ancenis and assessed the view that he'd seen earlier in the day. He turned 180 degrees to the west and began walking along the path back towards Champtoceaux.

"This way," he said.

He must have been on the same path this morning, Kim thought to herself. "Where are we going, Lee?"

"I know a place," was all he would divulge.

The leather of Lee's suitcase had absorbed water and was much heavier with the gun. He swapped hands every twenty seconds or so until Kim offered to hold it for a while. Lee thought about it for a few seconds and then handed it to her; he figured that he needed to maintain as much of his strength as possible. Kim was surprised at how heavy the case was to carry, which was made harder by having to walk the pathway barefoot. At least the boy was polite enough to stop each time Kim needed to pull a small stone from her foot. She could see that he was deep in thought but decided to ask the question that had been bugging her since she'd been in the water.

"At what point did you decide to fake your own death?" she asked with a hint of admiration. Lee coughed.

"Just before I pulled the trigger," he replied, without a trace of emotion.

As they walked further along the path, Kim asked more questions and Lee responded with some of his own. He asked her if she spoke French. When she answered in the affirmative, he asked her for the

French translations of a number of words, some of which he already knew. Other words he asked about were 'England, return and hiding,' so that he could tell if she was giving him up later. Kim had a sense of this already but played along anyway. It was interesting to watch the boy work things out, and it took her mind off the pain in her feet. As they joined the road that led to Champtoceaux, Lee told her to duck down behind the wall if they saw or heard any cars coming. Kim nodded, intrigued by the young boy.

It was starting to get late and visibility was declining. Kim's police chaperone had driven slowly along the road closest to the river but had seen nothing. When he eventually reached Pont de Mauves Bridge, the police there hadn't seen anything drift past either. In truth, the search had only been a half-hearted one, which was called off as soon as the light began to fade. The officer drove back to the station and put Kim's possessions in the storeroom.

Lee showed Kim the small entrance that led up the muddy bank to the church and where the campers were. They were both freezing and smelled dank.

"I'll see if I can talk to someone here to see if we can get cleaned up?" she suggested.

With Lee now in tow, Kim managed to locate a manager for the site, who could see they were a mess. She spoke in French, saying that their boat had overturned. She asked if they could use the facilities, and whether anyone had some spare clothing. The manager said that she could use the bathroom in his camper, and that he would ask around the site to see if anyone had anything to spare. He gave each of them a towel.

Lee kept an eye on them both. Their gestures and body language didn't raise any alarm bells, but he didn't really understand the language either. They took turns to wash with the little water available, which was tepid at best. The manager did what he could to rally the neighbours for clothing; Kim's seemed to fit better than Lee's, but at least they were dry, and he was thankful for small mercies. Kim explained to the man that she didn't have her purse and therefore had no money to thank him with.

"Nous devons nous entraider, non?" (*We all need to help others, no?*). Kim smiled and spoke to Lee.

"I don't have any money and the police have my belongings – so we'll need to go back to La Chapelle-Basse-Mer." Lee tensed.

"I'm not going back there; they'll put me in the cell again." He kept quiet about any money he had left in his case. Kim was exhausted, hungry and not in the best of moods. *It was time the boy heard a few home truths.*

"OK, Lee. Walk me through what happens next," she said, clearly showing her annoyance. Lee shrugged his shoulders. "You've been on the run for a while now. How much fun have you had so far?" Lee shrugged again. "The way you're going, all roads lead to you either being arrested, being hurt, getting ill or dying. Is there anything else I've missed off the list?"

"I might meet somebody nice and stay with them?" Lee countered.

"Oh, like Servane?" Kim suggested. *How does she know about her?* It was Lee's turn to be annoyed, but just as he was about to say something she continued. "Would you risk putting someone like her in danger for your own needs?"

"What are you talking about?" he muttered.

"OK, so someone takes you in – do you think that's the end of it? That it's all happy ever after? Of course not. People ask questions. Seven-year-old children don't just magically appear – people have babies first."

"I'm nearly eight!" Kim ignored his objection and continued.

"It doesn't matter. Once people ask questions, the authorities get involved. Once the authorities get involved, you not only cause a problem for yourself but problems for the person who's taken you and might have broken the law." Lee was about to interject again, but Kim held up a finger. "That's not all. If you keep on running, you'll either be put in jail wherever you end up or be sent back to England and get put in some kind of institution there. And what about your poor father and nan? They've been looking for you. Don't you want go back home and be with them, instead of all this?" she said, gesturing at their current clothing. Lee cocked his head to one side, thinking through what Kim had just said. "Just so you know, you won't be arrested whilst you're in my custody here. I have a plan to get you out of the country." Lee quietly relented. The woman's logic was hard to refute and, being honest with himself, running away was not what he had thought it would be.

Kim hoped she'd talked some sense into the boy but wasn't counting her chickens. He was clearly a slippery customer when he needed to be. She watched closely as he walked outside and deposited much of the contents of his suitcase into a waste bin. All of the food was spoiled, and he checked the pockets of all the clothes before throwing away anything that he felt would no longer be useful.

The manager didn't have a car himself, but he arranged for one of the other campers to drive the pair to La Chapelle-Basse-Mer – it was definitely better than walking at night. They arrived to find the police station closed. Kim had to think on her feet. Her hire car was still there, but locked – breaking into it was probably not the best idea. She asked the camper if he wouldn't mind taking them a little further and directed him to the bed and breakfast where she'd stayed before. The owner took them in without any problem but explained that they only had one single room left. Neither Kim nor Lee really cared; they were both so tired that they could have slept anywhere.

The room had a single bed which Kim offered to Lee. Kim slept on some spare cushions between the bed and the door, but not primarily to protect Lee. The owner had suggested that Kim sleep on the sofa in the living room, but there was no way she was going to let this boy out of her sight. She felt like an old Wild West bounty hunter – all she needed was the hat.

* * *

Nancy waited all day for Kim to check in. She knew that Kim wouldn't forget and knew by deduction that something must have happened. She felt completely helpless knowing there was nothing she could do, but in this game it was best not to jump to conclusions. You had to trust your agents when things didn't go to plan. She retired for the evening, hopeful to hear something from Kim soon.

In the morning, the owner of the B&B was kind enough to provide his guests with some much-needed breakfast, for which they were exceedingly thankful. They both smiled for the first time since meeting one another. As they walked back towards the town centre, Lee explained to Kim why he didn't want to go back to England. He told her that his mother hated him, the guy she married was nasty, his sister had been responsible for him being taken away, and that he wasn't sure that his dad actually wanted him to stay. Kim considered this for a while. She hadn't truly known what had gone on with the family before but sympathised with Lee's position in all the family dysfunction. *It must've been bad if he had to resort to this.* She didn't want the boy running away from her, potentially ruining her return to the active roster. Kim saw an opportunity to pursue something that had been on her mind ever since she'd arrived in the country.

"Look, I have a friend who lives a few hours away near Paris that we can go to whilst we sort this out. Would you let me talk this over with your nan? I'm sure that between us all we can work out a plan?"

"Sure." Lee shrugged, but he really didn't hold out much hope.

* * *

CHAPTER 20

TRUST

As they walked towards the police station at La Chapelle-Basse-Mer, Kim formulated a plan. She could see that her car was still there, but the station still looked closed. They both stayed out of sight in a disused car park by some overgrown bushes. Lee was to stay completely out of sight then, once she had retrieved her belongings and car, she would drive past and signal him to jump in the rear passenger seat.

"I intend to tell them I didn't find you yesterday. So you need to trust me when I'm in there. Do you trust me?"

Lee nodded.

"Can I trust you?" she asked in a more authoritative tone.

"Yes."

"Do you still have the gun? If you do, I need to return it."

"No, it ended up in the river when I fell."

Kim wasn't completely convinced he was telling her the truth, but she didn't think it wise to press him further at that point; she'd look for an opportunity to search his case another time. When Kim's chaperone eventually arrived, she walked over the road and caught him before he went into the station. The officer seemed genuinely pleased to see her.

"Avez-vous trouvé le garçon? Nous ne l'avons pas trouvé en aval" (*Did you find the boy? We didn't find him down river*), he asked.

"C'était très triste. Je n'ai pas pu rattraper le corps et je me suis presque noyé" (*It was very sad. I couldn't catch up to the body and nearly drowned myself*), she replied. "J'ai besoin de mes affaires pour pouvoir continuer vers l'ouest dans ma recherché" (*I need you to get my belongings, so that I can continue west on my search*).

"Je suis désolé madame, mais si vous voulez récupérer vos affaires, vous devrez obtenir la permission du patron lorsqu'il arrive dans quelques heures" (*I'm sorry, Madam, but if you want your things back you will have to get permission from the principal when he arrives in a couple of hours*).

Kim snapped. Angry at this stupid man's pettiness, and the fact that he had again addressed her as Madam, she grabbed him by the testicles and squeezed so hard that he fell to his knees. Lee watched and felt the sympathetic pain all men feel at some point in their lives.

"Vous me donnerez mes affaires!" (*You WILL give me my belongings!*)

Lee chuckled to himself as the pair went inside. He contemplated running off, but he actually wanted to speak to his nan to find out what she planned for him. *Maybe she'll let me live with her?* He opened his suitcase, pulled out the gun and hid it inside the oversized jacket he was wearing. Inside the station, Kim waited impatiently as the officer returned gingerly from the store and quietly gave her belongings back. It felt good to be in her own jacket and shoes again.

"J'ai besoin d'un stylo, du papier et d'une envelope" (*I need a pen, some paper and an envelope*), she barked. Kim wrote a note and instructed for it to be given to the station principal as soon as he arrived. It simply said, “Tout se déroulera comme prévu” (*Everything will proceed as previously planned*). She knew that he’d understand. Just as she was about to leave, the officer plucked up the courage to ask, “Où allez-vous maintenant?” (*Where are you heading to now?*).

“En aval! Où d’autre?” (*Down river! Where else?*). Lee watched Kim come out of the station unaccompanied, noting her top and shoes were different now. Although she couldn’t see him, she looked in his direction and gave two hand signals; the first a two-fingered walking sign, and the second giving the direction she wanted him to walk in. Lee did as he was asked while Kim got into the car and unlocked all the passenger doors. She drove off for thirty seconds in the opposite direction to where she’d instructed Lee to walk and then turned around. *That’s enough time for the police to lose interest.* She drove back to where she could see Lee walking and stopped to let him jump into the back.

Lee didn’t care too much about where they were heading; he just wanted to relax for a while. But, just in case, he still paid attention to some of the road signs. Kim asked him about his time in France, the good and the bad things, as well as how he’d survived. But Lee wasn’t really in the mood for a full interrogation and just gave short answers. Kim eventually got the message and left him alone for a while. Lee deliberately opened his still-damp suitcase in the middle of the back seat so that Kim could clearly see what he was doing in the rear-view mirror. He pulled out his wet roll of francs and started unravelling them on the seat to dry.

Kim saw this through the mirror and was initially angry that he’d not said anything about the money the day before. But then she thought about whether she'd have volunteered the information if the roles were reversed. *Again, smart kid.* Kim just wanted to find the signs to Paris. Once she saw those, she'd easily be able to drive north to Calais or continue east to the other location she had in mind. But that would be completely dependent on Nancy, so she thought about what she might say as she drove. After about fifty miles, Kim stopped for fuel and a break at the roadside services just past Angers. The last road signs had showed 290km to Paris and 510km to Calais. After refuelling, she parked outside the restaurant and suggested that Lee should put the money back in the case for now; he could leave it in the car. Before getting something to eat, Kim led them over to a phone booth. She had plenty of coins in her purse, and dialled Nancy's number. They both waited for what seemed like an age before Nancy finally answered the call. Kim said, "I have someone here that I think you'd like to talk to," and handed the receiver over. Lee's throat began to hurt with the emotion; he didn't really know what to say, so Nancy broke the silence.

"Is that you, my little detective?"

Lee smiled as his heart filled with warmth once again. The numb feeling of being completely alone washed away.

"Yes, Nan, it's me."

"I'm so relieved to hear your voice again, sweetheart. Are you OK?"

"I'm OK, Nan. But we're both a bit tired."

Nancy was happy that Lee was safe, but he didn't seem to have much life to his voice.

"I can't wait to see you again soon, my love," she said warmly. "And I can't wait to hear about all your adventures." Nancy continued. "Now, Kim is a very old friend of mine. I trust her completely to take care of you. But I also need you to trust her. Is that something you can do?"

"OK," he said, then added resolutely, "but I'm not going back to the children's home." Nancy thought about who would be able look after Lee when he finally came home. There was no way David could properly look after him and Nancy wasn't sure about taking on the full-time responsibility. But she'd worry about that later.

"I promise that's not going to happen and I'm crossing my heart as we speak." Lee handed the phone back to Kim who talked Nancy through what had happened.

"I've been thinking... would you mind if we stopped off in Paris for a couple of days to meet up with an old friend; it would give us both a little time to find some clean clothes and a chance for Lee to recover. Lee noticed that she had her fingers crossed when she asked the question.

"Is that to see who I think, Kimberly?" Nancy asked.

"Yes... I need to know." Nancy was briefly silent at the other end, whilst Kim put another twenty-centime coin in the coin slot.

"OK, but I want his address. How are you for money?"

"I probably have enough for a day."

"I'll have someone get in touch with you. They'll give you some money and you can take Lee to see the Eiffel Tower if you like. But Kim, make no mistake that you have two days in Paris only – your love life is secondary to my grandson," Nancy ordered.

"I understand and thank you, Nancy."

Kim gave Nancy the address, her ETA and the make and number plate of her hire car. Nancy asked Kim to put Lee back on before the call ended.

"There's something else I need you to do, Lee. Will you also look out for Kim for me?" It was a strange request and Lee wondered if his nan was just trying to amuse him, but the added responsibility made him smile anyway.

"Yes, Nan. I will," he promised. Whilst the idea of her request was to give a little distraction to the young boy, Nancy also knew Lee better than anyone else in the family. She'd spent a lot of time passively programming her little detective and, now that the seed was planted, she knew Lee would keep alert to any danger.

"What did your nan want?" Kim asked as Lee hooked the phone receiver into place.

"Oh, nothing… she just told me to be good." It was the quickest lie he could think of.

"Your nan's agreed that we can go to Paris for a couple of days!" Kim said excitedly. "We can even go and see the Eiffel Tower, if you like?" Lee didn't know what the Eiffel Tower even was but he agreed anyway. They both headed over to join the queue at the food counter.

"Is it OK if I go to the toilet while you order?" Lee asked.

"Alright. But you're not going to run away on me, are you?" Kim asked, genuinely concerned.

"Promise!" Lee said with a smile.

As Lee walked round the corner, Kim saw an opportunity to answer the question that had been bugging her. She quickly dashed out of the café to the car and searched Lee's bag; the belt and the holster were there, but the gun wasn't. *Guess he was telling the truth.*

After turning the corner, Lee waited ten seconds before popping his head back around to see Kim nip out to the car. *Thought so.* He smiled to himself and went back to the toilet. Kim dashed back to the queue, placed an order and paid the checkout lady. Lee came out just in time for them to pick a seat; they both gravitated towards the window, but Kim seemed further away somehow.

* * *

After the very pleasing phone call, Nancy informed The Chief of all the latest developments. They discussed new plans and agreed for a field agent to make contact with Kim once she'd arrived in Paris. It was a longer call than she was expecting. After listening to the stories that Nancy had filtered back, The Chief decided to make a proposal to her.

After the call with Nancy, The Chief had his assistant arrange contact with an agent based in Paris. Due to the nature of the contact Kim would be visiting, his orders were to discreetly shadow them and to make contact with Kim only.

* * *

CHAPTER 21

NO ESCAPING THE PAST

Agent 4 had been on a long-term surveillance operation when he received the orders for a short diversion to his current mission. He wasn't impressed to be doing a babysitting job, but orders were orders and disobedience towards The Chief's office would be career-ending. He'd been with the service for over 8 years and was considered a safe pair of hands. So, he decided to be professional, although not necessarily congenial.

The place he had to get to wasn't that far from his current location and he arrived long before his targets' expected ETA. It was a country house located in Férolles-Attilly, just south-east of the city. The house itself was on a two-acre plot, surrounded by wooded trees with two entry and exit points. With his car parked a half-mile up the road, Agent 4 took a backpack from the boot and discreetly walked the surrounding area; there were limited places that gave a good line of sight to the house, but something didn't seem quite right about one vantage point. As he looked closer, he could see that tree branches had been cut down deliberately to maintain the sightlines. He quietly crouched behind the nearest trunk and retrieved his CamBinox photo binoculars. He looked around fully 360 degrees, focusing more of his attention on following the sightline he was on, away from the house.

The situation looked safe for now, but he wasn't happy. *What am I into here?* Agent 4 stood up and followed the line back out to the road. There was no traffic, so he looked around for any other signs of surveillance. It wasn't long before he found what he was looking for – a discarded cigarette butt at the base of a bush by the side of the road. It wasn't new, but it wasn't old either – and it was definitely not French. As he continued to walk the perimeter, he could see the house was bordered by roads on two sides, with fields surrounding the other two. In all, there were three artificial lines of sight – one from the road and two from the fields. Agent 4 based himself in the most central position that gave him the best angles to view the house entry and waited.

Kim had been anxious for the whole journey but was excited at the prospect of seeing Ángel again. She had worked as an activist with him years ago in Spain as part of a mission to help uninstall Francisco Franco from power. Franco had reinitiated contact with the USSR via a French intermediary and Britain could not allow the Russians to gain a foothold in Western Europe – especially near Gibraltar. But Kim had made the mistake of falling head-over-heels in love with the charismatic man, which had ultimately compromised her situational awareness. Her cover had somehow been blown by a Russian agent, which led to her picture being posted in the newspapers. She'd immediately been recalled to England without having the chance to say goodbye.

After all this time, she wasn't sure what the reception would be like. For all she knew he might not even live there anymore. But she desperately wanted to see him again and this would be a good opportunity. Kim just hoped he would feel the same about seeing her too.

En route, she bought replacement clothes for them both so that they'd have something presentable to change into when they were cleaned up. On the journey she told Lee about Ángel, that he was a kind man and that hopefully he'd be able to accommodate them for a couple of days. Every time she spoke about him, Lee could see how happy it made her. But then, her face dropped and she became serious again.

"One more thing," she said before they arrived. "Let me do most of the talking and do not discuss any personal details." Lee looked at her quizzically.

"Like what?" he asked.

"Do not disclose anything about your family and why we're here. He's a nice man, but he also has a job where he's paid for information!" Kim looked at Lee with a very serious face. "Understood?" Lee didn't really understand why it was so important but agreed anyway. Besides, it was sometimes good to just observe.

"You'll do the talking; I'll just speak when I'm spoken to," he said.

"Yes, just do what you've been doing since I met you!" she chuckled.

Lee smiled back and went back to looking ahead again.

"But what if he does ask me why we're here?" Kim had been racking her brains for a decent cover story that wouldn't potentially implicate Nancy by association with Lee. But it was February – why would an

English woman and a young boy be in the country needing to change clothes?

"The best I can think of is that you were kidnapped by a lorry driver in England. I was called in by your parents and finally tracked you in France. We had a miraculous escape which required us both to jump off of a ferry and swim to shore. If he asks you where this all took place, just say that you don't know."

When they arrived at the house, Kim was a little nervous. She pulled the car in to the driveway and instructed Lee to stay where he was as she got out. The front door was opened by a short woman with thick dark hair and a stern expression. Initially surprised, Kim asked if Ángel was home. The woman looked her up and down and called out his name. She didn't smile.

At least he still lives here.

Ángel came to the door. Although initially shocked, he was happy to see her after such a long time. He recognised her instantly, even though she was wearing some very strange attire and smelled like 'eau de l'ancien étang' (*old pond water*). He invited her in without delay, to the chagrin of the woman holding the door open.

"I have a boy with me. Would it be alright for us to stay for a couple of days?" Ángel was a little taken back by the surprise request. He felt a little awkward but didn't feel he could refuse the woman who obviously needed some help.

"Of course, it's no problem," he said with a half-smile. "It's been a while since we had guests."

Kim beckoned Lee from the car. As they entered the house, Ángel introduced the woman as his wife, Nadine. Kim's heart instantly sunk like a plumb line, but she did her best not to show it. They waited downstairs as Ángel instructed Nadine to get the spare room ready for them and to run the bath.

"Bien sûr!" (*Of course!*) she responded tersely before heading upstairs.

"If you don't mind me asking, what happened to you both?"

Kim took the lead and repeated what she'd said to Lee. Their own clothes were ruined, and they'd had to accept the second-hand ones they were wearing. Ángel knew a bad cover story when he heard one but didn't want to push in front of the young boy.

Three minutes after the targets went inside the house, Agent 4 quietly approached the hire car using the trees for cover. He quietly opened the driver's door and placed a brief note in front of the instrument binnacle. He then traced his path back through the trees towards the road. He walked back to his car, which was on the same road that the target would have to pass along to get to where he wanted her.

Nadine came back downstairs and announced that the bath would be ready soon.

"OK," Kim said, "I need to get some bags from the car; we have new clothes to change into." After retrieving the bags from the back seat, she was about to close the car door when she noticed a note behind the steering wheel. She quickly read it and then placed it in the side pocket of the door. It specified a location, a time and to come alone. When she came back into the house, she gave one of the bags to Lee and suggested he should have the first bath.

Kim and Ángel spent a while catching up with each other. Ángel explained to Nadine that they were both political activists years ago in Spain and worked with the same newspaper. After about fifteen minutes of reminiscing that she clearly found tiresome, Ángel's wife made her excuses to head to the kitchen to prepare the evening meal.

Nadine had 'accidentally' met Ángel whilst travelling in Spain, not long after Kim had disappeared four years ago. She deliberately bought into everything he was fighting for and made sure to fill the void conveniently left by Kim's absence. After two years together, she'd even convinced him to marry her, such was her devotion to her country. But the last fifteen months had been fruitless. Ángel wasn't a bad husband by any stretch, but life had become boring and her brief had always been to find out more about his information network. He was considered to be still 'active' by her superiors, but she had yet to uncover anything of any use to them. They'd begun to lose patience with her and had been applying pressure for a while now, so the arrival of the two strangers was just the break she needed. She immediately recognised Kim the moment she opened the door, because she had taken the photograph and anonymously passed the story to the Spanish newspapers. But the last thing she expected was for the suspected MI6 agent to turn up on her doorstep.

In the living room, Ángel began to lower the volume of the conversation and motioned with his hand for Kim to do the same.

"That wasn't a very good cover story," he said in a questioning manner.

"It's actually not that far from the truth – we did actually go overboard."

"You might be putting yourself and the boy at risk by coming here." Kim sat up with a jolt.

"Why?"

"Let's go outside for a walk."

Outside Ángel explained that for some time now he'd felt a 'cold breeze' down his neck. He couldn't quite place it, but he'd noticed certain semi-familiar faces cropping at some of the locations he'd been to.

"You'll be ok to stay tonight, but it's probably best if you find alternative accommodation tomorrow," he warned. Kim understood and promised to comply. She now needed a reason to meet with Agent 4.

"I need to go and get the car fuelled up. Where's the nearest station?" she asked, as they were about to head back. Inside, Ángel wrote the directions on a scrap of paper.

"OK, that looks pretty straightforward. Tell Lee when he comes down that I won't be long."

Agent 4 waited patiently. The road he was parked on was hardly used; he'd only counted three cars in the last hour. He spotted the target's car exit the house from his rear-view mirror and let it pass, holding back a while before pulling out. She was on her own, so it was safe to assume she'd be heading to the rendezvous point. Knowing where your target was heading made a huge difference in covert operations. As she continued as expected to the dual carriageway, he overtook her to arrive at the fuel station in preparation.

* * *

Whilst preparing the evening meal, Nadine took a large rubberised torch from the store cupboard. She rested it on her shoulder and clicked the on/off button in patterns, trying to get a message to an agent that at times had them under surveillance. It took four attempts over twenty minutes to finally get a response.

Nadine: 'British agent former associate arrived to stay.'

Surveillance Agent: 'Sedate husband and agent for overnight removal. 2am.'

Nadine: 'Door will be unlocked.'

Lee was so enjoying being submerged in a bath that he didn't want to get out, but he was eventually forced to when the water became lukewarm. He couldn't wait to put his new clothes on; he'd managed to get Kim to buy things that his mother never thought him worthy of, and his new jeans had the deepest pockets ever! As he put on his new Star Wars t-shirt, something caught his eye from out of the bathroom window. He wiped away some of the condensation and peered out. He could see what looked like a blinking light flashing through the trees. He rubbed the window a little more and saw a car in the distance. Inside was a person flashing a torch in some form of code. He looked down and saw that there were flashes also coming from the kitchen below, which seemed very odd.

Lee quietly went downstairs to find the living room empty. He walked into the kitchen and stumbled across Nadine with a torch in one hand, making flashes to the car outside. Somewhat flustered, she immediately put the torch down when she heard the boy behind her. Lee pretended he hadn't really seen anything and just asked, "Have you seen Kim?" Nadine was as abrupt as normal.

"Non. Please wait by the fire in the living room."

He now knew that the woman could speak English.

* * *

At the fuel station, Kim went inside to pay for fuel and purchased both a local and a national newspaper. She walked back to the car to find a man sitting in the rear passenger seat.

"Please drive on, Miss Montrall. You can drop me off soon," he said. "I'm here on behalf of HQ."

"OK, but there's been a slight update. We'll be heading into central Paris tomorrow and finding alternative digs – my friend can't accommodate us for as long as I'd hoped," she said. The agent handed her a roll of French francs.

"Guess what? There's been another change of plan – you won't be staying in central Paris tomorrow; the house may not be clean." Kim knew what he meant, particularly after Ángel had warned her too. "That's courtesy of Her Majesty," he said, nodding towards the money. "Make sure you're on a ferry by tomorrow afternoon."

"Understood," she replied. The agent told Kim to stop the car and watched her drive away. The sooner she was off his plate, the sooner he could get back to his real work.

By the time Kim returned, Nadine had nearly completed the meal preparations. Ángel and Lee were talking about all sorts of things – football, cars, planes. She could see that Lee enjoyed his company. *He always was an interesting man*. She caught herself looking whimsically at the man and then saw Nadine looking in her direction. Lee recognised the uncomfortable tension between the two of them; it was the same between his nan and his mum.

Nadine said that there was now enough hot water for Kim to bathe before dinner was served. When Kim came down in her new clothes, Ángel gave her an approving smile.

"You look lovely," he said. Kim blushed a little. Ángel laughed and Lee was embarrassed. Nadine remained stoic, further cementing the frosty relationship between the two women. After what was a lovely meal, the two visitors went upstairs to sort out the sleeping arrangements, whilst their hosts cleared the dinner table. Ángel had provided an additional sleeping bag and cushions, so Lee said he'd sleep on the floor between the bed and window – it was only fair as he'd had the bed at the B&B. He went to bed before the adults; he took the gun from his suitcase and put it inside the sleeping bag – wanting to make sure he was prepared for anything.

The three adults chatted downstairs for a couple of hours over glasses of wine. It'd clearly been a while since Kim had last had a drink; she was beginning to feel a little drowsy. She made her excuses, thanked Nadine for the lovely meal, and headed off to bed. Ángel and Nadine followed shortly afterwards. When she entered the front bedroom, Kim quietly called out to Lee to see if he was awake. With no answer, she took off her outer clothes, leaving her undergarments on, and got into bed. Lee had woken when Kim opened the bedroom door, choosing to keep silent when she called out. As she de-robed, he tried to catch a glimpse, hoping to see something he shouldn't. But unfortunately, the bed and mattress were too high and obscured everything. Lee wondered how much she'd had to drink because she fell asleep five seconds after her head hit the pillow.

* * *

CHAPTER 22

CLOSE CALL

Lee's sleep was broken a number of times by the deep snoring Kim made next to him; there were times when it sounded like she was choking. She hadn't been this annoying at the B&B and he wondered why tonight was different. *Is this what happens when she drinks?* Once his eyes were acclimatised to the darkness, Lee finally got up and stood over Kim to watch. When she made the strange noises again, he shook her to see if she'd stop. He expected her to stir, but nothing changed. Just above the strange sounds emanating from Kim, Lee heard the distinct sound of footsteps on gravel outside. He quietly moved round the bed to the window just in time to see someone heading up the path towards the front door. He heard it open and wondered why anyone would be around so late. Something wasn't right. Lee heard whispering downstairs, so he went back to Kim and gave her another shove; but she was still in another world. Lee's heart began to race as he quietly stepped back to the sleeping bag and took the gun from inside. Resting his arms on the bed behind Kim's body with his eyes just above the mattress, he pointed it at the bedroom door. *Safety off!* he reminded himself.

Thirty seconds later the doorknob turned slowly and the door was quietly pushed open. A large shadow appeared. It was definitely the silhouette of a man with something small in his hand. A second, smaller frame followed in behind. Oblivious to everything, Kim's snores continued. As the man stood over her, Lee saw a syringe in his right hand. He tried to keep calm, but his heart seemed to be trying to escape from his chest. *Are they trying to poison her?* As the man bent over to administer whatever it was, Lee didn't hesitate. He fired the gun at the man's head from a metre away and then fired another round at the second person when he heard her scream. The 'Syringe Man' slumped over Kim's body as the second shot hurled the other person back against the wall then down to the floor. *Four bullets left*, Lee noted as his ears hissed from the aftermath of the gunshots.

Less than 200 yards away, Agent 4 was jolted awake when he heard the faint crack of shots fired. He quietly got out of his car and moved quickly towards the house, constantly scanning the horizon to make sure he wasn't being observed.

Kim moaned for a short while as Lee shook her frantically for what seemed like minutes to wake her, but at least she was alive. He walked round the bed to turn on the light and tripped over the second body, hitting his knee on the bedpost.

"Aaargh!" he exclaimed with gritted teeth. Cursing, Lee got up, stepped over the body and switched the light on. The room was now a completely different picture from when he'd gone to bed. Blood had smeared the wall above where Nadine now lay on the floor, twitching slightly. The big Syringe Man was slumped face-down over Kim with a two-inch wide flap of hairy skin folded over, exposing a blood-red hole in the back of his head. Lee winced a little but he didn't recoil, choosing to look around the wound for a few seconds. It was like the man's head had been sick. He could tell that it wasn't Ángel. *It must've been the guy I saw creeping up to the house.* Lee didn't shake and wasn't flustered. He'd had a job to do and he'd done what his nan had asked. He put the gun down on the bed and grabbed Kim by the shoulders, shaking her continuously until she finally regained consciousness.

"Wha... whaat's matter? Leave me alone."

"Get up, they tried to hurt you. GET UP!" Lee shouted at her. Kim remained groggy right up to the point when she looked down and saw the dead man lying across her body with his head barely intact. She immediately began kicking in fear, trying to pull away, but her legs felt numb.

It took both of them to push the dead weight off her pelvis, but they eventually manhandled him to the floor. Kim tried moving her legs and toes but needed Lee's help to avoid a pool of thick blood that now stained the sheets. To him, the blood smelled like the oilseed rape fields he'd been past in the car with his dad.

"What the hell happened?"

Lee picked up a syringe that was still on the bed and showed it to her, as her grogginess shifted to a state of alert.

"I think they were going to kill you, so I shot them first!" Lee said, as he was about to pick the gun back up. Kim got angry and snatched the gun away first.

"You told me you didn't have the gun anymore!" *Is that all you can say!* Lee thought. Well, enough was enough. He was sick of women ordering him around and being ungrateful.

"Well, it saved your life, didn't it? Most people would be thankful!" he snapped back with an anger that jolted her. He was right and she knew it. Kim said nothing, put her clothes on and went to both bodies to check the pulses. The assassin was clearly dead but Nadine was still alive – blood oozing slowly from her chest.

A sudden crash came from downstairs, followed by someone running up the stairs. Kim pointed the gun at the door and shouted, "Who is it?" Agent 4 identified himself with a code word. "Come in slowly," she ordered.

Agent 4 entered the room and saw the carnage.

"What the hell happened?" Kim went to speak, but it was Lee who spoke up and gave the man a concise but detailed account of what had happened. As Lee reached the end of the account, Kim stepped in to wrestle back some control of the situation. This was a right royal f*ck-up and she knew it.

"The assassin's dead, but the other one's still alive," Kim said, as if taking some credit.

Agent 4 threw her some handcuffs.

"Make sure she doesn't go anywhere!" he said with an air of sarcasm.

Kim moved Nadine around and secured the woman to the bed frame.

"Where's the other guy?" the agent asked. For a brief moment, Kim had forgotten about Ángel. Her stomach churned as a distressing thought crossed her mind. *He would've come straight to the room if he'd heard the gun shots*. The three of them headed across the landing to Ángel's bedroom and switched on the light. He was completely still, but small amounts of foam could be seen at the corners of his mouth. Kim desperately fought the urge to rush to the bedside and hold him in her arms – she knew what dead looked like. For now she needed to keep her emotions in check; they wouldn't be of any use now anyway. Agent 4 took charge and checked the man's pulse.

"Dead. I've seen this before. Get dressed and ready to leave in three minutes. Meet me outside at your car." They were both dressed and ready within two. Out by Kim's rental, Agent 4 checked the underside with a torch and gave her the all-clear.

"I'll clean up the mess here. Just get to Calais ASAP. Do you have the gun?" Kim gave it to him, with the butt first and the barrel facing downward.

"One last thing," he said. "No headlights for the first few hundred yards. Understood?"

"Understood," she responded appreciatively. She could barely see where she was going until she eventually switched the lights on. It was cold outside and the atmosphere in the car was subdued. Kim knew that Agent 4 would have to make a report and there'd be a lot of questions for her back in England. On top of that she felt devastated that Ángel had lost his life because of her. She didn't want to look back, knowing what Agent 4 meant by 'clean up the mess.' It wouldn't be pleasant.

Agent 4 was p*ssed off. He'd heard about Kim's reputation for sloppy work and leaving chaos in her wake. Cleaning up what she'd left behind meant leaving as few clues as possible to what had happened. He strode back to the house, putting a pair of leather gloves on as he did so. He picked up the syringe and placed it in a plastic bag for later and kept hold of the gun. He then checked the woman over to make sure she was still alive – she was, but barely. Confirming she was secure, he walked quickly back to his vehicle to locate a syringe kit of his own, a camera and a petrol can from the boot. Back in the house he injected truth serum into Nadine's neck and interrogated her for the last few minutes of her life.

From what he could ascertain, Nadine had put sedatives in Kim and her husband's wine that evening. But having had enough of her assignment, she'd also injected Ángel with a poison whilst in his sleep. She thought that eliminating the British agent would be straightforward. When Agent 4 asked about what they were going to do about the boy, she said drowsily that she would have let her superiors decide that. When questioned about who her superiors were, the woman eventually disclosed the information – "KGB." Agent 4's last question was about the man in the other room. Nadine told him everything she knew. Dazed, confused and loosing blood, the woman had served her purpose. Agent 4 placed his fingers around her trachea and crushed the cartilage in one swift and forceful action. After confirming she was dead, the agent turned the body over to check if there was an exit wound. He was in luck; he wouldn't have to get dirty digging into the body. He looked around the room and found what he was looking for – a small hole in the wall near the top of the bedroom door. He gouged the blunted round from the plaster and placed it in the bag. The other bullet that had killed the assassin was easy to spot and so he also gouged it out of the wall and put it inside the bag with the other items. He removed the handcuffs from the woman and placed her face-up on the bed, eventually manhandling the assassin the same way. Agent 4 took pictures of them both, and then saturated them with the petrol from the canister. He took a picture of the dead man in the other bedroom and went downstairs to switch on the gas. He completed a quick search of the place but found nothing of interest.

With a Zippo lighter, Agent 4 lit two pairs of the house curtains until they were well and truly alight. He closed the front door behind him and jogged back to his car to watch the fire take hold, making sure that there was still no other surveillance on him.

In the morning, after he'd disposed of all the evidence in his possession, Agent 4 coded a full report back to his case officer, gave the film to a courier service and went back to his original surveillance mission.

* * *

Kim kept driving without saying a word to Lee. She knew she should really thank him; after all, the kid had just saved her life. The silence grew more awkward by the minute, until she eventually plucked up the courage to say something.

"Thank you for saving my life back there," she said, looking straight ahead.

Finally the ungrateful cow said thank you... took her long enough! Lee thought. He said nothing in response until he'd formulated some questions that needed answered.

"Why did they try to kill you?"

Kim's instant answer was, "I don't know." She actually didn't know specifically, but she had a good idea after Lee explained what he'd seen to Agent 4. Lee followed-up.

"Who was that man that helped?"

Kim felt cornered. How was she supposed to answer this one? She thought fast.

"In my job, it's good to have contacts. I have contacts all over the place."

Adults always underestimate a child's ability to know when they are being lied to or given some soft soap to avoid harsh truths. This was one of those moments. Lee decided to press home his advantage.

"Who are you, Kim?" he asked calmly.

The woman was astounded and felt like she'd been kicked. *Does he know I lied?* she thought. She'd been taught to maintain her cover, no matter what.

"As I've already told you, my name is Kim Montrall and I have my own investigation agency." She stuck to her position. She wasn't going to change her story for a seven-year-old boy. Lee had listened to how differently she'd responded to the three questions, and he knew that at least two of her answers were lies. But it didn't matter to him now; he just wanted to get back to see his dad and his nan. Kim thought ahead as she drove.

"My car is still parked at Calais. I have to return this car back to the hire company to get mine. When we get close to the ferry terminal, you're going to have to jump into the boot, I'm afraid. You don't have a passport, and we'll get stopped if they find you. You might be in there for a while."

"As long as you let me out when we're on the boat," Lee negotiated.

"Of course," Kim agreed. "But it'll be the same drill when we get off the boat as well." Lee didn't care. The only thing he cared about was feeling the fresh sea air on his face and going home. But where was home going to be?

* * *

CHAPTER 23

INTRIGUE

After nearly two hundred miles, Kim pulled the car into a services area about twenty miles outside of Calais at just after 7 o'clock in the morning. She'd pulled off the autoroute partway to get some much-needed sleep, having twice nearly veered off the road en route. They both needed the bathroom and Kim had to check her plans with Nancy before catching a ferry. She thought about calling Nancy straightaway, but with the hour time difference thought it best to at least wait until 8 o'clock. The woman was going to be furious with her no matter what, so she at least wanted to avoid calling on an empty stomach. Kim bought them both a hot breakfast in the meantime; they sat by the window, watching the world go by with neither having much to say to the other. At 8 sharp, she made the call, giving Nancy a summary of the latest events and their current location. Nancy was livid, but deliberately stopped short of giving Kim the dressing-down she deserved... now was the time for keeping a cool head. There was to be no more latitude for her personal needs. Kim made no attempt to justify anything to Nancy; her goose was well and truly cooked. She said she'd aim to be on a ferry between 11am and 1pm. Nancy asked for her UK car make, colour and registration so that she could make sure Kim was waved through Customs & Immigration. Two loud revs of the engine would get the attention of the immigration officer. Kim was also told to make her way straight to Nancy's home afterward, even if she needed to adapt her plans.

* * *

The first thing The Chief was given by his assistant that morning was the transcription of the verbal report from Agent 4. It was short, punchy and to the point. The Chief's brow furrowed as he read about the incident in the house. He sat back, rubbing his bottom lip as he thought about the issues and ramifications. Three enemy agents had been eliminated in one night; two Russians and one communist sympathiser posing as a Spanish activist, who was really the French intermediary that had been right under the noses of MI6 for years. It was a short-term gain, but there would be consequences further down the line. They'd have to send out a bulletin to all field agents to be vigilant for any retaliation plays. Agent 4 had recounted Lee's view of the incident pretty much word for word. The Chief smiled to himself – he couldn't wait to meet this lad!

He instructed his assistant to get Nancy on the line so they could compare notes from the information they'd received. Nancy also gave him Kim's car details for the contacts at Dover.

"Should I make a reservation for tomorrow?" he asked. "I'd like to talk to this grandson of yours whilst everything's still fresh in his mind." Nancy thought about Lee and wondered whether he should have time to recover from his ordeal first.

"As hard a decision as this is for me, it's the only window of opportunity we have," she said. "What time?"

"Let's say 1 o'clock at the usual place?"

"Fine. I'll call you if there's going to be a problem," Nancy said as she put the receiver down.

* * *

Kim tried to relax her mind and let the effects of the sedative fully wear off whilst Lee played on the arcade games with the few coins she'd given him. She was tired but couldn't afford to fall asleep now; she might be able take a quick nap on the ferry. It was time to get moving, so she prised Lee away from his favourite tank game and bought some supplies for the trip home. When they arrived at the car hire location at Calais docks, she signed the paperwork, made her payment, bought a couple of tickets and walked Lee to her own car.

"I'm afraid this is where you get consigned to the boot," she told him. Lee hopped up and over the opening to get in. "The diciest part of this will be getting out of France. Make sure you're fully covered up with clothes and keep all the bags on top of you, facing the back of the car."

Lee nodded his agreement.

"When we get to England, it'll be the same arrangement, but we should get waved through Immigration. If things are going pear-shaped and I need you to be silent, I will beep my horn twice – understood?"

"OK." He lay on his back and watched the world go dark as Kim closed the lid. It wasn't the most comfortable place to be, but he'd slept in worse places. Kim did her best to minimise any jostling by not making any sudden movements on the road.

Commandant Marchand had obviously done his job at the French end because Kim had no trouble getting waved through to the ferry's car deck. Once the other occupants around her had vacated their vehicles, she let Lee out of the boot. Upstairs, Kim made herself comfortable in one of the lounges – but Lee just wanted to explore.

"You can go and explore if you like but stay out of trouble. Remember where I am and where the car is for when it's time to disembark."

"I'm going to need some money," he asked. Kim was about to say something but refrained and gave him a fiver from her purse – she'd get it back on expenses anyway. The ferry journey wasn't too choppy, and Lee enjoyed exploring the inside and outside of the boat. He especially liked standing as high up on the bow as he could to feel the wind through his hair. It was fun watching people being seasick. As the ferry approached Dover, he met Kim as agreed and snuck into the boot when no one was watching. With the hard part of the journey over, Kim revved the engine twice as she approached Dover Customs & Immigration. The immigration officer looked at a clipboard list and waved her through with a slight nod. Away from the port, and now safely on home soil, Kim pulled over in a lay-by to let Lee out and make a quick call to Nancy from the phone box to put her mind at rest.

Nancy waited by the window for forty minutes contemplating both her grandchildren until the car pulled up. She rushed outside to meet them and immediately gave Lee the biggest hug ever. They both felt the pang of emotion that came with not seeing a loved one for so long, and both tried their best to put on brave faces. She thanked Kim warmly for Lee's safe return, putting aside the procedural missteps of the last twenty-four hours and invited them both inside to the kitchen, where she made drinks for them all.

"And what would you like to do now, Master Walker?" she asked Lee.

Inside, Lee was overjoyed that someone remembered who he really was, not with some fake name of 'King.'

"Can we make cakes?" he asked. Nancy chuckled at his response. *I'm glad the old Lee is still there!*

"Of course! Give me two minutes and you can both tell me all about your adventures!"

She made a very quick one-word telephone call.

"Arrived."

Making cakes was definitely a great way of helping the boy relax. They spent the next couple of hours talking and laughing, whilst fitting all the pieces of each other's stories together. Nancy didn't hide how impressed she was. The escape from the French police station and jumping from a suspension bridge were exceptionally brave things to do. Even Kim was surprised at some of the missing pieces of the jigsaw puzzle. Lee asked his nan whether Dad would be coming round after work.

"Unfortunately, his promotion has taken him away on business, but he will be back in a couple of days."

"Promotion?" Lee asked.

"Oh yes, he's become a manager now. All of that hard work for the last couple of years has finally paid off for him," she added. Lee's demeanour changed and his thoughts became melancholic. *He's always at work.* Nancy could see that Lee didn't really like the explanation and so quickly diverted the subject. She signalled to Kim that it was time for her to go and they agreed to catch up in a week's time where Kim could present her report and invoice expenses for payment. She shook

Nancy's hand and then went over to Lee to give him a business-like handshake as well.

"Please don't run away again!" she said with a half-smile. After Kim had gone, Nancy asked Lee, "So, tell me what do you think of Kim?"

"She's alright. She did jump into the river to get me after all... the police didn't … but she's not a very good liar." Nancy smiled. His honest and accurate assessment was refreshing.

Soon after eating a large proportion of the cake they'd made, Nancy suggested that maybe Lee should go to bed and get some well-needed rest. Even though it wasn't particularly late, she could see he was tired. In the past, Lee would fight for every extra minute he could stay up – but not this time.

"Why don't you pop upstairs to wash your face and brush your teeth? I'll bring you up a nice hot water bottle and tuck you in."

Lee was already in bed when his nan came into the spare room. His face softened when she popped the water bottle under the blankets and stroked his hair.

"I'll make sure your clothes are all clean and ironed. We have a big day ahead of us tomorrow."

"Why's that then, Nan?" Lee said excitedly.

"We're going to London to get you some new clothes that fit, and there's someone I'd also like you to meet!"

"Who?"

Nancy winked and put a forefinger to the side of her nose in a playful way.

Lee liked the idea of being spoiled for once. He was also very intrigued about who they would be meeting.

* * *

CHAPTER 24

CHOICES

David hadn't heard from his mother in a few days and wondered if Kim had brought Lee back yet. It was difficult for him having this situation going on in the background whilst he was away on business. He managed to find a spare five minutes and called her at around 11 o'clock. He tried a couple more times that day, but to no avail; he wondered if she'd gone to meet Kim and Lee somewhere and decided he'd try her later in the evening.

Nancy and Lee jumped on the 09:36 train to London, just after peak time when the train would be less crowded. Seeing as the meeting expenses would be paid by HQ, she decided to treat them to first class. Lee had never been to London before, or on a commuter train, and was like a wide-eyed tourist. They even went on the Underground, which he found fascinating. In the West End, Nancy took Lee some mainstream shops and a couple of little boutiques as well. By lunchtime they'd both got their hands full with shopping bags, so Nancy suggested that they get something to eat.

"There's a nice place I know and, like I said yesterday, there's someone I'd like you to meet," she said cryptically.

"You haven't said who yet?" Lee probed, but Nancy just smiled and tapped the side of her nose twice. The grandeur of the restaurant impressed Lee, but what impressed him more was that they already knew his nan's name. He'd only ever been to a Wimpy before with his dad, and they certainly didn't remember your name there. A man escorted them to a private booth where the curved leather seating was plush and the table was set with silver cutlery and cloth serviettes. Nancy placed their order once Lee decided what he wanted. He had lots of questions for the waiter.

"Don't be worried about the prices, Lee. This one's on the house for both of us!" She smiled. They hadn't been seated too long when Nancy saw a man at the door and signalled their location. He was 6ft 3in tall, thin, clean-shaven and wore an impeccably tailored navy-blue suit. Lee couldn't work out his age, but he was definitely younger than his nan. He shook Nancy by the hand and gave Lee the exact same respect. Nancy introduced them both to each other. Lee felt the man had strength, but he didn't over-exert his grip.

"I've taken the liberty of ordering your usual," Nancy said.

"Your nan is wonderful, isn't she?" he said as he smiled at Lee. Lee looked at his nan and smiled in agreement. The Chief was very good-humoured towards Lee and complimented him on his resourcefulness during his time in France. After their food came, he decided that it would be best to talk to Lee as he would an adult - in an honest, relaxed and matter-of-fact way.

"So, you're probably wondering why I asked your nan to meet with me today?" he asked.

"Yep," Lee said, happy to play along.

"Do you know what your nan used to do for a living?" Lee looked at them both.

"No…" he said tentatively. The Chief leaned in towards him and lowered his voice.

"Well… you might be surprised to learn that your dear old nan here was one of Britain's highest ranking secret agents until she retired a few years ago." The man then proceeded to reel off a slightly rose-tinted catalogue of things that Nancy had done for her country over the years.

The Chief put his finger to his pursed lips, with a smile out of one corner of his mouth as if to say 'mum's the word.' Lee looked at them both sceptically. The Chief could see that the boy wasn't completely convinced, so with the briefest of nods; both he and Nancy took out their credentials. Lee took his time to read the inscriptions.

"Does Dad know you're a secret agent?"

"No, just you, young man." Lee beamed in awe feeling like he was part of a special club, as The Chief continued.

"Kimberly is technically one of us too but, from what I've been able to understand, she was compromised in Paris. Can you tell me what happened, from your perspective?" Lee liked being treated like adult. It was a level of respect he'd never received at home, school or anywhere else for that matter. He recounted all the key details about Paris whilst trying his best not to let emotions get the best of him – especially where Servanne was concerned. After listening until Lee had finished and glancing over at Nancy, The Chief leaned in and began to talk to Lee in a hushed tone again.

"Would you be prepared to listen to a proposal I have for you?" Lee shrugged, wondering if they were going to send him on a mission or something.

"Sure," he said coyly. The Chief now felt like a bit of a salesman – but that was the recruitment game.

"OK. So whilst I can't go into specifics, it would be safe to say that our recruitment strategy in the past has been somewhat narrow in its focus."

"What does that mean?" Lee asked.

"It means that we tend to recruit from the same sort of institutions like universities and other government agencies, with age ranges generally between nineteen to twenty-five. This strategy worked during and after the war, but it's now becoming a bit hit-and-miss. The world is changing and so our business needs to adapt to get ahead of these changes. We do also recruit from industry, and this will always be fruitful, but my plans are to recruit differently."

"When you say industry, do you mean like what my dad does... he's a manager now?" Lee said, looking proudly. The Chief gave a half-smile.

"Kind of, yes. We look for people from all walks of life, but more importantly people with good instincts... people who can adapt... people like you." Lee felt a little embarrassed. He hadn't been picked for anything important before. "One of the biggest problems we have is people not being able to adapt quickly in the field. But when we learn things at a young age they become second nature to us as we get older. To use one of your own examples – when did you know you were going to jump from the bridge?" Lee's eyes darted upwards. "At what point did you make the decision to not shoot yourself?" As Lee thought about what the man was saying, he began to smile in realisation. "Am I right in saying they were split-second decisions?"

"I guess?" Lee said questioningly, as he shrugged his shoulders again.

"But what made you choose that path, after all; you could've given yourself up to the police?" Lee's face took on a resolute frown.

"I wasn't going back to a jail cell, I wasn't going to be taken back to the home and they had guns pointed at me." Lee didn't feel like any addition explanation was needed. The Chief wanted probe further, but experience had taught him it could wait – besides, he much preferred it when the boy was smiling... although he knew this may not be for long.

"So, what I'm proposing is that you'd be enrolled in my new programme. To anyone on the outside it will look like you're leading a normal life, but you'd also receive the type of special training that only a select few ever get."

"What sort of training?" Lee asked.

"All sorts, weapons, fitness, self defence, electronics, photography, elicitation, surveillance detection and avoidance, bumps, drops, brush passes... the list is endless." Nancy could see the slightly confused expression on Lee's face.

"Don't worry my darling, over time everything would become second nature to you; just like the way you ride your bike." She said knowingly. Lee smiled. He hadn't ridden his bike in ages and missed accelerating down hills, skidding around corners and the wind through his hair. Nancy had always been around to patch him up if he fell off; and she knew that never made the same mistake twice. "I think what The Chief is saying is that he believes in you, and I definitely think you have what it takes." Lee smiled again whilst pondering his next question.

"Where will I live, will it be with you or Dad?" He asked excitedly. Nancy looked over at The Chief for help. It was the one question that cut through her heart like a Japanese Tantō blade and a question she couldn't bring herself to answer... and still look into the eyes of the child sitting next to her.

"I have a boarding school west of here in mind." The Chief cut in. "It means that you'd spend most of your time living there during each term. You'll probably have to fit in with older children, but we'd make sure you were looked after. For your sacrifice, we would make you the first of a new breed of Elite Agent." Lee smiled again. The man made him feel special. His mind wandered briefly to secret spy missions and James Bond films.

So far so good, The Chief thought.

"I see you're smiling, but now I'm going to tell you the downsides to what I'm proposing. The first is that to be an Elite Agent will require unwavering dedication and hard work. Life will not be easy, but I can promise you it will always be interesting. The second is that only your grandmother, Kim and I will know of your existence. Everybody else will be told that you drowned when you ran away to France – including your father."

The Chief paused and deliberately said nothing for what seemed like minutes. Both he and Nancy kept their gaze fixed firmly, but kindly, on the boy to gauge his reaction. The realisation of what the man had just said changed the look on Lee's face.

END

ABOUT THE ALBUM

This book was always meant to be combined with the album of music that was written for it. If you've read the book without having had the chance to listen to it, I hope you'll take the opportunity to do so. If you have listened to the album, I thank you, and have provided a brief guide to where each song fits into this story.

TRACK 1 THE EDGE

Having run away from England to France, Lee has been cornered by the police on a bridge. Determined not to be arrested again, in chapter 1; he stands on the edge of a heavy girder about to jump into the cold river below.

This soundscape explores the tiredness and confusion of Lee's situation. He is prepared to die!

TRACK 2 WHEN I LOOK IN THE MIRROR

Having been given a letter written by his six-year-old son, David Walker and his mother hire an investigator, who confirms that his wife is having an affair. When David confronts her, a heated argument ensues and he eventually walks out of the family home – leaving the two children with their mother.

This song explores David's feelings towards his cheating wife and how something so good turns so bad.

TRACK 3 HAPPY BIRTHDAY

As time moves on, Lee's sister, Laura, is spoiled by being given a guitar for her birthday. But when Lee's birthday comes around, he gets... well not a lot really. His whole family barely acknowledges his birthday at all.

'Happy Birthday' reflects the solemn feelings Lee has when treated unequally and as the unwanted one in the family. At seven years old, he doesn't understand why.

TRACK 4 GOOD DAY

In order to make life impossible for David to see the children, Louvaine Walker and her new partner move the family miles away to a new home. David and his mother reengage the services of the investigator to find them. David's mother, Nancy, is not one to be trifled with, and when she is given the location; pays a visit – which leads to an interesting situation unfolding where Louvaine and Laura end up in trouble with the police.

This song looks at the outcome from Lee's perspective, as it's good to see his nan again and good for others in the family in trouble for a change.

TRACK 5 SAY GOODBYE

After another move and a whole host of trouble for Lee, he is removed from the family home and sent away to a children's home.

'Say Goodbye' catches Lee at the specific morning of his removal, where his now stepfather calls from work and when his mother sends him away with a social worker. The song is written almost as if there was a spirit talking to Lee.

TRACK 6 A HOME, NOT HOME

After Lee arrives at the children's home he feels desolate, forlorn and gloomy for the future – wouldn't you?

This is a culmination of Lee's reflection of what's happened and where he now is, as he unpacks what few possessions he has in his case and watches Lynn Franks drive away.

TRACK 7 RUNAWAY

After a number of run-in's at the children's home and news that he will never be returning home, Lee decides to run away.

This song takes us through his decision making process and whether he has anything to lose.

TRACK 8 NOT GIVING UP ON YOU

Purely by chance, Lee's grandmother, Nancy, finds out Lee has runaway. Enlisting the help from the investigator again, she is determined to find him. She knows that a seven year old on the streets has little odds of surviving... especially during winter.

This song explores Nancy's anxieties about finding Lee alive. She wishes she'd acted sooner to help him and vows to make sure she finds him.

TRACK 9 STAY OUT OF SIGHT

It's a soaking wet day with few places to shelter. Lee is now in France and has been beaten up in a small town by some older kids. He retraces route back to Servane – a woman who had originally picked him up while hitch-hiking. The kindest woman he'd known in recent times.

The song explores the pain and fatigue felt by Lee. Running away is not the adventure he thought it would be.

TRACK 10 WATER FALL

We're now back to the beginning of the story where Lee is cornered on the bridge.

With no other choices he can see, this is the deciding moment for Lee to jump off the bridge and take his chances.

TRACK 11 OVERNIGHT REMOVAL

When the investigator catches up to Lee and finally has him in her custody, they go to meet with a contact she has in Paris (with permission from Nancy). Little does she know that she has just placed both their lives at risk because of her past.

Using a form of Morse code, Nadine makes contact with a KGB assassin. The assassin instructs her to prepare the guests for 'Overnight Removal.'

TRACK 12 HEADING HOME

After Lee saves Kim (the investigator) from certain death, there's an atmosphere between them on the journey from Paris to Calais.

The song represents Kim's stubbornness/inability to apologise to or thank Lee for saving her life. The journey is just two people in a car, not speaking to each other as the lights go by.

TRACK 13 WAITING AT THE WINDOW

When they reach English soil, Kim calls Nancy with an ETA to bring Lee to her home. Nancy waits by the window for Lee to arrive.

Nancy reflects on her longing to bring Lee back home and the song builds to her relief when he finally arrives. But it is also tinged with a dark side, her subconscious knowing of the meeting she has set up for the next day.

TRACK 14 WHAT PAST, WHAT FUTURE?

As Lee lies in bed, he thinks about what his nan has planned for him the next day.

What Past, What Future? Is an amalgamation of Lee's memories from the past year... until he finally falls asleep, bound tightly in clean sheets warmed by a hot-water bottle.

TRACK 15 SAY GOODBYE (REPRISE)

After receiving a proposal, 'Say Goodbye (Reprise)' is a reflection as Lee thinks about never seeing his father again.

ABOUT THE AUTHOR

Born in the county of Essex in 1970, Autolemy left school in 1986 and dropped out of college in 1987 to pursue a career in music remixing. Within year he went from selling remix tapes in the local record shop, to being asked to produce regular monthly creations for the then prestigious DMC DJ only record label. Over the years, he's gained notable success in many walks of life, from DJ to accountant, and from business transformation to pilot. With notable achievements under his belt, Autolemy is set to become an underground sensation in his new venture as an author and producer.